CW01512673

Acknowledgements.

It has been written a thousand times before, that writing is a lonely occupation. This is true. I sit, uninterrupted by another human for hours at a time, however the writing is but a fraction of the whole process of getting to print and it would be a failing if other people did not get a mention as they helped in large, or small, ways to get this novel, my first, to where it is today. Without such help, no book would ever be read. So I am grateful to the following, beautiful, friends. Ade Wildsmith for the photograph that started the madness. Kelly Brotherhood, with me from the start, her encouragement was limitless and she gets a special mention for providing the character 'Taff Stone.' Nat Shaw for reading and pointing out my errors in the first draft with a smile, whilst drinking Pina Colada on a beach. Amanda Martin for the proofreading and putting me back on track with character names. To anybody else I have missed, you know who you are and how you have helped and I thank you all.

Frank Castle. Lincoln, June 2020

2 Tigers Revenge

TIGER'S REVENGE

FRANK CASTLE

4 Tigers Revenge

DERBY

ENGLAND

1969

ONE~

Petricek Dvorak stood in the shadows.

His stolen fedora slouched low over his brow and despite the fug of cigarette smoke that curled up from his brutal Czechoslovakian cigarette, his eyes, ever alert, never wavered from the girl at the end of platform three.

Three days earlier, Petricek had been sitting on a bed with damaged springs in a seedy hotel two blocks from Derby railway station; it was teeming down with rain and the occasional sound of thunder rattled the cheap window frames.

He hated England. He hated Derby even more. Petricek carried a lot of hate, but that was the exact reason why he had been chosen from the handful of his brothers who served in the dreaded StB.

The Státní bezpečnost was controlled by the Communist Party of Czechoslovakia, a ruthless organisation despised by the inhabitants of that troubled country, an organisation that prided itself on secrecy and domination, glorifying in its visceral methods of obtaining information from every strata of society, both home and abroad.

He raised his heavy body from the battered bed, the tired springs now thankful for any respite, and headed for the door. He never bothered locking it behind him, what was the point? A small child could have bypassed the flimsy lock with ease.

Tramping heavily down the threadbare carpet that barely concealed the creaking wooden staircase, he openly cursed the fact that he'd lost his hat the previous day to a gust of wind whilst crossing a dreary bridge in London. He hated London.

With the collar of his cheap mackintosh turned up high, he turned right and trudged into the night. He had two full hours before his meeting, but the majority of that time would have to be filled as he carried out the necessary tradecraft. Anti-surveillance was an art form commonly known as 'dry cleaning.' Some of the most basic manoeuvres included going up an escalator then down the same one, getting on a bus for one stop, crossing the road and getting the next bus back to where you started and walking through a busy retail premises.

He could not afford to be followed.

Ninety minutes later he entered the dimly lit interior of The Red Cow Public House. The rainwater from his mac dripped onto the stone flags creating small pools behind him as he walked to the bar.

'Whisky,' he ordered.

'Certainly Sir. Irish or Scottish?'

'Large.'

The bored bartender turned to the meagre array of sprits hanging mournfully at the back of the bar muttering to himself, unknowingly signalling that he too hated where he was and what he was doing. Petricek handed over a soggy £1 note and received his change with no other communication and headed for a table where he could keep an eye on the front door.

And he waited.

Twenty minutes had passed with nobody leaving or entering the pub. Petricek's large tumbler of cheap whisky stood untouched on an injured table. He was tired, he was aching for his wife back home in Kolin, 55 km east of his Capital city and on the bank of the glorious Elbe river.

His quiet musings were halted as the front door opened and his contact entered the premises. 'Basketcase' he muttered under his breath. He'd recognised him from his earlier meeting at Arboretum Park in the City centre. The large man heading for the bar was definitely the man he was here to meet. It had taken him by surprise that afternoon, that such a scruffy looking individual with a weight problem could possibly be in the service of his Crown, a Sergeant in the Air Force no less, but the protocols had been met and that was good enough.

Adrian was ordering of a pint of Scruttocks Old Peculiar beer and a large bag of Pork Scratchings and looking around the lounge area. As he glanced across the room, his gaze fell upon the man in the wet mackintosh and, after receiving and paying for his goods, he falteringly strode across the open space clutching his ale and snack, one in each shovel sized hand.

'Strange old day,' said Adrian.

'Yes it was,' replied Petricek, his Eastern European accent dripping from his lips like a third rate 1950's spy movie.

'Fancy a Pork Scratching old boy?'

'Pork? I am of the Muslim faith and it is forbidden.'

'It's your loss mate, I'm only trying to cheer you up.'

Petricek wasn't a Muslim at all, he'd never set foot in a mosque in his life. He fancied a bowl of hot steaming Svickova and some home-made bread, proper food, not the devil's food, and besides, the crunchy snack that 'Basketcase' was feasting on looked suspiciously like a pig's nipple. Disgusting.

'Do you have the photographs?' asked Petricek.

'I do,' stated Adrian, reaching into the depths of his overcoat and retrieving a thin plastic file and handing it over. 'Here.'

Petricek removed the thin rubber band and pocketed it - rubber bands were in short supply back home. He scanned the contents of the package for thirty seconds or so. 'These are good.'

'I try,' came the sardonic reply as the big Englishman crunched on his snack and gulped down a large portion of his bitter.

'No I mean they really are good, we can use pictures like these. Shots of your current aircraft are extremely sought after,' adding wistfully. 'Especially if the planes are upside down and trailing plumes of red white and blue smoke.'

Adrian rolled his eyes and sighed. 'I have some of our flora and fauna if you're interested, and a cracking set of robins in flight.'

'You have an aeroplane called a Robin? I have never heard of this. These I must see, this is great news.'

'We haven't got an aeroplane called a Robin.'

'Ah code name. We like that. I will take them all from you Basketcase, everything you have, and I must have them all. You can, I hope, get them for our next meeting?'

Adrian thought ' "Basketcase?"' That's a bit rich mate, there is only one basket case at this table, and it's not me', but answered. 'Probably.'

The two men looked at each other with neither really knowing what to say next, so in time honoured fashion, reserved for use in uncomfortable situations, Adrian swiftly demolished the remnants of his pint banged it down on the table, wiped his mouth with the back of his hand and belched. Petricek didn't look impressed and waited several moments before he spoke.

'You want the money? No?' He lifted his left hand with his finger and thumb rubbing together in the internationally recognised signal of payment required.

'Of course.'

Petricek reached into the innards of his mackintosh, produced a battered brown envelope and slid it across the table top stating. 'It's all there.'

'Then we are done for now old boy,' said the big Englishman scooping up the package before thoughtfully stroking his chin. 'Are you drinking that?' He asked, pointing at the whisky in front of Petricek.

'No.' As soon as he finished the word, Adrian had scooped up the tumbler and slid the raw amber liquid down the back of his throat with a belch whilst uttering a word that sounded uncannily like the word 'bollocks' at the same time.

Petricek's brow furrowed as he frowned his displeasure at such boorish behaviour, although he managed a weak. 'Na zdravi!' as 'Basketcase' lifted his ample frame from the shabby chair, pocketed the envelope and left the building without a backward glance.

'That didn't go so well,' pondered Petricek, as he tried to gather his thoughts. 'Things can only get better.'

13 Tigers Revenge

He left the Red Cow in torrential rain.

~TWO~

The next morning, fifty miles to the North East, John 'Tiger' Stripes was up and about in his converted farmhouse in rural Lincolnshire. It was 7.30 am and he'd awoken to an empty house an hour earlier. He had forgone his usual ritual of thirty minutes of Tai Chi on the back lawn. He didn't have the time today, his schedule wouldn't allow it, and to be honest he was getting fed up standing on one leg in a rain soaked field with only a group of bored crows as an audience. 'Daft exercise anyway,' he thought. 'It'll never catch on.'

With the small transistor radio on the kitchen windowsill tuned into the news on BBC Radio 4, and wearing only a dressing gown, he wolfed down a couple of slices of toast and marmalade with gulps of strong white tea whilst listening to a piece on American actions in Vietnam. Halfway through, he raised his hot mug and uttered 'Semper Fi, my friends.'

There followed a soft interview by Jack de Manio with some professor or other warbling on about the Prague Spring in Czechoslovakia; nothing too exciting, so time to go.

Upstairs in his spartan bedroom, he slid his lean body into a pair of blue denim jeans and a white tee shirt.

He sat back down on his bed and pulled on a pair of burnished black engineer boots. Opening a cupboard he ran his finger along a rail where half a dozen leather jackets of different styles were hanging and scooped one seemingly at random. He then picked out a motorcycle crash helmet from a choice of four, a pair of leather gloves, and a set of steel and glass goggles before heading down stairs.

He closed, but didn't bother locking the door and headed for the out buildings where he parked his vehicles. Today's choice was his favourite motorcycle and he threw open the double doors of the garage to reveal a gleaming black painted 1968 Triumph T100S.

He wheeled her out into the early morning sunshine, the light dancing on the chrome exhaust pipe, and leaned her on the side stand whilst he donned his helmet, goggles and gloves.

His right boot crashed down on the kick-start and 500cc of pure British engineering thundered into life before settling down to a steady, satisfying rumble. After pulling in the clutch, he lifted his right foot, snicked the machine into 1st gear and rode slowly across the courtyard. He raised his left hand in silent greeting to his immediate neighbour, the elderly, worldly wise Miss Polly

Richardson, who he knew would be watching out for him as he left his property and turned towards Lincoln City.

Up into second gear, no need for the clutch if you get the engine revs matching the road speed. Third gear, then fourth and Tiger was buzzing along at sixty miles per hour, his Triumph begging for more fuel but he eased off the throttle slightly as he approached the first bend. Slight pressure forward on the left handlebar and the machine rolled easily into the left hand corner, covering the back brake with his left boot as he was leaning over, in case a tractor and trailer full of potatoes appeared and he needed to scrub off speed - only learners and idiots went anywhere near the big front brake - then back on the throttle and feel the rear suspension crunch down under the thunder of acceleration as he lifted upright and exited the corner quickly - approaching the next obstacle, in the shape of a Ford Anglia, whose driver had the temerity to be traveling at the regulation speed limit, he passed the car in a blur of light blue.

The weather was fine at the moment, but as a motorcyclist he always had an eye on the weather and large black clouds were lounging about in the skies ahead, probably a spot of rain over Newark. He hoped it would clear, as he was heading that way and his favourite battered black leather jacket and blue jeans were as waterproof as a sponge.

After 45 minutes of riding he was clear of the Lincoln and Newark traffic snarl ups, heading Southwest on the A46. He was drenched. He had called it wrong on the weather.

As he approached the small mining village of Cotgrave in Nottinghamshire he decided to make a telephone call from the next callbox and have a smoke until the rain passed. The large Koepe towers at the pit head were clearly visible above the newly built miners' cottages as he found the familiar red box and made his call to a private address in Derby, his eventual destination.

The call was short and to the point, his smoke was long and leisurely, he was in no rush.

Tiger had a meeting with an old flame, an on-off relationship that had started at the Odeon Picture House in Lincoln some 12 years earlier. A red haired lass named Margaret Thornton, a match for any man on a motorcycle. She currently rode a 1966 Velocette Venom, and that motorcycle was magnificence personified. Alloy rims, BTH racing magneto, Amal TT carb, rev counter, rear sets and a close ratio gearbox which could rocket the rider to 105mph in seconds. Sometimes Tiger wondered who he preferred, Margaret or her motorcycle.

Back in Derby at the cheap hotel, Petricek Dvorak was also making a call. His was long distance, international and was far from short and to the point. His attitude to the international female operator attempting to put him through to the exchange in Prague wasn't helping. The exercise was no doubt frustrating for her, but infuriating for the Czech spy.

'You are a stupid idiot.'

'Calm down, Sir, this won't take much longer I'm sure.'

'Shit, I hate this country.'

'That's not for me to say Sir.'

'Hurry, hurry you imbecile.'

Eventually the connections were made, the scratchy voices tumbling up and down a long length of thick copper wire deep under the surface of the English Channel, were of course being monitored, and although Petricek was fully aware of this, his temperament that morning had got the better of him and he wasn't sticking to the protocols.

'Your call has ended Sir. May I help you with anything else?'

'Yes,' growled Petricek. 'Find my hat.' Then he slammed the phone down shattering the Bakelite.

~THREE~

Margaret Thornton ran a brush through her hair. She was stood in front of a full length mirror in the master bedroom eyeing her nakedness. At 38 years of age she was confident in her body, she knew how to move it, and how it affected men, and more often than not, other women, yet there wasn't the slightest flicker of arrogance in her eyes.

Her friend Johnnie Stripes had just called and would be arriving within the hour and she wanted to look good for him. She actually loved Johnnie, or 'Tiger' as he was more commonly referred to, but had no idea how he felt about her, something of a dilemma at times, but as an old fashioned girl, she was not the one to be asking the delicate questions. That was the man's job. A Tiger's job.

The telephone call had been brief. A mutual friend called Adrian was in a spot of bother, something to do with a fat foreign man who was buying photographs. She and Tiger had helped to sort out the 'Moroccan' incident the year previously, with a bit of help from Daddy and his team of bad boys from the Secret Intelligent Services, so dealing with some dodgy bloke from overseas didn't seem like it would be too much of a bother.

Although there was something she couldn't put her finger on just yet that was bothering her.

Two minutes later she had pretty much pushed the call to the back of her mind whilst she concentrated on more pressing matters, like what to wear? Answering the door to Tiger fully naked definitely appealed, but that could get awkward if one of Daddy's bad boys turned up uninvited, as they often did.

The weather outside was frightful, so anything by Christian Dior was out of the question and her favourite Hermes outfit was at the cleaners following a simply ghastly evening at Dominic's Bistro the previous Friday. Tarquin 'Double Barrel Something' was such a bloody clumsy arse and why on earth he had decided to balance two fully loaded champagne flutes on his stupid little head was anybody's guess.

She opted for the Lise Charmel blue silk dressing gown with baby blue La Perla panties. French and Italian, perfect.

~FOUR~

Adrian, who, for reasons he hadn't quite yet grasped, but was now apparently known as 'Basketcase' was having difficulties of his own.

Comfortably sprawled, taking up pretty much every inch of his battered favourite sofa, he eyed the unopened envelope he'd placed on his mantelpiece the previous evening. Despite his nonchalant approach to this whole mess, he was way out of his depth. And he knew it.

He'd been scared witless when meeting the stranger at the Red Cow, and it was only the three pints of Abbots Ale he'd drunk at the Pig and Whistle before the meeting, and the one pint of Scruttocks Old Peculiar when in the Red Cow with the fat foreign bloke, that had got him through the situation. The late night call to his good friend Tiger in Lincoln had helped enormously, but a cloud of unease had made for a sleepless night and it wouldn't go away. He had convinced himself that his flat was now under surveillance by a foreign power and he would check the place for listening bugs if he knew what one looked like. But he didn't, so he hadn't.

The needle on the record player started scratching. He wrestled his large frame up from the sofa and carefully replaced the needle at the start of the 33 ⅓

Long Playing vinyl record on the turntable. The splendid, matchless voice of Joan Baez hit his speakers and the album, 'Baptism, a journey through our time' played for the fourth time that morning.

~FIVE~

Petricek Dvorak had vacated his room. He hadn't bothered settling the bill, the hotel was a flea-bitten shit hole, and he guessed that his next lodgings were not about to live up to his expectations either.

He was hungry. Turning right off Wellington Street, he entered London Road and spotted a cafeteria on the other side of the road. Without pausing, he stepped into the road and was startled from his thoughts by an irate driver in a sporty red Ford Capri punching the horn as he came to a sudden stop, followed immediately by the sound of rubber screeching on tarmac, a dull thud and the tinkling of headlight glass. Non-plussed, he continued his crossing, arriving at the instant realisation that not only was this country really shit, he'd forgotten that they drove on the wrong side of the road as well. Idiots.

Up until now, his orders had been quite clear. He ran through the simple checklist in his head as he sat at an outside table of the little café waiting for the coffee and toast he had just ordered from an overly keen young waitress inside.

1. Meet the photographer code-named 'Basketcase' in Arboretum Park in the centre of Derby City.

2. Ensure that 'Basketcase' has the photographs for sale.

3. Arrange a meeting with 'Basketcase' later that same evening.

4. Pay for the photographs.

5. Enquire if there are any more photographs to be had.

6. Meet again if required.

We'll he'd met the Englishman at the park, noted that he'd been a photographer, swapped code words, looked at some pictures, been invited to the shithole of a pub called the Red Cow later that night, once more inspected the photographs and then paid for them. There would be one more meeting and that was that.

He now wondered when his contact would let him know when he could leave for his wife back home in Kolin. It was now a matter of some urgency. His earlier, rather irritating, call to his superior Officer in Prague had been very worrying. The British Secret Service had somehow got wind of the mission and there was a high likelihood that the both the Royal Air Force photographer and himself were under surveillance. If the job went wrong - if any part of the job went wrong - he wouldn't have a family to go back to.

~SIX~

Tiger placed the Triumph into neutral and reverse parked his motorcycle onto the kerb, his long muscular legs making it look easy. He sat for a moment or two with the rain dripping from his crash helmet, forming rivulets down the sides of his face as he gathered his thoughts. He turned off the engine, patted the fuel tank, pulled off his helmet and goggles and eased himself from the saddle and across the pavement.

He was stood at the front of a modest looking townhouse on Midland Road, a stone's throw from Derby Railway Station.

He pressed the brass button next to a solid looking front door, and waited, letting out a silent curse to the rain gods, his leather jacket and favourite pair of jeans were sodden and he was sure his engineer boots were at least half full of rainwater.

Margaret heard the soft tinkle of the front doorbell and rushed down two flights of stairs before taking thirty seconds to compose herself, get her breath back and get her racing heartbeat down to somewhere short of stratospheric.

She slowly opened the heavy oak door to see her love standing on the threshold. He was dishevelled, his short early greying hair bedraggled, wet and plastered to his face, but his cheeky grin put paid to that. He looked utterly gorgeous.

'Well hello there Miss Thornton,' he drawled in a poor imitation of a Deep South Texan Park ranger. 'How are you today?'

She blushed. Damn, she was sure she blushed.

'I am just fine and dandy Sir. Please, please come in.'

The door shut silently behind him, he parked his helmet and goggles on the George III style serpentine mahogany hall table and he took Margaret into his long lean arms, and kissed her gently on the forehead.

'Missed you Maggie.'

'Missed you Tiger.'

Without another word, she pushed him away, looked into his deeply unfathomable blue eyes, grabbed his hand and ran with him up two flights of stairs to the master bedroom.

Margaret's arms locked around Tigers neck, her breasts pushed hard into his chest and she kissed him, hard and wild. He responded, both hands on her hips, his tongue slipping into her warm receptive mouth and kicked the door shut.

Margaret pulled away, breathless and whispered, 'wait.' She disengaged from him and without losing eye contact backed into the room and fell backwards onto her bed. Her gown opened and exposed her firm breasts and rock hard nipples. She placed her thumbs either side of her panties and lifting her derriere, slowly wriggled them down her thighs.

Tiger leaned against the door jamb and watched the show, his erection jammed hard between the denim of his jeans and his muscular thigh.

With finger and thumb Margaret stretched her baby blue La Perla underwear and catapulted them towards Tiger who caught them with one hand and slowly brought them up to his nose, taking in her scent.

With their eyes locked, Tiger pushed himself away from the door and walked slowly to the side of the bed and removed his tee shirt. His pectoral muscles rippling as he put his arms over his head, causing Margaret to moan softly and move her fingers from her nipple towards the soft dampness between her legs.

Tiger whipped his belt from its loops on his jeans letting it coil around his hand and popped the buttons on his fly, one by one, releasing his hard shaft and allowing Margaret take him into her open mouth as he shivered with excitement.

Two minutes later Margaret pulled her lips from his manhood and whispered, 'take me Tiger, take me now you horny bastard.'

He wasted no time, kicking off his boots and ripping off his jeans he stood naked in front of his prostrate lover. Then the Tiger pounced.

~SEVEN~

Adrian opened up a small crack in the curtains and nervously took a peek outside. He noticed three things. Firstly it had stopped raining. Secondly, there did not appear to be anyone taking the slightest interest in the front of his property. Thirdly he realised, apart from his socks, he was naked.

Getting dressed wasn't too much of a problem for Adrian. His wardrobe held more wire coat hangers than actual clothes. He had a fine suit, sure, that was for weddings though. Work. It was important that he looked smart when he worked weddings.

He grabbed the same pair of royal blue cotton twill trousers he'd worn the previous four days, they were clean enough, and a blue collarless shirt that had been pressed at some stage in the last three weeks, the sharp creases along the arms had long given up the struggle, but he wasn't going to a job interview today. A pair of brown brogues and his beer stained maltreated, 'drinking' sports coat finished the ensemble. Everyone should have a drinking jacket; he'd tell anybody who cared to listen.

The telephone conversation with Tiger the previous night was straightforward. He was visiting Maggie at 10am, going for a late breakfast, and they'd both be meeting him at the entrance to the Arboretum Park at 11.30am where he was to show them the precise bench he'd hooked up with the Eastern European the previous day. He was told to take his camera and best lens with him.

~EIGHT~

The waitress, Jackie, at the cafeteria on London Road was exasperated. The only customer in that morning was a fat foreigner. She didn't have a problem with foreign, she didn't necessarily have a problem with fat. She did however have a problem with rude. Her customer that morning had passed beyond any boundary of civilised rudeness. She lived on the Sidney Street Estate, not exactly renowned for its residents' use of genteel language and "Queen's English" turn of phrase. Not by a long chalk. But that man was, well, disgusting. The coffee apparently tasted like shit. The toast definitely looked like shit, the service was too slow, (at least that wasn't shit, she'd thought) and there was a smell of bacon in the air which somehow offended his nostrils. Christ, everybody she had ever met liked bacon, correction, everybody she'd ever met loved bacon.

Her boss, Maureen, the owner of the café, had a Doctor's appointment at 10am, (her ankles had flared up again) and knowing the surgery she was visiting, Jackie knew she wouldn't be back until midday. She was on her own. She was in charge. The last time this had happened was a disaster. Two months earlier, a group of Americans, (they could have been Canadians) entered the café en-masse and ordered pancakes and grits and refried beans.

Jackie hadn't been on the pancake course, if there was such a course, and she sure as hell didn't want to put bits of gravel and second-hand beans on a customer's plate, even for a joke, as she was sure this was. And she said so. She didn't use genteel language, nor anything approaching the Queen's English.　　　With all this in mind, she was absolutely not going to let another disaster like that happen again, so she meekly turned the other cheek, made up a fresh pot of coffee, opened up the rear fire door in order to remove the (lovely) smell of bacon and popped two slices of the freshest bread into the toaster.

~NINE~

The big oak door closed behind Margaret and Tiger as they exited the Midland Road townhouse. Arm in arm they strolled to the end of the road, turned right, and headed east on London Road.

Tiger was sporting his favourite hat, motorcycle crash helmet notwithstanding, a rather spiffing fedora, a present from Margaret's father following a mopping up operation in Morocco the previous year. He kept it at Margaret's place. 'Wherever he lay his hat could someday be his home,' he often chuckled. It looked an odd combination with the blue jeans and his worn black leather jacket, but that thought had never occurred to him. Margaret on the other hand looked stunning in a leather mini skirt and a mink fur bolero jacket and white hipster boots.

'Something's made me ravenous darling.'

'I have no idea what could have caused that Maggie.'

Margaret smiled, she loved this time with Tiger, and they hadn't been together properly for nearly 6 months now, but surely they were meant to be together now, forever? There had been other men, of course, she was an attractive woman, with needs and Tiger was, well, he was Tiger. Often abroad on work she wasn't supposed to know about, and when he was back in Blighty he was on the road with his motorcycle and his pals.

She never felt guilty when dating other men, but she always felt uncomfortable the following morning. Life could be so bloody complicated, and she had no idea if Tiger was seeing another woman. Perhaps she'd ask him today. Yes, that would help, she'd ask him today. But she knew, deep down, that she wouldn't.

'There's the café I was telling you about darling, there, across the road.'

She pointed at the neat little cafeteria nestling rather uncomfortably between an empty plot of land and a butchers shop, proudly telling the world on a rusty old sign that it had been in business since 1897. It was closed.

They crossed the normally busy London road with ease, there appeared to have been an accident or perhaps a breakdown a little further up the street. At any rate, a few smartly dressed young men were milling about on the road with raised voices.

A portly gentleman was seated to the front of the café. He had a dour looking expression and was poking at a slice of toast with a gnarly finger, an undisguised look of contempt on his face. A small valise was tight up to the side of his chair, as if the owner was afraid it could be stolen from him at any moment. His soaking wet, cheap looking mackintosh finished off the picture of a man who appeared to be having a bit of a bad morning. He didn't look up as Tiger and Margaret passed him and entered the cafe.

'Margaret! How nice to see you again,' said the young waitress as soon as they had entered.

'Good morning. Jackie isn't it?' replied Margaret. She'd obviously been here before and probably recently, Tiger thought.

Tiger just nodded, grunted and pulled out a chair at the back of the room. He had seen the man outside pretending not to notice them as they came in. A subtle, shifty glance was all it took. That man is very aware of who is around him, thought Tiger. Is he a man after my own heart?

'I see you do pancake now Jackie, very upmarket.'

'And grits with refried beans,' laughed Jackie.

'Can't smell any bacon though,' Tiger chimed in, 'and pancakes? What's that all about? What happened to good old bacon?'

The question was obviously taken as rhetorical, as Jackie slid behind the counter without offering up an answer.

Margaret joined Tiger at the table. Seating for four, with a freshly cleaned plastic tablecloth in red and white check, a chrome dispenser for paper napkins, and little glass condiments for salt and pepper neatly finished off with tomato ketchup in a large plastic tomato.

'I won't be moment Margaret,' Jackie's voice reduced as she headed for the front door with a pot of coffee.

'Presumably for the chap outside,' ventured Margaret.

'Well unless she's made a pot for those lads outside arguing down the road, I presume that you'd be correct.' countered Tiger. Something was troubling him. His guard was up and he was being feisty, a situation that only ever occurred when there was an imminent threat of some sort.

Jackie re-entered the café, tears streaming down her face. 'I'm sorry, I'm so sorry, I have to close up.'

Tiger eased from his seat and approached the distressed waitress. 'What's up Jackie?' he asked.

'That man outside. He's been so rude all morning.' She was blubbing now and could hardly get her words out coherently. 'Shit toast, shit coffee… I'm sorry I have to close. Last time it was the American pancake crowd and now that rude man. I can't do this, it's too much.'

Tiger had no idea what she was gibbering on about. Pancake crowd? How does that fit in? But he recognised a lady in distress four times out of five, and he knew how to recover a lady's honour. (As well as take it.) So with three large strides he was out the door to face the shifty looking bloke outside intending to drag him in by the scruff of his cheap mackintosh and make him apologise. He'd probably even get a chance to dispose of the dodgy looking plastic tomato filled with ketchup, in some non-chivalrous way.

Fat man had gone. No sign of him. Tiger stood on the pavement and looked up and down the London Road. Nothing. Nada. He turned to re-enter the cafe when he noticed the small black valise next to the now vacant chair.

He toe poked it with a heavy engineer motorcycle boot. It shifted slightly, obviously heavy. Crouching down, he took a closer look. Black in colour, plastic looking with some sort of metal on the rounded corners and a handle. It didn't smell dangerous, and he had a very good nose for any type of danger.

He picked it up with both hands and stood up. It was heavy, perhaps 40 pounds? Like a very large bag of potatoes maybe? A couple of human heads? He placed it on the table and noticed Margaret and Jackie peering nervously over the mid placed net curtain of the front window. He motioned for them to step back and had another look at the case before he carried it into the café.

'Where's the fat man?' This from Jackie.

'What did you do to him darling?' added Margaret.

'I don't know.' 'I didn't touch him Maggie, he was on his toes before I got outside.' Tiger liked to keep his answers in the correct order to the questions posed. It saved time, and confusion.

'Well he left in a mighty hurry,' replied Margaret, 'and he's left his valise behind...'

'If you've quite finished ladies, shall we see what's inside?'

'Are we allowed?' asked a nervous Jackie.

'I'm pretty sure we can,' answered Tiger. 'We need to know who it belongs to so we can return it, you see?'

'I vote we open it.' Margaret said with some authority.

'It's not a debating society Maggie. I'm opening it,' said Tiger, adding, 'now stand back, we have no idea what's in there. Jackie, lock the front door and put the closed sign up.'

Tiger unbuckled the two small straps on top of the valise whilst Jackie fumbled about with the front door lock, nervously looking left and right over the top of the net curtains. The buckles parted easily and Tiger eased down the two zippers that were now exposed. The two ladies inched closer to Tiger; he could feel Margaret's breath on the back of his neck. He glanced up at Jackie. Her earlier character totally reformed. Her tear stained face now replaced with a flushed glow of rampant expectation. Tiger had seen that look once or twice in his life. Oh yes.

He looked back down; the zippers ended their journey, allowing Tiger to gently prise open the valise and reveal any prize within.

He slowly and deliberately began to open the plastic material...

RAP! RAP! RAP!

Three sharp knocks on the front window of the cafeteria.

Tiger cursed under his breath, Margaret almost fainted and Jackie broke wind.

Scooping up the valise with one hand and grabbing Margaret with the other he walked to the rear of the café. 'See who that is Jackie, don't let them in. Tell them to bugger off, tell them you're closed.'

Jackie walked hesitantly towards the door and asked in a pathetic little voice, 'who's there?'

'Get a grip woman,' hissed Tiger from the shadows at the rear of the café.

Jackie ventured nearer the door and asked again, more firmly 'Who's that? We're closed.'

An exchange of voices then continued for about a minute, it was a man on the other side of the door. Tiger could guess that, but couldn't hear the words clearly enough to make a decision that would involve clear and incisive injury to the unknown voice. He placed the valise on the floor. Tiger was evaluating, conducting a high speed danger appraisal. Why wasn't the man outside looking over the curtain? It wasn't that high. Why was the conversation so quiet?

He felt movement at his feet.

Looking down he couldn't believe it. Margaret had opened the case and was having a good rummage around. 'For Christ sake woman!' He whispered, 'what are you doing?'

'There may be a gun...Or a knife we could use.'

'For God's sake Margaret, I'm a trained killer and we're in a bloody café surrounded by sharp bloody knives and...'

He never finished his sentence. Jackie walked over to join them and said,' it was the butcher next door. He was late getting in this morning, huge traffic jam on the London Road. Gridlocked apparently and all the way back to the City centre. Nobody knows why. He just fancied a 'cuppa and a bacon sandwich before he opened his shop.'

Tiger let out a long, slowly controlled breath. 'Why didn't he look in over the curtain?'

'Oh. He's only five foot tall, tiny little old man. I've told him that the grills and pans are switched off, that Maureen the manager is at the Doctors and I am on my way home. He was okay about it,' and in the same breath, 'let's look in the case.'

'There's nothing in the case,' stated Margaret. 'It's empty.'

And so it was.

~TEN~

Petricek Dvorak realised as soon as the pathetic waitress went back inside crying like a mouse with no cheese that the fit looking guy in the fedora would be straight out, and he didn't have the time, or the inclination for a public scene. He stood up and ran as fast as his legs would operate, right on the pavement, right again into Litchurch Street, around the left hand bend and towards the London Road Community Centre. Just twenty seconds of breathless activity and he was in the clear.

He'd taken no more than five further steps when he realised that he had left his valise behind.

'Shit! Shit! Shit!' He shouted, just as an elderly woman was leaving the Community Centre. She had obviously heard him cursing and began to harangue him.

'Shame on you, a man of your age as well. You should be ashamed of yourself swearing in public like that, there should be a law against people like you, where's a Policeman when you want one? That's what I want to know. Probably cutbacks if you ask me. They cut back on the buses, cut back on the buses I tell you! How am I supposed to visit Ethel if there are no buses? Bloody liberty if you ask me. Not that you're asking me, oh no! You're too busy running around with a dirty mouth you are. No good asking you anything is there? Worse than my old Stan you are God rest his soul. Now he knew how to swear properly did my Stan, and no mistake. He'd have you on Market day in a fisticuff mark my words. Who won the flaming war anyway?'

With a last defiant poke of her umbrella in the general direction of a stunned Petricek, she was gone.

'Shit,' repeated Petricek, although a whole lot quieter. How in the name of Gods Holy teeth was he going to sort this out? He couldn't go back. He couldn't even keep an eye on the damned café without being spotted and he needed that valise.

~ELEVEN~

Tiger didn't believe her. Couldn't believe her, the valise was far too heavy to be empty. He crouched down, picked up the valise and placed it on the table and peered inside. Empty.

'Right Maggie we have to go,' said Tiger.

'Are we taking the valise?' She replied.

'Are you taking the valise?' Echoed Jackie.

'Yes to both questions, and we have to go now,' adding forcibly. 'Right now.'

Tiger handed Jackie a business card, bent down and kissed her lightly on her cheek and,dragging the valise behind him, exited the café, followed by Margaret only two steps behind. Jackie closed and locked the door behind her strange guests and set about tidying up and going home - probably for the rest of the week - and seriously considering never washing her face again.

~TWELVE~

Adrian had an uneventful trip to the Arboretum Park. He entered via the Reginald Street entrance, located the nearest bench and sat down. His camera bag held closely to his side. A rustling in the tree behind him caught his attention; he turned his head slowly whilst slipping his hand into the leather bag beside him. A red squirrel sat at the bottom of an old oak tree munching on an acorn, not three yards away and seemingly oblivious to its human neighbour.

Very slowly he removed his camera, his favourite, an Asahi Pentax Super Takumar with the 50mm f/1.8 lens already attached. He had removed the tacky plastic strap as soon as he had purchased it on a recent trip to Thailand, and hadn't got around to replacing it.

With practiced hands he adjusted the focus as he raised the camera to his eye and fine-tuned his instrument as soon as he had the squirrel in his viewfinder.

'Click.'

The squirrel barely glanced up as it continued to gnaw furiously on its midday dish.

'Click.'

Again the little beast ignored the photographer, so Adrian took a chance. He was sure both his previous shots had been spot on, but he would love a close up. Without taking his eye from the squirrel, his right hand entered his bag again and found the Super Takumars 135mm f/3.5 lens sitting in the correct pocket. Single handed, he unscrewed the steel lens cap and prepared the camera body for a quick lens change. A fairly simple procedure nowadays with the M42 screw mount.

He guessed the aperture speed using the tried and tested 'Sunny 16' method and again raised the camera to his eye to fine tune the focus and…

'Click.'

The squirrel then winked at him, kicked the acorn husk into the crowd and gracefully retired from the field of play.

Unfortunately for Adrian, his relaxing afternoon was about to get less a little less relaxing and a little strange. Tiger and Margaret had entered the Park through the same entrance and were marching purposefully toward him. He carefully placed his camera back in its bag and stood to greet his friends.

~THIRTEEN~

After a frustrating thirty minutes, Petricek had risked a walk past the café; it appeared to be closed. The sign in the front door window certainly gave him that snippet of information. However, nothing was ever as it seemed in his type of work. The unofficial motto at the Státní bezpečnost Headquarters back in Prague was, 'Never Punch an Elk.' It wasn't as snappy as some of those Latin mottos, he realised, but it was what it was.

A second walk past a few minutes later gave him more hope, and after gaining access to the rear of the café by way of the plot of empty land next door, and quietly jemmying the fire door with a length of scaffold pole he found there, he was pretty convinced that the property was, for the time being anyway, vacant.

Once in through the door he stood stock still.

Listening.

For ten minutes he stood near the broken doorway in case of a silent alarm, or more probably anybody hearing his efforts at the rear door with a scaffold pole, and giving the Police time to get there, if they were on their way. Satisfied that he had the place to himself for the foreseeable future, he began a thorough, systematic search.

After forty minutes he was sure that the valise was not there, the big guy in the fedora must have… The fedora! There, on a hook by the door hung the very same hat. He was sure of it. He picked it up and inspected the inside of it looking for a name and address that quite evidently was not forthcoming.

He had lost his valise, but now? Now he had a hat! This euphoria only lasted a nanosecond, it could have been a picosecond but he really wasn't counting. He was still in deep trouble and he pondered this situation as he made his way out of the burgled premises and unnoticed into the Derbyshire afternoon.

~FOURTEEN~

'Pick this up,' ordered Tiger to a confused Adrian.

'What is it?' enquired Adrian.

'What does it look like?' asked Margaret.

'A valise?'

Tiger chastised him, 'stop behaving like a school boy and pick the damn thing up.'

Adrian picked up the valise and placed it on the bench saying, 'crikey! What's in there? Part of a dead body?'

'There is nothing in it Adrian my old mate, that's the point I am trying to make.'

'Well if you say it's empty, I am sure that it is. But it isn't…have you got a pocket knife?'

Adrian unzipped the valise and Tiger handed over his antique, pearl handled 'Grandpas Market' steel folding knife from Germany, and watched as his friend dug into the lining of the valise.

'It's lined with bloody lead old boy, look!' Exclaimed Adrian, and three heads bobbed forward and eyed the dull grey, thin slabs of metal that made up the interior.

Tiger made a decision. 'Right, this is not the time to dissect this thing. We have got work to do on it, but not here. Adrian, show us the exact bench you were sitting on when you met your friend the photo album collector, and we'll need a complete description, a rundown of what happened, who said what to whom, time durations, which person left the park first and directions of travel, are you okay with that?'

'I sure am,' replied Adrian, 'so follow me.' Then he turned on his heel and walked further into the park.

'Here we are,' stated Adrian. They'd arrived at an unremarkable bench about one hundred yards away. They all sat down.

'Why were you sat here?' Asked Tiger.

'It was random really,' answered Adrian. I come here maybe twice a week, it's fairly quiet and I can get some half decent shots of the wildlife. It's not the Serengeti, but it has its moments.'

'We passed three benches to get to this part of the Park,' noted Tiger. 'Maggie, if you lean forward we can see two subtle lines, and the word 'Elk' scratched into the back rest behind you.'

She complied, and as Adrian leaned over and peered at the marks, Margaret appeared to speak for them both. 'Kids! Kids scratch stuff onto park benches all the time, they have done for generations, so what?'

Tiger thought for a moment and stood up. 'Aye, they do, but the three benches we just passed had no marks at all. Graffiti free, so I'm asking myself why has this bench been marked, and not the others? And I have come to the conclusion that this bench is special. The two lines are not random, and the word 'ELK' has significance.'

'Ere Lies Kilroy?' Ventured Adrian, giving Margaret a friendly punch and grinning from ear to ear at his little joke... until Tiger frowned at him.

'Significant? In what way? asked Margaret.

Tiger was talking and thinking on his feet at the same time. He spoke slowly. 'Significant in the way that the Czechoslovakian Secret Intelligence Service uses the word 'Elk' in its motto, but I am unsure about the two lines. I'm thinking this is a meeting point and those lines indicate the number of days until the next meeting or the days since the last one'

'Wow!' Exclaimed Adrian. 'I met the bloke yesterday, and again last night and he definitely mentioned another meeting so the next meeting will be today or perhaps tomorrow?'

'Maybe, maybe not old friend, there are two scratches though…what did you do whilst sat here yesterday? Were you taking photographs for example?'

'Nope, it was quite busy and any wildlife would have been scarce. I was quietly sitting, minding my own business flicking through a portfolio of pictures I'd taken at last week's air show at RAF Scampton, when I was joined by the fellow I met last night. He just plonked himself next to me, we remarked on the weather and he whispered 'Basketcase.'

Margaret stifled a giggle. 'He knew you quite well then…'

Adrian laughed, 'I'd never seen the chap before in my life, but you know what it's like around these parts, bloody weirdoes for the most part.'

'So, you can't remember exactly what was said then?' Adding, 'can you recall if anything sounded a bit coded, out of the ordinary?'

'I can't recall if I did or didn't. I may have said something along the lines of it's a grand old day, and he mentioned some nonsense about a long hard winter ahead, but that was only to avoid a confrontation with the bloke.' He then asked to look at my photographs, which I reluctantly handed over.'

'Dear God Adrian, you stumbled across the contact password! And then?'

'He gave them back to me and said that they were very good, and that he wished to buy them. Frankly I was stunned. The chap was obviously a fruitcake, so I stalled for a bit, gave him the name of a pub I last went into ten years ago and said I'd meet him there that evening if he was serious about buying them. He just got up and left, I didn't take any notice of where he went as I honestly never thought I'd see him again.'

'But you did turn up at The Red Cow last night?'

'I did. After I got home I thought long and hard. You know I have been trying to make money outside of my wedding stuff, that side of the business is really slow at the moment, so I thought what have I got to lose? He'll either be there and I'll make a couple of quid, or he'll be a no-show and I get to have myself a mini pub crawl.'

Adrian then gave Tiger and Margaret a ten minute outline of the conversation he'd had the previous evening in the Red Cow Public House.

'He's got the wrong bloke,' said Tiger. 'He thinks you're a contact named 'Basketcase' and he thinks he's buying photographs which he really shouldn't have.'

'Blimey!' replied an astonished Adrian.

'Give us a description of this fellow,' Margaret butted in.

'Well, he was about 5'10'tall heavy build, muscled maybe but turned to fat, scruffily dressed in a ratty looking mackintosh that belonged in a flea market bin. Spoke in a heavy foreign accent.

'Eastern European?'

'I've never heard an Eastern European speak'

'Think really bad spy film.'

'Yep that would do it. Maybe he could be Eastern European.'

'Do you think it's possible that it's the same man we saw in the café on the London Road this morning, Tiger?'

'Well that stretches the bounds of coincidence!' exclaimed Adrian.

'Maybe,' stated Tiger. 'But how many foreign spies are there in Derby this week? Not many I'd wager. He certainly fits the description, I wasn't happy with the man at the café, he was so shifty he made the hairs on the back of my neck stand on end, and now we have his valise...And it's lined with bloody lead. We need to get back to Maggie's place and have a proper look at this valise.'

His two friends nodded their agreement, before Adrian peeled off to his apartment and Tiger and Margaret headed for her house on Midland Road.   It was then that Tiger realised he had left his hat at the London Road cafeteria.

~FIFTEEN~

Petricek Dvorak had checked into another run down hotel, this time on Railway Terrace. He was asked to pay a deposit for two nights in advance, a paltry sum that he reluctantly handed over and curbed his anger when his request for a receipt was curtly denied. He had caused enough problems in the area that morning and didn't want to exacerbate his situation.

He was supposed to be undercover, slinking about the area collecting general information and photographs, not causing young waitresses grief and arguing with hotel staff. Up until the loss of his valise he'd been doing just fine, and he really needed to get that back before his next meeting with 'Basketcase' at Arboretum Park the following day.

A train entering the nearby station sounded its dual tone horn and rattled the windows. He swore in his native language, laid back on the flimsy mattress, pulled the stolen fedora over his face and began to think.

~SIXTEEN~

Back at Margaret's, Tiger suggested that they go for ride, take advantage of the break in the weather, and it would give him some time to think and, although he never mentioned it, it wouldn't hurt to check out her '66 Velocette Venom. Damn, that motorcycle was beautiful.

Margaret donned her tight leather jeans and a somewhat unladylike pair of bike boots; a black leather jacket, with a white silk scarf tucked in, finished the ensemble. Motorcycling clothing was not designed to win any fashion awards but she was giving it a damn good go.

Once outside, she tossed Tiger a set of keys and he opened the garage door to the side of her house whilst she donned her crash helmet. There, right there under a brown dust sheet the fast little motorcycle was sleeping. Tiger whipped off the sheet and wheeled the machine across the pavement and onto the road next to his own. Painted gloss back, it showed no sign of actual use since it had left the showroom two years earlier, although a glance at the speedometer mileage reading of 4000 miles told a different story.

Tiger booted his Triumph into life and watched Margaret as she tickled the carburettor float needle valve, pulled the clutch in and slowly booted the kick-start a couple of times building up a bit of compression and allowing lubrication to prime the important bits. Once she was happy that the piston was at its highest point in the cylinder - a skill not every biker had mastered - she flicked on the ignition and kicked down hard with her right booted leg. The engine crashed into life and settled into a steady gurgle. Tiger doubted very much that he could start her bike first kick, it was a difficult procedure. He was impressed.

Above the noise of the two British motorcycle engines Margaret laughed and shouted at Tiger. 'After you, big boy!'

Tiger obliged, pulled in the clutch, hoisted the gear change into first, winked at Margaret and pulled off with a showboating rear wheel powerslide that lasted about twenty yards. The rear of his bike threatening to pull to the left as Tiger gently counter steered to the left to compensate.

Margaret was more composed -she didn't need to show off. The real skills would be shown out on the open road and she had those skills nailed. It took around twenty minutes of steady riding to get to the point where they could see Derby in the rear view mirrors and hit the open road. Tiger had taken the lead up until this point when Margaret dropped down into third gear and opened her throttle. At 6,200 revs per minute her machine poured out 34 brake horsepower and every one of those horses were currently stampeding past Tiger as she changed up to fourth and roared past him.

Tiger was not surprised to see her pass him and was content to follow and listen to the sound of the engine whistling through the fishtail exhaust. Her body was poised, moulded to her motorcycle, her road position was inch perfect around every corner as she shifted her weight from left to right and it was an absolute joy watching Margaret in total control of that magnificent machine.

Two hours later they were back at Margaret's town house on Midland Road, both riders flushed with adrenalin. Tiger pushed his goggles to the top of his helmet and let out a lungful of air. 'You haven't lost the art Maggie. That was a cracking ride out.'

'I enjoyed it Tiger, I love riding with you and we'll do it again soon, but now let's get cleaned up.'

~SEVENTEEN~

Tiger had phoned Adrian to let him know he was welcome to pop over and have a closer look at the valise and knowing that it would take him some 40 minutes he shared the shower with Margaret, where they practiced a different type of riding, with Tiger taking the lead role.

Adrian had arrived and work had begun on the valise. Maggie had cleared some space on the kitchen table for it and was preparing tea whilst Tiger and Adrian set about dissecting the innards. Using his trusty pocket knife, Tiger carefully started cutting away the interior cloth lining whilst Adrian held the material to one side slowly revealing more and more lead.

Maggie placed two cups of Earl Grey tea on the table. 'Here you go chaps' she said. The two men were so absorbed in their activity they didn't appear to hear her.

'I said here you go chaps.'

'Thanks Maggie,' they chorused.

'We could do with a break. I'm pretty sure this thing is empty, there's obviously a reason why it's lined with lead and that's a concern,' said Tiger.

'Shoplifting?' ventured Margaret.

'I'm fairly certain it's nothing to do with shoplifting. It's been constructed very carefully by someone who knows what they're doing,' said Tiger.

'Smuggling?' Queried Adrian. 'I reckon it's for smuggling photographs past customs.'

'Smuggling is probably right on the button,' said Tiger. 'But you wouldn't use lead slabs to hide photographs from the boys and girls on the border. You'd use lead slabs to hide something made of metal. A weapon maybe.'

'Jeez,' whistled Adrian. 'A gun! This is more serious than I thought. My life could have been in danger last night. I don't like this. I do not like this one little bit.'

'It's only an educated guess my friend,' replied Tiger.

'Your educated guesses have a nasty habit of turning out to be deadly bloody accurate facts old boy.

Tiger remained silent. He looked up at Margaret but she pointedly avoided his gaze. He took a mental snapshot of that moment. It's what he did.

Margaret's phone started ringing in the hallway. Unlike a standard phone this gave off a sort of warbling noise. Margaret stood up and said. 'I'll get that,' as she moved towards the hallway.

'Is that a phone?' asked Adrian.

'Aye, it's a Trim phone.' Replied Tiger. 'A new-fangled thing, it won't catch on but Maggie loves all these new gadgets.'

'Trim phone?' Another question from Adrian.

'It's an acronym my friend.' he spelled it out. 'T. R. I. M. it stands for Tone Ring Illuminator Model,' Tiger explained.

'Every day's a school day,' retorted Adrian as he leant back and tasted his black tea-leaf and bergamot oil beverage.

Tiger was straining to hear the muffled one sided conversation that Margaret was having on the phone. He picked up the words, 'yes it's safe,' and 'he has no idea,' before Margaret gently closed the hallway door shutting off any more access to her hushed conversation.

~EIGHTEEN~

Petricek was desperate. He fully understood his orders and he was under no illusion as to how his masters back in Prague would pick apart every detail of this mission once he returned. They always did. The cross-examinations he'd undergone after previous missions would have broken even the most hardened spy. Indeed, many had simply disappeared after an operational de-brief. Petricek could hazard a guess as to where they had gone, but was in no mind to dwell on the subject.

With all this in mind, he exited the red public telephone box outside his hotel. His UK contact could only be called upon in the gravest of situations. He considered this situation fairly grave and so had made the call.

~NINETEEN~

'I need to pop out,' said Margaret, when she re-entered the living room. That was Daddy on the phone. He's coming over tonight and I need to stock up on food.'

'Bit short notice,' said Tiger.

Margaret had sensed a belligerent tone to Tiger's reply.

'He's my father, Tiger, he paid for this place and he can come over whenever he pleases.'

'Fair enough Maggie. We need to get out anyway. We have to make a plan for tomorrow. I am convinced that matey boy is going to be the park tomorrow and we don't have much time.'

Tiger and Adrian stood and headed for the door. Tiger held the valise tightly to his chest.

'You're not taking that thing with you are you Tiger?' asked Margaret, pointing to the valise.

'Aye, I am. I have plans for this,' replied Tiger.

'Surely it'd be safer here?' suggested Margaret.

'I think that whoever is near this valise, is not safe at all,' replied Tiger.

'Where are you going?' Another question.

'To find my hat.' Another answer.

~TWENTY~

Petricek entered a busy little building called The George Hotel on Midland Street. He idly noted that they offered accommodation, but it was a little pricey, and anyway it was far too busy for his needs. His contact had picked the place for the meeting and he was surprised at how close it was to his seedy run down place on Railway Terrace. It would've been a mere five minute brisk walk, if he'd done 'brisk', which he didn't, so it was a fifteen minute amble. He waited for two or three minutes to be served. The young couple beside him at the bar had no idea what they wanted to drink. Petricek guessed they were under age. Or idiots. A bottle blonde girl in her mid-twenties with an enormous cleavage eventually got around to serving him with a large cheap whisky and asked him to cheer up.

He ignored her attempt at pleasant banter and paid for his drink without any pleasantries. He really wasn't in the mood. He carried his drink across the wooden floor of the bar area and dropped his ample frame into a faux leather armchair where he could command a view of his surroundings, and the main entrance.

She walked into the bar. He noticed her immediately. Smartly dressed and confident, she made no attempt to purchase a drink and headed straight for him.

'No need to stand,' she said.

'I wasn't going to,' he thought. 'All this standing up on account of a lady being present was utter lunacy. Women should be in the kitchen making Potato Soup, or in the bedroom making babies. Either way it didn't involve him standing up. Well, apart from once, and that was a disaster, and he wasn't trying to make soup at the time.

But he said nothing.

She took a seat opposite him.' This is a huge break in procedure,' she said.

'This is a huge problem I have,' he replied.

'I understand that you fool, and I am going to have to report this meeting and your total imbecilic approach to this mission.'

Petricek spluttered his indignation.

'How dare you speak to me like that' he hissed.

'I'll speak to you in the manner you deserve and keep your voice down. You're not in some Prague whorehouse.'

'I don't go to whorehouses,' he simpered, 'I have a loving wife. You know that.'

'I really don't have time for this,' she retorted, 'and here, this belongs to you.' She slid a white plastic bag across the table and Petricek slipped the heavy item beside him out of view.

'Thank you,' he whispered, truly grateful, 'and the valise?'

'Just that for now. I am working on getting the valise.'

'Thank you.'

'Well, that concludes our business for the time being.' She stood up and turned to leave then stopped herself and pointed at his untouched drink. 'Are you drinking that?'

'Later.'

She reached down, picked up the tumbler of cheap whisky and swallowed it in one gulp and slammed it back down on the table.

'Disgusting,' she commented, and strode towards the exit.

'Why do these shitty people insist on drinking my whisky?' he said out loud.

~TWENTY ONE~

Tiger and Adrian walked North along the London Road. 'Where are we headed?' asked Adrian.

'I'm hoping to find a café,' replied Tiger, a little self-conscious of the stares he was getting from other pedestrians and the odd car driver as he wheeled along the valise.

'Well we have passed two already old boy, so you obviously aren't that thirsty,' said Adrian.

'That's the one I want,' he replied, nodding his head at the café nestled between a butchers and an empty plot of land.

They crossed the road and approached the café, Tiger wasn't sure it'd be open and was pleasantly surprised to see that it was.

Just as Tiger was about to open the door, it opened for him, and a large uniformed Police Officer stepped onto the pavement.

'Evening Officer,' said Tiger, giving the lawman a curt nod.

'Evening Sir.'

'Has there been some trouble?'

'Are you gentlemen regulars here?'

'No Constable,' butted in Adrian, 'I've never been here before in my life.'

'Well there appears to have been a break-in earlier today, the owner is a bit shaken up but she's still serving tea.'

'Thank goodness, I'm parched,' answered Tiger, 'I hope nobody was hurt. Was anything taken?'

'Not for me to say Sir,' replied the Constable. He held the door open and allowed Tiger and Adrian to squeeze past his portly frame and enter the café.

'Hang on a minute Sir!' The Police Officer held onto Tigers arm. 'What's that thing when it's at home?'

'It's just an empty valise,' replied Tiger, not at all pleased with the prospect of being apprehended whilst a nosy bluebottle inspected the valise. A suspiciously heavy valise. One that he didn't own, and didn't wish to explain the circumstances of its coming into his possession.

Tiger looked the lawman directly in the eye, a sign of honesty. A few seconds passed.

The Police Officer released his grip on Tigers arm. 'A valise you say? Well, have a good evening gents.'

Tiger smiled and breathed a sigh of relief as he entered the café. It didn't actually look at first glance as if it was actually open. The lights were off, there were no customers and it was very quiet. The two men stood at the counter. 'Hello! Service!' Tiger called. 'Is there anybody at home?'

A frail looking lady of indeterminate age appeared from the kitchen area. Tiger noticed that she looked worn out and could do with a good night's sleep. Or a three week Caribbean cruise.

'Good afternoon.' said Tiger, I gathered from the Police Officer that has just left that you are still open for tea?'

'We are open,' she replied, 'but only for tea, I can't be making food I'm afraid. It's my ankle you see.' She shuffled around the counter and offered up a spindly leg for her latest customers to see a bandage wrapped around her right ankle. 'Keeps flaring up you see. Been to the Doctors, but they're not interested. Nobody is interested anymore, I don't know what's come over people in the last thirty years. They've even cut back on the buses, cut back on the buses I tell you! How am I supposed to visit Ethel if there are no buses? Bloody liberty if you ask me. And what with my Stan no longer with us, it's a struggle I tell you.'

Tiger smiled, he felt some empathy for the woman. Trying to run a small business nowadays was an uphill task and he wanted to keep on the right side of her.

'I thought you had staff to help you here?' asked Tiger, 'young lass called Jackie? She's the reason I popped in really, she knows a friend of mine.'

'Jackie isn't here,' the café owner stated, 'she was here this morning as I was around the corner at the Community Centre having my ankle seen to by a Doctor Patel. I'm no racist but Doctor Patel? I tell you it's not right, I doubt if he's even qualified. Where did he come from? What happened to Doctor Smith…?'

Tiger gently interrupted, he didn't want to get involved in a dialogue about the Government's immigration policy, Lord knows how long this woman would be banging on about it if he didn't steer the conversation along a more fruitful route.

'I saw Jackie this morning,' said Tiger, 'a nice lass, very helpful, although she never had time to make my tea.'

'She doesn't have time to make anybody's tea!' retorted the woman. 'I get so many complaints about her. Do you know not long back, four Americans came in, they might have been Canadian, I mean they all speak the same don't they? They spend a lot of money wherever they go, I know that much. My Stan couldn't stand 'em. The war you know.'

Tiger didn't know, and had very little inclination to find out.

'My friends call me 'Tiger' and this here is my good friend Adrian. What do you say if we sat down and you made us a large pot of tea?'

'I can do better than that Tiger. You can call me Maureen and whilst the kettle is boiling I'll open a fresh packet of biscuits as well.' She walked back behind the counter muttering, 'Tiger indeed.'

Tiger and Adrian planted themselves at a table whilst Maureen busied herself in the kitchen.

'I do believe you have a plan,' said Adrian, absently fondling a large red plastic tomato.

'I do believe I have,' replied Tiger. Adding, 'can you put that ketchup container down, they're not the most hygienic of things.' Privately thinking the top of that thing looks about as clean as a teddy bear's arse.

'Ketchup?' Good God man, whatever next?' He said as he replaced the condiment and pulled a napkin from the dispenser to wipe his hands.

'Tea's next I believe,' noted Tiger as Maureen cleared her counter and hobbled towards them with a loaded tray.

'Tea for two gentlemen I fancy,' stated Maureen placing the tray between the two men, 'and Ladies Fingers, opened fresh just for you.

'I love a Ladies Finger,' smirked Adrian, who then looked suitably chastened as Tiger glared at him.

'Thank you Maureen,' said Tiger, 'just what we wanted, something to wet our whistles. Why don't you join us and tell us about the break in?'

'Who told you about the break in?' Asked Maureen suddenly looking alarmed.

'The Policeman as we were coming in,' replied Tiger.

'Oh,' said Maureen looking confused for a second, and then catching herself, 'of course. It happened sometime this afternoon. I left the Community Centre, the one around the corner, at about 12 o'clock and went home. I only live around down the road on Canal Street. number thirty six. It was the only house on our street that got bombed during the war you know. We're very proud of that. Me and Stan. Stan's not with us anymore but he took that shrapnel wound to his head to his grave as a proud man you know...'

She looked as if she was about to start crying. Adrian offered her the napkin he was clutching.

'You don't get shrapnel like that anymore,' she whispered as she wiped a streak of crusty tomato ketchup across her forehead.

'Did anything get stolen?' asked Tiger, once again glaring at a bemused Adrian.

'I don't think so,' said Maureen. 'The till wasn't damaged, not that there was much in there, we don't seem to get any big spenders in here, and the Americans and Canadians haven't made an appearance since, well, since Jackie was rude to them...'

~TWENTY TWO~

Twenty minutes after his contact had left him staring at an empty whisky tumbler Petricek exited the George Hotel and walked back to his hotel on Railway Terrace. Once ensconced in his tiny room, he removed a small handgun from the white plastic bag his contact had handed him. The Russian designed Zastava Tokarev pistol M70A, weighed in at just one kilogramme when loaded with a nine round magazine, and the 4½ inch barrel was all that was required to steer a 9mm copper coated steel projectile towards an intended mark.

It wasn't an accurate weapon by any means, so if Petricek wanted to play the really ruthless man for a couple of minutes, he'd have to get within bad breath distance of his target. This had never been a problem for him in the past and he had no particular reason to think it'd be a problem in the future.

He struggled to pop the magazine off as the Serbian built model he was handling wasn't built to the exacting standards of Western small arms and had a tendency to jam, but he eventually succeeded and removed nine deadly looking bullets placing each one on the rickety little table beside his bed.

Removing a clean handkerchief from one of his pockets he thoroughly removed any trace of his fingerprints from each round before clipping them back home against the spring in the magazine.

Automatic weapons had an awkward by-product. After each shot the exhausted brass cartridge was ejected from the weapon and sent spinning away to the right, and they had a propensity to roll into little spaces that an experienced Police investigator could find and use as evidential gold dust.

He was not in the habit of leaving evidence lying around, but sometimes a quick exit was called for after a target had been eliminated, meaning there often wasn't the time to go shuffling around on his hands and knees looking for spent brass.

A train noisily rattled its way into the railway station as he lay on the bed and attempted to get a couple of hours sleep, silently cursing British Rail and anything else British.

~TWENTY THREE~

'Would you mind if I left this valise with you overnight?' Asked Tiger, 'Jackie knows all about it.'

'I'm sure we can do that for you young man, I'll put it in the back.'

As Maureen wheeled the valise to the stockroom at the rear of the café, Tiger glanced up at the coat rack by the front door.

He turned to face Adrian and said, 'There was something stolen.'

'Really? What would that be old friend?'

'My bloody fedora, that's what. Now, who would break in here during daylight hours, have a good rummage around, not bother with a couple of quid in the till and steal nothing other than my hat?'

'Are you thinking about our Czechoslovakian friend?'

'I most certainly am. He came back here to retrieve his valise I'm sure of it.'

'Then we'd better get cracking and find your hat old boy,' said Adrian, getting to his feet and craftily pocketing the last of the Ladies Fingers.

~TWENTY FOUR~

Margaret Thornton once again was stood in front of the full length mirror in her bedroom. The maid had been in earlier and made good the tangled mess of sheets and blankets that had been scattered across the room following her bedroom antics with Tiger Johnnie some hours previously. This time she was fully clothed and was talking to her father in the reflection.

A tall thin reed of a man, he carried a very serious face. Clean shaven and with piercing, inquisitive eyes that never missed a trick, Sir Andrew Thornton was impeccably dressed in a bespoke three piece blue pinstriped suit, made to his exacting specifications by the master tailor at Huntsman & Sons from their premises at 11 Saville Row in London. His highly polished Oxford brogues poked out from beneath the turn ups of his sharply creased trousers.

Leaning casually against the door jamb he said, 'I noticed a crash helmet and goggles in the hallway, Margaret, so I presume that Tiger isn't far away?'

'He's out and about Daddy,' replied Margaret as she put the finishing touches to her make up. Adding, 'he'll be joining us for drinks after dinner.'

'How is the young gallivanting so-and-so? I haven't heard from him since that awful Moroccan business. Still scooting about on his motorcycle and destroying ladies' hearts I suppose?'

Margaret blushed. She had not told her father of her affection for Tiger, although he had probably guessed, and she thought he'd throw a blue fit if he knew they were actually (sort of) full time lovers.

'He's fine Daddy. As I told you on the phone, his friend Adrian is in a spot of bother with a Czechoslovakian spy and he is here to sort it out.'

'That's what I'm afraid of darling, I know of this Czech fellow, he's called Petricek Dvorak and he's a nasty piece of work, had some dealings with him when I was on the East European desk back in '58. Word back at the office is that he's over here on a covert mission collecting photographs from an Air Force Sergeant called Jack Dean, code named 'Basketcase.'

'And I thought you'd travelled up from the City just to see me?' Margaret purred.

The old spymaster didn't miss a beat. He knew his daughter well.

'Sergeant Dean has been on our radar for about nine months now and we'd love to catch him at it. We're pretty sure he's done nothing technically wrong with regard to the Official Secrets Act as yet, but we can't have our servicemen meeting up with chaps like him and not reporting it through the proper channels. It's just not cricket.'

'Daddy dear, why don't you go the kitchen and pop open a bottle of wine or something, all this talk about work is simply too much.'

'Why certainly darling,' replied Sir Andrew, making no effort to move from his position in the bedroom doorway.

'Well what are you waiting for Daddy?'

'I'm just a little curious,' he replied, pointing at the lampshade hanging from the centre of the ceiling, 'as to how on earth a piece of your underwear managed to get up there...'

~TWENTY FIVE~

Tiger and Adrian parted company outside the cafeteria as Maureen locked the door behind them, after blowing them each a cheeky kiss.

'See you in the morning Adrian.'

'Are you sure there isn't anything I can do tonight?

'Positive old friend. Get home, lock your door, put some Joan Bakewell on and relax. I'll see you at 10am.'

'Joan Baez.'

'What?'

'You said Joan Bakewell. I listen to Joan Baez.'

'I know you do. I'm thinking about the television my friend, she's on Late Night Line-Up tonight on BBC 2. I heard that she's 'thinking man's crumpet' surely you don't want to miss that...?'

Before he'd finished speaking, his old friend was practically running down the road.

Tiger walked the short distance back to Margaret's house, stopping short when he spotted the black Daimler Sovereign parked on the street outside her property.

Keeping to the shadows, he approached the sleek luxury vehicle from behind. Moving stealthily up to the passenger door, he opened it and swung into the passenger seat in one fluid motion.

'Now then you old bugger,' exclaimed Tiger to the startled man behind the steering wheel.

'You bloody idiot!' 'You want to be careful pulling stunts like that, I'm bloody armed tonight,' replied the man behind the wheel.

'Gruff' Wetherspoon and Tiger went back ten years or so. They'd served as cooks in the Army Catering Corps. At least that was what they told strangers who asked about their military history. It kind of killed any conversation stone dead, which was pretty much the whole point.

In reality they had both been members of 'G' Squadron, the elite inner unit of the Special Air Service reserved for Guardsmen who had left their respective Battalions, passed the gruelling marathon known as 'selection' and entered a place where their lives would be for ever challenged.

In all that time, Tiger had never known his mate's real first name. Gruff was never actually gruff - it wasn't in his nature - he was a very quietly spoken man, so why he was so called had been lost in the mists of time. What was known about Gruff was that he was an expert in hand-to-hand combat. Under a pseudonym, he'd represented Great Britain with his mastery of Judo and Karate. He could speak four languages fluently, and had declined a commission with the Grenadier Guards opting instead to join the proud Regiment as a Guardsman, a basic soldier.

He'd sailed around the world single handed. Twice. He'd saved Tiger's life. Twice. But he couldn't ride a motorcycle...much to Tiger's everlasting amusement. He just couldn't get to grips with it and had long since given up trying.

'I suppose old Thorny is in with Margaret then?' Tiger was using the wholly unofficial nickname of Sir Andrew Thornton, head of second directorate Russian desk at Century House on Upper Thames Street in London. Headquarters of the Secret Intelligence Service, Military Intelligence Section 6, or MI6 as it was more commonly referred to.

'Well seeing as I'm sitting in his car outside her house, I'd say you're wearing Sherlock's cloak tonight, Tiger. Did you bring a deerstalker and a pipe?'

Tiger smiled, 'and where are you off to tonight Gruff?' Or would you have to kill me if you told me?'

Gruff laughed, 'I have no idea mate, I just go wherever the old man tells me to.'

'Well I'm having drinks with him and Maggie at 10'clock at the Old Grey Whistle.' Tiger was referring to a top end club on the 'right' side of the town. It was the sort of place that he felt uncomfortable in. There was always some 'Hooray Henry' acting like a fool, someone who'd be fawning over Maggie, generally being a pest and begging for a dig in the throat. He really did try his best to avoid such places.

'You're not popping up to say hello then?' asked Gruff.

'Nope,' replied Tiger. 'Things to do, people to see, you know how it is.'

'I certainly do mate.'

Tiger exited the car, bade his friend goodnight, told him to lock the passenger door and faded into the shadows.

~TWENTY SIX~

Sir Andrew was sat in the back of his car next to his daughter Margaret. He'd earlier asked Gruff to take them to the Patterson Club in the middle of the City. The Patterson Club was a private members club situated behind the John Lewis department store on St Peters Street. The entrance was an anonymous, heavily painted black door covered by a discreet security camera and it would be an understatement to say that it was not a well-known address.

Gruff guided the powerful 2½ litre V8 Daimler North through the Derby City streets with skill and precision and was ever alert to his passengers' conversations.

'Where are we going Daddy?' Margaret asked her father.

'Oh, it's just a little club restaurant owned by a friend of mine,' replied Sir Andrew, 'I don't think you've been there before.'

'It's not the Patterson is it, Daddy dear?'

'How on earth do you know about the Patterson?' Replied her Father.

'Er, I suppose I must have heard you mention it,' answered Margaret.

An awkward pause followed this brief dialogue. Sir Andrew was pretty damn sure he'd never mentioned the club in his daughter's presence, and Margaret silently cursed herself for blurting out the name. Gruff saved them from further embarrassment as they pulled smoothly to a stop.

'Here we go Sir, safely at your destination.' Gruff stated whilst looking directly at his boss in the rear view mirror. 'I'll go and 'do the business' if you'd both like to sit tight."

He exited the vehicle and approached the black painted door. To the left, a brass bell push was situated about 5 feet up. To stop kids messing about with it he presumed. There was a complete absence of locks, door handles, letter boxes and other paraphernalia that usually accompany a business front entrance. He pressed the bell for about 3 seconds and waited.

A lock clicked and the door opened slowly, revealing a short stocky man in his sixties wearing a dinner jacket and black bow tie.

'Evening Sir,' a pleasant welcome from the well-dressed guardian of the door.

'Good evening,' Gruff replied. 'I believe you are expecting Sir Andrew Thornton, up from London with his daughter.'

'Indeed they are expected and if you'd like to escort them to the door I'll see to the rest of the proceedings.'

Gruff nodded and turned back to the Daimler. He opened up the offside passenger door, had a careful look around the area, including the rooftops, and nodded at his boss. Sir Andrew exited the vehicle and had the briefest conversation with his driver before taking his daughter's hand as she slid along the seat to exit from the same door.

Sir Andrew entered the building together with his daughter and the heavy black door silently closed behind them.

Gruff took a packet of Marlboro from his jacket pocket, he put one of the cigarettes into the corner of his mouth, found a Zippo lighter in another pocket, snapped it open and lit his smoke. 'Well that was a bloody weird journey,' he said to himself. The whispered chat that

Thorny had with him just a moment ago, only added to his unease. He took a last drag of his cigarette, ground the half-finished smoke under his heel before getting back into the Daimler, and went in search of a phone.

~TWENTY SEVEN~

Tiger was sitting at the end of the long bar at The Old Grey Whistle. It was a bit early for the posh idiots that usually frequented the place, and he was just killing time whilst he waited for Maggie and her father to show up.

A pretty looking girl in a red velvet mini dress, sitting alone halfway down the bar, had been eyeing him up for at least twenty minutes as he sipped on his pint of Worthington White Shield IPA. He was dressed in the same clothes that he'd worn to ride his motorcycle that morning, and although his jeans had long dried out, and some girl was flirting with him, he still felt underdressed.

He was aware of a telephone ringing somewhere in the building but couldn't place it as 'Louie Louie' by The Kingsmen was playing quietly on a juke box in the corner. Tiger loved this version, and tapped his engineer boot on the wooden floor to the beat, as the almost incomprehensible words of Jack Ely floated around the bar.

The bartender approached Tiger.

'Excuse me Sir. Are you the gentleman known as 'Tiger'?

Tiger hesitated. Only a handful of people knew he was coming to this particular establishment at this particular time, and the bartender was definitely not one of them.

'Who wants to know?' Asked Tiger.

'You have a telephone call Sir, a gentleman calling himself, er, Wetherspoon.'

'Then that's me, where's the phone?'

'End of the bar Sir, it's off the hook.'

Tiger stood and walked the length of the bar. His leather boots thudded into the wooden floor with every casual step. The lady in the red dress never took her eyes off him as he approached her, turning her head as he passed her, and continued along the bar counter.

He located the phone and picked up the handset.

'Tiger.'

'Hello mate, it's Gruff. I took a guess that you'd be in the Old Grey Whistle about now, you were always up for an early drink if business had finished for the day.'

'Well business hasn't finished for the day and I'm sipping on some Godawful pint of beer called White

Shield. They don't serve Double Diamond in here, the posh gits. Anyway, what's up mate?'

'There's been a change of plan regarding your evening get-together with the Thorntons. The Old Man had a quiet word with me about twenty minutes ago, I would have called earlier but the first two call boxes had been vandalised to within an inch of their lives.'

'Typical, What did he have to say then?'

'The meeting with 'Thorny is still on, at the Old Whistle, but Margaret won't be attending. He never elaborated as to why, but I have a funny feeling that he doesn't trust her. It's all a bit odd.'

'Everything's odd in Old Thorny's line of work mate. I presume you'll be driving him here?'

'I will, and I'll be joining the meeting.'

'I'm sure there's an innocent explanation to all this mate and I'll see you later then.'

'Roger that, be careful Tiger.'

'Will do.' Tiger ended the call by placing his finger on the cradle. He kept a hold of the handset as he pondered the conversation he'd just had with his most trusted friend, before carefully replacing it and heading for his seat.

'What's your name handsome?' The young lady in the red mini skirt sounded like she'd just completed her final four months at the Institut Villa Pierrefeu finishing school in Montreux, Switzerland.

Tiger was tempted to give her the brush off, but held himself in check as a plan started to slowly develop.

'It's 'Tiger' sweet cheeks, what's yours?'

'I'm Amanda, my friends call me Mandy though.'

'Well in that case I'll call you Mandy. You don't sound as if you're from around here Mandy?'

'Good God no! I live in Kensington.'

'Kensington London?'

'Oh you are funny Tiger! Is there another one? If there is I am completely unaware of it.'

For a reason Tiger couldn't initially comprehend she started giggling furiously. His look of bafflement made her giggle all the more.

'What's so funny?'

'Nothing really,' said Amanda between giggles, that were dangerously starting to sound like hiccups. 'I just giggle when I'm a bit nervous.'

'Do I make you nervous?'

'A bit,' her giggling/hiccup fit had started to ebb. 'Just a bit, you're so handsome it's taken me three stiff Martinis just to speak to you.'

'I see. Well there really isn't any need to be. I'm just an ordinary chap about to have a great couple of hours with a very attractive young lady called Mandy.'

There followed a pause of about five seconds where Tiger looked straight into Amanda's hazel eyes. Her mouth gaping, she looked as if she was about to drown.

'Oh. My. God,' she whispered. Then, still open mouthed she gasped. 'Really?'

'Aye lass. Let's split this dump and go and find ourselves some Double Diamond!'

~TWENTY EIGHT~

Petricek Dvorak awoke around 9.30 that evening. He'd managed to grab a couple of hours of troubled sleep. He needed to get his valise back because its absence troubled him greatly. His life depended on it. He was getting nowhere here in Derby and would have to get to London in order to work out a plan 'B'.

A quick glance out of the window informed him that the rain still persisted and he dressed accordingly, stuffing the small Tokarev pistol deep into the pocket of his cheap mackintosh. He donned Tiger's fedora and without bothering to lock his room door, he left the crummy hotel and headed for the railway station.

The station was closed. 'This country is shit,' he muttered and was about to leave when he spotted a uniformed porter exiting a side door and locking it.

'Excuse me!'

'Yes Sir. How may I help?'

'I need to get to London in the morning. What time is the first train?'

'You'll want the express from Manchester, arrives here at 8.45 and arrives at London Euston at around 11.30 Sir.'

Petricek doffed the fedora, bade the porter good evening and continued along Railway Terrace, heading North towards the River Derwent where he knew a little pub in the area that sold cheap whisky, and where there was very little chance of anybody drinking it for him.

~TWENTY NINE~

Amanda and Tiger had strolled no more than fifty paces from The Old Grey Whistle when Tiger spotted a taxi cab heading towards them, its yellow 'For Hire' sign hardly distinguishable in the light misty rainfall.

Placing his right thumb and forefinger into his mouth he managed a shrill whistle whilst lofting his left arm in order to catch the driver's attention. Amanda couldn't believe it when the taxi slowed and executed a 'U' turn and pulled up alongside them.

'How do you do that?'

'Do what? Whistle?'

'No silly, how do you get a cab like that? It's like we're in a movie or something.'

Tiger chuckled and held the rear passenger open for her before 'shooing her up the bench seat and swinging in beside her.

'Connaught Hotel please driver, and don't spare the horses.'

Amanda had explained earlier that she had planned on visiting a couple of friends and had booked a room at the Connaught, but one of them had been taken ill that morning and their plans for the day and evening had been cancelled. Amanda was travelling back to London the following morning. First train.

The taxi cab ride lasted a mere ten minutes. Tiger paid the fare and escorted Amanda up the steps and into the warmth of the Connaught Hotel foyer. There was nobody on the large wood panelled reception desk, so unimpeded by awkward questions they headed directly to the bar area where Tiger ordered and paid for a pint of Double Diamond bitter and a large Gin & Tonic for Amanda. He thought that might stop her giggling. Glancing in the large mirror behind the bar, he noticed that the big breasted barmaid was busy undoing a top button on her blouse as she sorted out his change.

She returned to his position with a beaming smile, he didn't need to glance down, the overspill of cleavage was clearly on show a minute or two earlier and he really didn't need to see any more. He pocketed his change and gave the barmaid his biggest, cheekiest smile and raised his eyebrows as he picked up the drinks.

She blushed.

Tiger moved on.

He joined Amanda at a corner table, away from a handful of men who he presumed were on business, and from where he could keep an eye on the doors. Old habits die hard.

Tiger started the conversation. 'I'll be quite truthful with you Amanda.'

'Please call me Mandy. What do you mean truthful?'

'Well to start with Mandy,' he said, looking directly into her eyes. 'You are a very attractive young lady who really shouldn't be out and about on her own. Then there's a problem that I have, which I was rather hoping that you could help me with.'

'I'll help if I can Tiger.'

Over the next thirty minutes Tiger explained what he wanted her to do, and after another round of drinks he gave her a peck on the cheek and he took his leave from the Connaught Hotel bar.

He walked across the empty foyer out the doors and down the steps into the chilly night rain. He pulled up the big collar of his leather motorcycle jacket and headed for The Old Grey Whistle, hoping he'd be as lucky with a cab ride as he'd been earlier.

105 Tigers Revenge

~THIRTY~

Sir Andrew Thornton was deep in thought. His driver bodyguard, Gruff, was seated two tables away from his chief in the lounge of The Old Grey Whistle, and whilst he appeared to be in deep in conversation with an attractive woman who was at least twenty years older, his attention was concentrated on his boss.

The old Spy Master unconsciously rotated the glass of 12 year old Castarède Cognac in his left hand, the dark amber liquid looking as if it should be sticking to the walls of his warm brandy snifter.

The Camacho Robusto cigar of dubious integrity sat unlit in the glass ashtray in front of him. Margaret was playing silly buggers again, he was sure of it. He had no proof other than some circumstantial events that she may be batting for the other side. After the Morocco incident she had promised him that nothing was amiss. She had promised, and a Thornton's promise was far better than a copper plated contract.

The door to the bar opened, allowing a blast of cold air to enter the warmth followed by a bedraggled looking Tiger. One or two people looked up momentarily before returning to their own business.

Tiger had fully scanned the premises within three steps of his entrance. Sir Andrew sat on his own, to the left, an unlit cigar in his ashtray. Gruff was seated two tables from Sir Andrew and nearer the door. He was chatting to some bit of mutton dressed as lamb and appeared not to notice him, although there was fat chance of that happening.

Two chaps sat on stools at the centre of the bar, one of which had been occupied some ninety minutes ago by Amanda. They had both looked up sharply as he entered and then looked away to carry on their conversation less than a second later.

No threat.

There wasn't anybody at all to his right. Not a big crowd of Hooray Henry's in this evening then, so it was looking just fine and dandy.

He approached the bar; the same bartender he'd met earlier was polishing glasses and watching him as he approached. He eyed Tiger with a mixture of disgust and apprehension, perhaps he fancied Amanda? He'd obviously seen them walk out together, not that long ago either and here he was back again. The cad! Tiger laughed to himself. No threat there either.

'What was I drinking earlier?' Tiger politely asked the barman who was in danger of polishing a beer glass into oblivion.

'Er, White Shield Sir, would you like another?'

'White Shield, that was it. Terrible stuff, made me a bit horny. Have you got something with less of an aphrodisiacal punch?

Tiger could spout out the big posh words when the occasion demanded, and he was enjoying the look of horror on the bartender's spotty face.

'I'm teasing you,' stated Tiger. 'I'll have a large brandy, no water no ice.'

'On the rocks then?'

'No. Over there at the same table as the distinguished looking gentleman who I presume is drinking Cognac.' Tiger smiled again. He loved using that 'on the rocks' line.

He strolled over to join Sir Andrew, who stood up and greeted him with a firm handshake.

'Sit down son you look like a drowned rat. Don't they have taxicabs in this godforsaken City?'

'I think I saw one earlier this evening Sir, and thanks for the offer of a seat, my drink is on its way to this table so that'll be very handy.'

'You're not so funny Tiger. I can't possibly see any trait in you that would lead me to believe that you have any good intentions towards my daughter.'

Tiger wasn't sure if the old boy was laughing at him or being deadly serious. 'Talking of which, will Margaret be joining us?'

'No Tiger she definitely will not be joining us, that's why I'm here and Gruff is over there.'

They both looked over at Gruff, who put his arm around the lady next to him, looked over at Tiger and winked.

'Good God,' harrumphed Sir Andrew, sitting down and taking a large swig of his drink. 'Sit down son, your drinks on its way and we need to talk.'

~THIRTY ONE~

Margaret Thornton ran a brush through her hair. She was stood in front of a full length mirror in the master bedroom; she was eyeing the sleeping, naked body of a man who was lying at full stretch on her bed. She was in a good mood.

———————————————

Petricek Dvorak was wide awake, his tongue was thick with cheap alcohol and he had nearly gagged after testing his breath, by breathing into his hand and smelling the disgusting cocktail of the previous night's drinking. He was in a foul mood.

———————————————

Gruff was putting on his suit in a hurry. The older woman on the bed in the small bedroom was likely to wake up at any minute. He didn't have the time to be in any sort of mood.

———————————————

Adrian was peeking through a small gap in the curtains at his lounge window. Nothing seemed amiss but he couldn't help feeling edgy. He really wasn't looking forward to today, and if his old friend wasn't in town he probably wouldn't even go out today.

_____

Tiger was pretending to be asleep, he could see the shadow of a woman through his eyelashes as she prepared herself for the day. He wasn't feeling too proud of himself.

_____

The sun was out, the forecasters on the radio were informing their listeners that it was going to be an Indian summer and to take advantage of a break from the dreary last couple of weeks.

The Manchester express train had left Manchester Piccadilly and was heading south. It was due to stop at Derby Central in sixty minutes before continuing on to London Euston. Its driver, Eddy Francombe, had been with the train company for thirty two years and was due to retire at the end of this one.

_____

The man who'd shared Margaret's bed opened his eyes and blinked away the Sandman. He asked,' who's the owner of the helmet and goggles on the table in the hall? They don't look like yours.

'Just a friend,' she replied, adding, 'they'll be gone today, don't worry.'

_____

Petricek Dvorak was famished. The cafeteria he'd broken into wasn't that far away but he daren't risk going back there, and the food was shit anyway and the staff there were lazy and tended to cry, and they stole stuff. He'd have to see if there was anything worth eating at the Railway Station before his train arrived.

Gruff had managed to sneak out of the woman's apartment without waking her. He was missing a sock and without his regimental tie. She could have them, a souvenir of his visit. He headed for the secure car park where he'd parked the Daimler and hoped that he could purchase some socks and a tie before picking up Sir Andrew.

~THIRTY TWO~

Tiger was showered and dressed and waiting with Amanda at the front of the Connaught. He had used the fire escape again to exit the building, the same way he had been let in. Amanda cleared checkout and the concierge had ordered a taxicab to the Railway Station.

'Let's get some breakfast first Tiger,' said Amanda.

'We'll divert the taxi to the cafeteria I told you about Mandy, It's only a short walk to the Station from there.'

Once safely ensconced in the back of the taxicab, Tiger explained the situation to the driver and settled back for the ride. He was dog tired and had so much to do but had to keep Amanda on-side.

'I feel so good when I'm with you Tiger, nice and safe. It's such a shame you can't come with me to Kensington. I know you said that you'll come down next week to pick up this special valise thing, but I do so wish it wasn't this way.'

'Trust me Mandy, if I didn't have pressing business here in Derby today, I'd be jumping on that train with you.'

The taxi stopped at the little cafeteria on London Road, it was open for business and the smell of bacon emanated from the kitchen, wafting around a couple of tables before storming out through the open front door and reaching the nose of the cab driver.

'If I wasn't so busy Sir, I'd let you buy me breakfast instead of the fare.'

'Next time my good fellow,' Tiger had replied giving him a good tip and escorted Amanda into the cheerful interior of the café.

~THIRTY THREE~

Petricek Dvorak had purchased a second class return ticket from the booking office at the Railway Station. He had checked the timetable, twice, and was now sitting on his own in a dreary corner of the departures hall, eating what had been advertised as a cheese and pickle sandwich, and a hot drink that had been advertised as coffee, but were in fact just shit.

So much for breakfast, he had thought as he idly scanned the hall checking out the commuters, the beggars and railway staff as they all carried on their business. He wasn't looking forward to the journey, but it was a necessity that couldn't be avoided.

He needed to hand over the photographs he'd received the previous day to his contact at Euston and pick up any fresh instructions, should there be any, work out an alternative plan should the valise become impossible to retrieve and he needed to be back in Derby that afternoon for his next meeting with 'Basketcase.'

There! He couldn't believe it! There in the short queue at the booking office he saw a tall athletic looking man in a leather biker's jacket. He was sure it was him. It had to be! Yes! He noticed that standing directly behind that man was a pretty young lady wearing a red baker boy-style cap. She was holding a valise.

His valise.

Leaving the soggy remains of his simple meal on the table, he shoved the fedora on top of his head and got up to watch from a better vantage point. The man had purchased a ticket and given it to the woman.

'Right, here you are Mandy, I've got you an upgrade to first class on your ticket, as promised, now I really have to fly. I've got your Kensington number and I'll call you tomorrow evening. Make sure you're in!'

'I'll be in Tiger. Don't you worry about that.'

A muffled announcement bounced its way around the Station halls.

'Train announcement. Manchester Piccadilly to London Euston. Train arrives in five minutes at Platform three.'

They hugged for a moment and Tiger lifted her red cap and planted an affectionate kiss on Amanda's forehead, before heading for the exit. He didn't look back.

Petricek was thirty yards away, eyes alight with anticipation. They were hugging and now the man was going. Damn, he'd like to get the valise and sort out the tall thief, but the valise, that was more important and he had to get to it before his train. He had five minutes.

He followed the girl.

Platform three was very busy and Petricek had a little difficulty in keeping the diminutive stature of his quarry in sight. Fleeting glances of her between jostling men and women who also headed along the same platform were unknowingly hampering him, but he was getting closer and closer to her.

Amanda found herself slightly crushed between a large woman hanging onto two unruly children and a large man with disgusting breath. An odd mixture of sour whisky and cheese and pickle.

She felt a slight tug on Tiger's valise so she gave a slight tug back, 'one of those pesky kids' she thought.

The express train was approaching now and although it was slowing down it still carried some speed. And a lot of mass.

Another tug on the valise that she firmly resisted, there was no point looking down at it as it was all just a sea of kids and bags. She resolutely stared at the approaching train and the people jostling for position, some of whom were standing perilously close to the edge of the platform.

A whistle blew, an official sounding one presumably one from a train employee, followed by a shout that she couldn't hear properly as the noise from excited passengers and closeness of the train drowned out everything around her. Petricek tugged on the valise again, the bitch wouldn't let go. He had to have that case. The train was only a couple of yards away. He could clearly see the driver, an old man with a shock of grey hair. He looked calm and in control.

Petricek made another grab for the valise handle, placed his right foot behind the girl's leg and pushed.

Somebody screamed, the sound piercing through the hubbub of the station, clearly heard above the sound of the train.

Eddy Francombe might have been an older man with a shock of grey hair but his reactions were lightning fast. He hit the emergency brake lever and eighty mighty drum brakes responded as one. Metal on metal screeched as the wheels locked and juddered under him.

Underneath the train, hot oil and water dripped onto a twisted, broken, fragile body in a fashionable red cap. Amanda whispered what could have been the word 'Tiger' and a weak giggle, but nobody was there to listen, and even if they were, they would never hear Amanda utter anything again.

~THIRTY FOUR~

Tiger returned to the café on London Road. He didn't need refreshment; the large tea, and the bacon and toast he'd devoured earlier had quenched that particular need. He just wanted to use the phone to speak to Margaret, as he sure as hell wasn't just going to show up at her house without calling her first, not after hearing what her father had to say about her.

'Morning Maggie.' She'd picked up the phone after only three rings so she must have been sitting in the hall, or about to leave the front door Tiger surmised.

'Well, good morning, Tiger. What happened to you last night?'

'I was going to ask you the same question, Maggie,'

'I had a spat with Daddy at the restaurant and decided to have an early night.'

'Well my night was a bit more interesting I must say, however I need to pop over and pick up my helmet, is that okay?'

'Where are you?'

'Top end of town, I stayed in the Connaught.' He didn't feel like he was lying, he did actually stay at the Connaught Hotel last night, it was just that he wasn't actually there at this precise moment and something worrying at the back of his mind had stopped him from telling the truth.

'Well that's a bit posh for the likes of you Tiger' she retorted. 'Give me an hour would you, I need some breakfast, say 10 o'clock?'

'Ten's fine Maggie, that'll suit me.' He hung up the phone and ordered a cup of tea. He was suddenly thirsty.

~THIRTY FIVE~

Petricek Dvorak managed to escape the commotion on platform three. Some people were stood stunned, others were running from the platform, some were actually attempting to board the train. It was a chaotic scene. He couldn't have cared less though. He had his weapon back, the valise, and he was back on track. His contact in London wouldn't like the fact that he wouldn't make the meeting in Euston, but these things happen. He started whistling as he traipsed along Railway Terrace and was actually singing as he entered the dismal portal of his hotel.

~THIRTY SIX~

From a table right at the back of the café Tiger watched as Margaret Thornton and another man entered. He had a large build, but was flabby looking though; he didn't visit the gym that was obvious. Hatless and clean shaven he looked to be about forty years old and had a small scar on his right cheek. They were obviously together. Tiger wasn't sure that he fitted the profile of the gentlemen friends that Margaret kept for company, but he did knew that for reasons beyond his ken, some women liked men with scars. Tiger was sure however that he recognised the man but couldn't put a name to him.

Yet.

'Two teas please Jackie,' Margaret chirruped, 'and your finest breakfast menu.'

'I'll just have toast if you don't mind Margaret.' The man sounded Welsh, but there was something missing, as if he hadn't lived in Wales for a long time.

Jackie said something to the man that Tiger couldn't hear and at that point Margaret turned to look directly at Tiger.

She didn't blink for at least ten seconds, never taking her eyes off him before turning to Jackie and saying, 'I'm terribly sorry Jackie love, I never realised it was so late, I really have to run.'

She whispered something to the man and together they made an undignified and hasty exit to the street. Their sudden exit clearly wasn't planned.

At 10 a.m. precisely, Tiger rang the doorbell to Margaret Thornton's house. The front door was opened after a short pause and Margaret invited him in.

Margaret was shedding her clothes as she walked up the stairs. She timed it perfectly, wearing only her 4" heels as she reached the top step. She turned to face Tiger who was only halfway up the stairs and didn't appear overly excited.

'Are you okay Tiger?'

'I'm good Maggie, it's been a long day.'

'Well get your lovely arse up here, I'll improve it for you darling.' She turned on her heel and entered the bedroom.

Tiger was a few seconds behind her, and watched as lay on her back playing with herself.'

'I'm hot and wet for you Tiger, come on get those jeans off.'

Tiger sat on the side of the bed and slowly removed his tee shirt jeans and boots and rolled onto the bed alongside a panting Margaret.

'I'll soon get you going lover, lie back and think of England Tiger.'

That of course was the problem for Tiger, he actually was thinking of England and was about to get fucked by a gorgeous woman who didn't give a rat's arse about her Country. He propped his head on a pillow and watched as Margaret slid down the bed, gently kissing his chest and stomach before arriving at his semi erect penis. He felt the warmth of her mouth envelop him and was finding it very difficult to resist the pleasure. He could see the knelt form of Margaret in a mirror on a wardrobe door, two fingers playing with herself as she attempted to arouse him.

'Stop Maggie, that's enough.'

Margaret lifted her head and looked straight into Tigers eyes, he wasn't joking. She slid back up the bed, lay on her side and whispered, 'what's wrong Tiger? Is it me?'

Her red lipstick had smeared, her mascara had started to run and she was breathing heavily, still in the throes of arousal. Tiger thought that she looked like a tramp.

'I have to go Maggie, I shouldn't have come up. I only wanted my helmet and I need to go now.'

'But, but Tiger,' Margaret spluttered, 'we are great together, we always have been, I love you, you must know that? What's gone wrong? What's happened? Are you angry?'

Tiger had dressed. He turned to Margaret.

'No Maggie, I am extremely sad.'

Tiger made for the door and was halfway down the stairs when Margaret showed her true colours.

'You bastard Tiger, you utter bastard.' Tiger ignored her and carried on down the stairs and stopping only to retrieve his helmet and goggles, he heard Maggie screaming, 'get the fuck out of my house...' as he closed the door behind him.

Tiger sat astride his 500cc Triumph, the steady, satisfying rumble usually gave him a sense of calm, a sense of purpose and a sense of well-being, but whilst waiting in traffic a short distance from the Railway Station, none of these emotions had opened a door. He felt uneasy, his sixth sense had never let him down, and in fact it'd saved his and his mates lives on more than one occasion.

The reason was the ramshackle parking of half a dozen emergency vehicles just ahead of him. There were at least four Police cars and two fire engines, the blue lamps atop each vehicle turned lazily, somehow giving a lie to the seriousness of the situation. Whatever it was, the throng of people pouring from the side doors of the station had given him pause for thought as well, but he had no business there, he had no authority and like any other member of the public he would have been given the brush off by those that needed to work.

'Sod it,' he thought to himself and gunned the motorcycle in a smooth 'U' turn having decided to take the scenic route for his meeting with Adrian.

To be honest, he didn't think that Derby was at all scenic. The county of Derbyshire however, was an absolute joy to throw his motorcycle around but his journey today was rather more mundane. He pulled up outside Adrian's apartment block, switched off the ignition and paused for a second to gather his thoughts before dismounting. Removing his helmet he walked to the communal entrance and rang the buzzer for flat number 14. He knew that his friend would look out from his lounge window, he always did when his doorbell rang, so Tiger stepped back a couple of paces and without looking up gave a cheery wave.

~THIRTY SEVEN~

The doorbell sounded in the hallway. Adrian nearly jumped out of his skin. He was expecting Tiger twenty minutes or so ago, but still, his nerves were definitely heading in the direction of the place that offered 'jangling' or 'shredded.' He looked briefly from his lounge window to see Tiger nonchalantly waving at him three floors below. 'Flash bastard,' he correctly surmised before buzzing down to open the communal door lock.

'Come in, come in,' shouted Adrian as Tiger knocked on the door to his apartment. 'It's open!'

Tiger opened the flimsy wooden door and, stepping into a narrow hallway that led directly to the small lounge some four paces away, he closed the door behind him. He walked into the lounge and saw that Adrian was in the small kitchen to the right busying himself with the makings of tea.

'Morning mate.'

'Morning old boy. How the devil are you?'

'Well, I've been better chum, so hurry up with that brew, nothing fancy for me, just tea and come and sit down.'

Tiger had plonked himself onto the sofa that had clearly seen better days. The sponge seats were completely flattened, the velour cover hanging on by a thread, literally, and the springs had long since given up supporting anything human. Tiger looked awkward and slightly comical, sat down with his knees at head height cuddling his motorcycle helmet.   With a commercial metal teapot that looked like it had been stolen from a cheap truckers transport café now sitting on a small occasional table, accompanied by a couple of chipped mugs full to the brim with some brownish coloured liquid, the two men began to talk.

'I bumped into Maggie this morning.'

'Lucky you, I was up here on my own wondering what the hell is going on.'

'Luck doesn't come into it, and I am going to try and explain what's going on now.'

'So?'

'So, I had an interesting meeting with Sir Andrew Thornton last night during which time he informed me that his daughter is batting for the other side.'

'What?!'

'I spent the night with a nice lass from London, Mandy's her name. I trust her completely and she agreed to act as my courier and get that valise well away from Derby. I have people in London that would like to get a better look at it and I haven't got the time to get it down there myself.'

'I don't know if that was wise old boy, you have said yourself that the valise was a dangerous thing to be around.'

'It is a dangerous thing to have around as apparently it's got a bloody bomb in it.'

'What?!'

'It's perfectly safe until a switch is activated to arm it and as we don't know where the switch is I was ordered not to fiddle about and try and find it.'

'Does this Mandy girl know? Is she safe?'

'She'll be okay, and we actually have some mutual friends from Kensington. Anyway she's off on the train as we speak. More importantly mate, I popped back to the café on London Road and who happened to walk in?'

'Knowing you old friend it was probably Sophia Loren.'

'Old fool. No, it was Maggie, and she had some bloke in tow that I reckon I've seen before, but I can't place him.'

'Crikey! That's a turn up. I'll make a note of this. He proceeded to imitate a newsprint reporter scribbling on a notepad... Tiger the great memory man admitted to me that he cannot recall a face...'

'It'll come to me.'

'Was he in the game with you? Was he involved in Morocco? Is he ex Army?'

'No... No...No...Wait a second...Yes old boy. Army. He was one of the Instructors at Hereford when I was on my selection course for the SAS.'

'Name?'

'Tony...Tony...Anthony. Anthony bloody Stone.

'Rank?'

'Colour Sergeant, from the Welsh Guards. Taff! That was it Taff bloody Stone. Well done old man. Terrific interview skills.'

'I do my best.'

Tiger then went on to explain what he knew about 'Taff' Stone, and it wasn't good news. Anthony Stone was a relic from the past. He came from a small Welsh mining village, Tiger couldn't recall which one, but he did remember that he was a hard man and he'd had a grudge against Tiger. He'd tried to get him thrown off an arduous military course that was notoriously easy to fail anyway. He had been continually goading him, telling him that he would never pass the course in a month of Sundays. During a 24 hour rest period towards the end of the course, Tiger, along with the few remaining candidates in his squad, had spent the morning cleaning their kit and were sitting around the radio in the barrack room listening to Spike Milligan and his pals goofing off in a series called The Goon Show. There was much hilarity in the barrack room; the lads had done well to get through to this part of the selection process and up to now it had been anything but hilarious.

Colour Sergeant Taff Stone, now badged as a Special Air Service, Senior Non Commissioned Officer from a little valley in Wales, had chosen this moment to burst into Tiger's barrack room. He'd ordered the lads outside as if on parade and barked and yelled at them in an unwarranted abusive tirade. It was obvious that he had been drinking heavily, and Tiger had told him so. This of course had riled the big Welshman up even more because he then singled out Tiger for some physical abuse and had attempted to punch him in the face, a clumsy manoeuvre that Tiger had evaded with ease. He might as well have sent Tiger a telegram of his intentions. On the third attempt at physical contact, Tiger dropped to one knee as the punch was about to make contact, spinning around and getting behind the drunken NCO, he'd grabbed hold of his webbing belt, stood up and kicked him hard in the back of the thigh.

As the man fell to his knees wincing in pain Tiger stepped forward one pace and had him in a brutal headlock. One small twist to the right and the Welsh bully had slumped to the floor unconscious. Tiger had looked down at him and said, 'there is a massive difference between a hard bastard and a complete bastard,' he had then calmly stepped over the prostrate body, walked back to the barrack room and started to pack his gear, convinced that he would be classed as 'RTU' meaning Returned To Unit, and that would be the end of his military career as far as he was concerned.

He had been in the process of packing when the Company Sergeant Major had entered and had asked some basic questions about the drunken, sleeping NCO to the side of the barrack room. Questions that appeared to surprise the men in the room and to which they all stated that they had no knowledge of anyone asleep outside. The Company Sergeant Major had taken one good hard look at every man before spinning on his heel and marching back towards the barrack room door. With one hand on the door handle he had turned to look directly at Tiger before shouting, 'Well don't just stand there you horrible lot...Carry on!'

'So you managed to finish selection then old boy? asked a stunned Adrian.

'Aye I did, and I never saw that bastard again until this morning.'

'What was he doing with Maggie?'

'I have absolutely no idea. My plans didn't cater in the slightest for the arrival of ex Colour Sergeant Taff Stone.'

~THIRTY EIGHT~

Margaret Thornton felt stunned. She leaned back against her front door and listened to the sound of Tiger's powerful motorcycle engine as it started and continued listening long after it had receded down Midland Street.

'What a bloody mess,' she thought. She hadn't told her current lover Anthony that she had seen Tiger in the London Road cafeteria. She had said her goodbyes to him after their hurried exit. She would tell him later though, at their next meeting as she thought it was inconceivable that their lives hadn't crossed at some point during their respective times together in the 'Regiment' as the SAS preferred to call itself.

Firstly though, she had to sort out that imbecile of a spy she was supposed to be running. She too had seen the commotion at the Railway Station and although she didn't yet know for sure if Petricek Dvorak was somehow involved, she intended to find out pretty damned quickly if he was. She rushed upstairs and made a phone call. She glanced in the mirror, noted that her coiffured hair was still in place, then grabbed her handbag and left the house heading for the station.

Amongst the chaos of the ticket hall, Margaret spotted Detective Chief Superintendent McIntosh, a dour faced Scot with a liking for expensive whisky and fine wines that were well above his pay range. Her father knew him and indeed they had all dined together on numerous occasions.

He was stood in an area of relative calm now reserved for important people by way of the blue and white striped crime scene tape that had been stretched along the entrance to Platform 3 and was viciously guarded by a couple of overworked uniformed Police Constables. She caught his eye, waved and mouthed that she needed to speak to him. He walked over to one of the custodians of the tape and had a quick word with him. This magically turned the Officer into Prince Charming himself.

'Come on through Madam,' he said as he winked at her.

Margaret lightly gripped the senior Detectives elbow and steered him effortlessly a few yards away.

'What's going on Mac?'

DCS McIntosh was a canny fellow, he knew exactly who he was talking to and was in no doubt that any misinformation or lack of cooperation with Margaret would lead directly to Sir Andrew Thornton, and his expensive drinking habits would wither and die.

'There's been a death, Margaret. Some poor lass from Kensington has fallen under the Manchester Express as it pulled into the platform. Most unfortunate. Most regrettable. Lessons will be learnt.'

'I'm sure they will be Mac. Now what is this young 'lass' from Kensington called? Does she have a name?'

The DCI hesitated, he hated being in this position but his appreciation of the nicer things in life quickly outweighed his civic duty.

'According to the identification we found on the, er, on the... young lady's body, it is Amanda Horseferry. This obviously has to be confirmed before any public announcement is made, Margaret'

'Naturally. Were there any witnesses?'

'Quite a few, we have spent the last hour taking statements.'

'What about the train driver? What's happened to him?'

'He is in fact our best witness. We're looking after him at Derby Central nick.'

'And what has he got to say for himself?'

'He clearly saw Miss Horseferry fall. There was nothing he could do to save her. One second she was standing between a woman with a couple of kids and a large man wearing a battered looking fedora hat. Next thing she was under the train's wheels. We located the woman and her kids, but we haven't found fedora man yet.'

'This is good work Mac. It sounds very much like a tragic accident. I'll let my father know that you are on-side.'

'Thank you, Margaret. Please give him my fondest wishes, and if he ever needs free tickets to the next Policeman's Ba...' He never finished his sentence. Margaret was on her way across the concourse for a brief chat with the tall good looking Police Officer who had a nice line in winking.

~THIRTY NINE~

Back in his room Petricek Dvorak was dressed in just his vest and grey baggy underpants and he was livid. On opening his valise he could easily see that someone had been checking it out. The lining had been cut open and pulled apart. His precious valise had been violated. Someone would have to pay for that. His fat fingers unconsciously crumpled Tiger's fedora. He was bent over and rinsing his face at the small ablution area in the corner of his room. He looked up at his obscured reflection in the broken and rust stained mirror, and gasped.

Margaret Thornton was stood directly behind him. He was certainly surprised to see her, but he was truly shocked at how she had gained such a silent entry to his shitty room and managed to get so close without him being aware. She was obviously very well trained and... Shit! She had a gun pointed at a spot close to the back of his head.

'Don't you move a bloody muscle you imbecile.'

'Margaret. How nice to see you again.'

'Don't you 'Margaret' me you cretinous individual. Just what the bloody hell do you think you're playing at?'

'Playing Margaret? Playing? I haven't been out to play since I was seven years old.'

'This morning. At the train station. What did you do?'

'Ah! I can see why you would be upset Margaret, she was so young, and so pretty...'

He suddenly spun around with a speed that didn't match his bulk as he grabbed the small pistol with his left hand and twisted it from Margaret's hand. With his right he open slapped her across the face with such force she staggered across the small room, reeling from the blow and ending up spread-eagled on the unmade bed.

Petricek never even glanced at her, his attention focussed on the firearm he was now holding.

'Beretta M 1934. Italian. 9mm with a box magazine. I can feel by the weight that it's loaded as well. All seven rounds in the magazine Margaret? I wonder if there is an eighth one?'

Within the next 3 seconds, he'd made the weapon safe by depressing the magazine release button with his right thumb, popping the magazine out, pulling back the top slide one quarter of an inch and having a quick glance. In the next two seconds he'd replaced the magazine, pulled back the top slide and snapped a round into the barrel making the weapon very dangerous indeed.

'Well Margaret, only seven rounds in the magazine and nothing in the chamber, nothing that could have hurt me.'

'Fuck you.'

'Ah yes. 'Fuck'. He savoured the word for a moment. 'One of your good old Anglo-Saxon words... and that reminds me...'

He slowly brought the weapon to arm's length and pointed it at her prostrate figure.

'Take your clothes off.'

~FORTY~

Anthony Stone had just finished in the shower. He stood on the plush white carpet of the executive suite belonging to the Excelsior Hotel. The drips of water from his shoulders had so far to travel that they had evaporated before they reached the top of the towel that he had wrapped around his ample waist.

He was a big man.

Margaret Thornton had called him at his office the previous day with a proposition. It was a proposition that he was inclined to refuse, until money was mentioned.

Big money. For a big man.

Although he'd been raised in the mining valley of Merthyr Tydfil about 20 miles to the North of the Welsh capital Cardiff, and at one time in his life he had been universally known as 'Taff,' he'd not been anywhere near his home town, or indeed his home Country for over a decade.

He hated his roots. He'd even lost the most part of his thick Welsh brogue due to his attending elocution lessons after leaving the British Army. Well, to be honest, he didn't actually leave, he was asked very politely to hand his kit back to the Quartermaster and take a bloody hike. His Commanding Officer at Bradbury Lines, the Headquarters of the Special Air Service in Hereford, had been taking a keen interest in his career following an allegation of misconduct whilst serving in an elite Sabre Squadron in Aden. It was all nonsense of course, a perfectly reasonable explanation would have ended the situation he found himself in, but that damned goat herder's daughter wouldn't let it lie. And the goat herder? Well he was just after easy compensation from the UK Government. Every Tom Dick and Mohammed knew it was easier to get recompensed by an invading force than it was earning a few dinar scrabbling around a weed patch on a barren desert, it was the talk of the Wadi.

'Removed from Active Service' they called it. He'd apparently now 'done his bit' and was posted back to Hereford as an Instructor. A position he loathed. He had turned to drink, had very few friends in the Regiment and his wife of three years had left him after discovering, alas too late, that he had a venereal disease. This fact alone hardly gave his 'reasonable explanation' any weight whatsoever, coupled with the scar that the young Arab girl had caused when she had raked a dirty fingernail deep into his right cheek.

The fit young men that had volunteered to join the worlds most coveted Regiment, the fit young men that he now had control over, caused him deep resentment. They were about to have it all. They were the ones who'd go on to have outstanding career opportunities, the glory, the medals and the stories to tell the Grandchildren. Sure, he'd done some of that, but now, even in part disgrace he was in a position to challenge the fittest of the fit, the best of the best that the British Army offered and by God he intended to show them that an old soldier was a force to be reckoned with.

His underhand methods of destroying a soldier's spirits were, up to a point, working. That is, until the day he met a Guardsman called John Stripes. What sort of name was that anyway? And no prizes for guessing here...what was he known as?

'Tiger' for God's sake!

The man was fit, he'd give him that. He was bloody good in the gymnasium when it came to unarmed combat and he was a decent shot out on the ranges as well. But 'Taff' had decided that this fellow was far too cool for school and needed bringing down a peg or two. The problem was he was popular. The Directing Staff on the course liked him, his fellow candidates liked him, despite their being in direct competition with the man and there was even talk in the Sergeants Mess about his outstanding qualities, that he was a 'shoe in' for the vacancies in 'G' Squadron. Taff wasn't privy to the actual conversations, nobody bothered talking to him in the Mess, but he had bloody good hearing.

Despite his best efforts, 'Taff' had failed to break Tiger's spirit. He had to be careful when in barracks, but out in the field, up and down the brutal hills of the Brecon Beacons he had tried his best. But his best simply wasn't good enough. The man was a war machine, a born hunter and natural survivor.

He couldn't actually remember the exact events of the afternoon when he visited barrack block 17. This was the accommodation block containing half a dozen of the candidates in the last throes of the ruthless selection course. He couldn't recall as he was full of drink, but what he did recall was 'Tiger Stripes' assaulting him and despite his protestations to the Commanding Officer during the inevitable interview without coffee, the following morning he was out. And the Guardsman with the stupid name was still in.

'Tiger Stripes.' A name he would never forget.

Or forgive.

~FORTY ONE~

Margaret Thornton ran a brush through her hair. She was stood in front of the nasty little mirror in the crappy little bedroom in the cheap Hotel on Railway Terrace. Petricek Dvorak was lying on the soiled bed eyeing her nakedness.

'You were magnificent Petricek. A beast.'

'I try my best Miss Margaret.'

'What time are you meeting 'Basketcase' today?'

'I'll be at the Park rendezvous at around one o'clock this afternoon. He should be there at two o'clock.'

'Excellent, keep me informed. Usual channels.'

'I will of course.'

'There is something else that I suppose I should pass on.' She reached into her clutch bag and retrieved a slip of paper. 'This order came through from Prague. High priority.' She handed the note to Petricek who received it with a slight tremble in his pudgy hand.

'I don't understand,' said a bewildered Petricek. 'Why? What have I done to warrant this? It doesn't make sense, this is suicide.'

'Your cover has been blown, the SIS know all about you and your double dealings, they have even tracked you down to this dump of a hotel, it wouldn't surprise me if that door came crashing down right this minute.'

'No,no', whimpered Petricek, 'this is madness - how can I ever survive this?'

'You have your orders, you fat mess. Just make sure you are at that park.'

Margaret turned to leave.

'And tell me...' she waved a lazy arm in the direction of the room door, 'where did you get that disgusting fedora? It looks familiar.'

~FORTY TWO~

'That brew was disgusting, how do you survive drinking sewage water?'

'One gets used to it old boy.'

Tiger and Adrian were still sat in the small sitting room of Adrian's simply furnished flat. He had always insisted that he would never be a fashion victim, always a financial one. He had been trying to take that 'perfect' photograph for fifteen years. The one that would sell and sell again, then resell through the intricate nuances of syndicated photographic agencies.

Fifteen years was not such a long wait.

He dreamt of taking pictures of enemy Generals being executed, capturing that moment of essence, the last breath of another human being captured forever on film. He dreamt of taking a photograph of a yellow robed Monk so absorbed with his own bitter angst that he had self-immolated in front of a chanting mob and of a vulture creeping ever closer to the ruined starved body of a child somewhere on the African Continent.

He knew of course that no matter how dreadful those dreams were, they could never happen in real life.

It was difficult enough capturing a squirrel eating nuts in a park.

They were waiting for a telephone call from Gruff.

'He's bloody late.' Tiger glanced at the 1962 Rolex Oysterdate timepiece fastened to his right wrist. He'd known it was a cheap fake when he haggled with a market trader in a downtown souk in Marrakesh the previous year whist working with Thornton's lads. He wore it on his right wrist in order to gain a couple of valuable seconds knowing that a potential combatant in a close up scuffle would think he was left handed.

'He's probably trying to find a phone box that hasn't been vandalised. Where is he anyway?'

'London somewhere.'

'Then we'll be here for some time I expect...'

The phone rang. Adrian stood and walked to the hall table where a black coloured Bakelite telephone was sliding around on a wobbly table, it was moving closer to the edge and telephone heaven with each successive ring.

'Derby 24409,' Adrian had saved the phone. 'Not today thank you.' He replaced the handset and nudged the machine back to the centre of the table.

'Not Gruff then?'

'Nope, that was a cold call seller asking if I wanted to upgrade my Hotpoint washing machine.'

'You don't have a washing machine.'

'This is correct, and that is why by simply replacing the handset those hideous callers will never succeed. I'll give it 6 months maximum and if we all do it cold calling will be dead in the water.'

Tiger was about to give his opinion on that but was interrupted yet again by the phone, and this time it was Gruff.

'Tiger. Hello mate.'

'Morning Tiger, greetings from the Smoke.' He was referring to the bad old days of a smog-bound capital city.

'Aye, it's the morning here alright, what have you got for me?'

'Old Thorny is hopping mad. He has confirmed that Maggie knows this Royal Air Force chap, Sergeant Wossisname.'

'Jack Dean, aka Basketcase.'

'That's the fella, anyway there's now clear evidence that Maggie is up to no good, and he wants you to sort it.'

'Really?' Tiger rubbed his chin thoughtfully. 'I am not sure I want to get that involved.'

'Don't shoot the messenger mate. Of more importance, there is an experienced Czech operator working with this Sergeant Dean character. He came out of Prague about five days ago. The watchers picked him up as he came ashore as a foot passenger at Harwich docks...' He paused, 'they lost him at Colchester Railway Station.'

'I think I know where he'll be this afternoon. What's his name?'

'Dvorak. Petricek Dvorak. D.V.O.R.A.K.'

'Got it mate. Is he a big bloke, looks like he fell from the ugly tree and hit every branch on the way down?'

'That sounds like the bloke, Tiger'. I only have the surveillance notes. I haven't got any pics mate. He's a bit camera shy if you catch my drift?'

'Well aye, and I reckon I've seen him kicking about the Derby café scene.'

'Be careful, Tiger, he's a right rum bastard.'

'Thanks mate, I'll be okay. Now listen, I have something for you.'

'I'm all ears mate.'

'Colour Sergeant Taff Stone.'

There was at least thirty seconds of silence along the telephone lines before Gruff answered.

'Christ mate, what about him?'

'Can you ask your boss to get a handle on him? I need to know what he's been up to this last ten years. I'd like an address, vehicle details, the whole nine yards.'

'That's a big ask, Tiger.'

'You can do big asks.'

Another thirty seconds of silence. Tiger waited patiently, he knew his friend was still on the line, he could hear him breathing.

'I can't do that one mate. His boss is my boss.'

The following silence was genuine. Gruff had abruptly ended the call.

~FORTY THREE~

Detective Chief Superintendent McIntosh had a problem. A handwritten note on a page of Connaught Hotel notepaper simply stating, 'Tiger Johnnie Kensington 33540' had been recovered from the body of Miss Amanda Horseferry.

One of his Detectives had called the operator service at the General Post Office that covered the London area switchboard for Kensington and was transferred to a Police Liaison Manager, from there it was established that the number 33540 was indeed a live telephone number but it had been 'red flagged.'

The 'red flagging' of a telephone number meant that it is very expensive to run, is password controlled and more likely than not, belonged to a Government department, a department that nobody should really know about. So every time the number is dialled, someone, somewhere, is notified and a little red flag is raised leading to the callers' identity being very quickly ascertained.

There was no chance whatsoever of getting any help from the GPO. This really had to be passed up the chain of command, official channels through Police

Headquarters and maybe landed very gently on the desk of the Chief Constable.

Sat behind his expansive desk, the head of Derby City Criminal Investigation Department Detective Chief Superintendent McIntosh thoughtfully rubbed his chin. Perhaps there was another way?

~FORTY FOUR~

If Tiger was shocked at hearing the news about Taff Stone, he was thunderstruck that his old mate Gruff had put a phone down on him without an explanation or even a simple 'cheers mate.' He absently watched Adrian faffing about in the kitchen area and hoped to God that the man wasn't attempting to make tea.

Adrian was attempting to make another brew. He was aware that Tiger's tea preference was not demanding but he was determined to make a special effort this time and his friend seemed genuinely upset after the call from Gruff. If the truth be known though, he needed to keep busy. His nerves were shot to pieces.

~FORTY FIVE~

Margaret Thornton was back in her town house on Midland Road taking a shower. The steaming hot water cascaded down her body, her ample breasts heaved as she lathered scented soap over them causing her nipples to tingle. She was killing two birds with one stone in a way. Washing away the scent of Czechoslovakia and preparing herself for the imminent arrival of a tall handsome Police Officer called Dave something-or-other who had a terrific line in winking.

_____

Sergeant Jack Dean, Royal Air Force, was sat in his motor car. His fingers drummed on the steering wheel as he tried to think things through. His Czech contact had mysteriously stopped meeting him although he was positive he'd read the coded instructions from the last 'dead letter' drop correctly. He had a package on the passenger seat, a compendium full of restricted photographs that if he was caught with, would mean a lengthy prison sentence. He made a decision and started the motor. He'd go to the Park again. He hadn't managed to put the vehicle into gear before a Police car slammed to a halt in front of him closely followed by another one behind to stop him reversing.

Petricek Dvorak had checked out of the Railway Terrace dump of a hotel in his own unequivocal way, he just left his room open and walked away making no effort to pay the balance of his paltry bill. The scent of a recently conquered woman and the animal musk of hard sex drifted to his nostrils. It put a spring in step as he carried his valise towards his rendezvous with Basketcase.

Anthony Stone was sat at the writing bureau in his Excelsior Hotel room. Now dressed in blue pinstripes with his carefully tailored jacket hanging over the back of the chair, he was taking a telephone call from his boss, Sir Andrew Thornton of Her Majesty's Secret Intelligence Service. It was a brief but interesting call.

Miss Kelly had taken the day off work. Her black and red Triumph Bonneville motorcycle was due an M.O.T at the local garage. She hadn't told her boss that, obviously, she'd just mentioned the magic words, 'Doctors surgery' and 'woman's internal plumbing problems,' and like a typical bloke he'd dropped her from the daily shift pattern faster than she could have ever hoped.

_____

Sir Andrew Thornton had just finished a telephone call with 'that odious fellow Stone' when his secretary, Mrs Fillfinger, entered his office and informed him that a Detective Chief Superintendent McIntosh from Derby City C.I.D was on line three and wanted to speak with him urgently and wondered if he had a spare ten minutes.

~FORTY SIX~

Wonder of wonders! Petricek Dvorak had accidentally stumbled across a small chintzy Czechoslovakian restaurant. On glancing in through the window it was apparently empty and this suited him. He was in no mood to be making pleasantries with anybody. Not today. He entered the building and took a seat where he could see the front door.

'Jste připraveni objednat?'

He looked up from the two day old Czech newspaper. The 'Lidové Noviny.' The People's Paper, a serious centre right publication that he wouldn't normally read because most of the commentary he found within its pages usually bored him, but it was nice to read something in his own language and it was free, so he'd helped himself to a complimentary copy on the way in.

The waiter tried again. In English.

'Are you ready to order Sir?'

'Knedlíky.'

'Will that be all Sir?'

Petricek just glared at him until the hapless waiter turned tail and headed for the kitchen.

Five minutes later, the waiter returned to Petricek's table with a steaming bowl on a tray.

The old spy moved his newspaper 3 inches to his left and nodded at the table. The waiter attempted a shrug and placed a bowl of traditional Czech dumplings in front of his indifferent customer who he knew spoke Czech. He'd ordered his meal in the language, even though he'd only grunted one word, he could place him to within fifty kilometres of his birthplace. He had left his home Country because of people like the man he'd just served. Assholes.

'Enjoy Sir.'

Petricek waited until the surly waiter - who was surely an Englishman with a basic knowledge of his language - had moved away before putting the paper to one side and picking up a fork. It looked good and it tasted like home. It made him sad. His life had totally unravelled, and it didn't matter how may times he denied it to himself, there was no going home now, not after Margaret's little speech.

He had about ninety minutes to kill before his meeting. Like any good spy he would normally be there at least an hour beforehand to scope the place out; this afternoon though he couldn't really be bothered - nothing was going to happen until everybody had assembled at the Park and it didn't matter if he was first or last. The Arboretum Park was a five minute stroll away, which meant it'd take him fifteen, meaning he had a leisurely forty five minutes to enjoy his food. The valise was parked between his legs and thereby hidden from view under the table. There was no way he was going to let it leave his side.

Until later.

~FORTY SEVEN~

Sir AndrewThornton was on the phone to the Chief Detective in Derby City.

'How are you Ian?'

'I'm fine Sir.'

'How's the good lady wife? Rose isn't it?' Thornton flicked through the green file on his desk as he spoke. The one marked 'Detective Chief Superintendent McIntosh.'

'Thank you for remembering, Sir Andrew. She's in good spirits. She's still trying to raise money for her start-up company.'

'Ah! The children's soft toy-company the one that specialises in cuddly birds?'

'Aye that's the one Sir.'

'Excellent. Excellent! 'My-Crows-Soft?' Is that the one?'

'Unfortunately Sir, it is.'

'So Ian, how can I help you?'

'Tiger Johnnie.' It's a name that has cropped up in relation to a delicate matter here in Derby...'

'Platform 3 this morning? Manchester Express?'

Detective Chief Superintendent McIntosh actually spluttered into the phone.

'There are no leaks in my department Sir Andrew. I must ask in the most strenuous terms how...'

'I have the ear of the Prime Minister, Ian. The Home Secretary is my squash partner, the Lord Chief Justice fails to beat me at poker on a Tuesday night and the Speaker of the House looks after my bloody tomato plants when I am out of the country. I don't need 'leaks' Ian, old boy. As far as Tiger Johnnie is concerned, I've never heard of him, and by the way...neither have you. I hope that clears the matter up?'

'Yes, yes it does Sir Andrew, I appreciate the time you have given me and may I say you are most welcome to attend...'

Sir Andrew had disconnected. He was speaking to himself.

~FORTY EIGHT~

Adrian was sat on the back of Tiger's Triumph T100S, he wasn't wearing any sort of protective headgear other than a band of sweat and it wasn't particularly comfortable. The tails of his beer stained 'drinking' sports coat were flapping behind him as he'd forgotten to button it up before climbing aboard. Riding with a pillion passenger opens up a lot of interesting scenarios, not least the fact it can be uncomfortable, if not downright dangerous for both parties. Tiger was aware that Adrian was in a position to actually steer his machine simply by shifting his weight about causing him to make slight alterations though the handlebars to counteract this, never the less Tiger manoeuvred his machine with ease through the busy streets of the city, fully aware of his friend's discomfort and enjoying every minute of it.

Adrian's camera case was strapped to the rear luggage rack and he hoped to God it'd still be there when they arrived at Arboretum Park. Tiger had briefed him on the meeting that he hoped was not going to happen, but in his heart of hearts knew that it would. Tiger was rarely, if ever, wrong about such matters. He'd been told to establish a vantage point on the far side of the Park, but in such a position that he had a clear view of his least favourite bench. He was to check that he had a fresh roll of film in his camera and to make sure that the bench was in crystal clear focus. Tiger had promised him the photo of a lifetime.

Fifteen minutes later Tiger had found an empty space and parked his motorcycle a short distance from the entrance to Arboretum Park and offloaded his passenger. He removed the camera bag from the rear luggage rack and handed it to Adrian.

'Right my old friend, let's do this,' said Tiger, as they walked towards the entrance.

'Piece of cake, I've been looking forward to this all day old boy.'

'Hang on a minute, you're looking a bit green around the gills, are you sure you're up to it?'

Although Tiger took some satisfaction from his friend's awkwardness on two wheels, he wasn't a complete sadist and he genuinely felt some sympathy for him.

'I'm good to go Tiger, stop fussing.'

'I'll see you on the other side then chap. Good luck.'

'Whoa there Tiger, what do you mean 'on the other side?'

'The Park Adrian, the Park, I'll see on the other side of the Park. Are you sure that you're okay?'

Adrian just nodded and walked slowly towards the entrance, entered the Park and headed for the far side where he'd look for an appropriate location as briefed. Tiger turned away from the entrance and crossed the road. He'd spotted something interesting.

~FORTY NINE~

Ten minutes before Tiger had left for the Park, Margaret Thornton had stepped into the waiting Taxi and ordered the driver to take her to Arboretum Park where he was to park up and await further instruction. She had rid herself of the tall handsome Police Officer called Dave something-or-other who had a terrific line in winking. He was lousy in the sack and she doubted that she'd ever see him again. However, on the positive side, she had managed to learn that Tiger was wanted by Derby City C.I.D for questioning in relation to events at the Railway Station that morning.

'Tap. Tap. Tap.' Startled by the rapping on the glass next to her head, Margaret Thornton flinched, looked round and wound down the rear passenger window of the taxi.

'Tiger! Fancy seeing you here?'

'Yes Maggie, fancy that. Are you going to open the door?'

The taxi driver looked into the rear view mirror at his fare. Margaret nodded and the security bolt on the door lock clunked. Tiger opened the door and slid onto the rear seat next to his erstwhile lover whilst looking at the drivers' eyes in the rear view mirror. 'What's your name driver?' Tiger asked.

'Who's asking?' Came the cocky reply.

'You have two choices my friend.'

'Really? What two choices are they then?'

'You tell me your name, or you'll enter a world of pain.'

The driver paused for thought and looked at Tigers eyes properly.

'Eric.'

'Thank you Eric, nice to meet you. Now listen carefully, and putting it bluntly there are no choices here, I want you to get out of the vehicle, leaving the keys in the ignition and go and find a uniformed Constable and bring him back here. Have you got that?'

'I do, but what do I tell him?'

'I don't care. Tell him I threatened to break your neck, tell him that you've got some sandwiches in the boot of your car that you'd like to share with him, I really don't care but you will do it NOW.'

Eric took one more look at those obviously maniacal eyes, and exited the cab a hell of a lot faster than he did getting in it at the start of his day.

'So what happens now?' Asked Margaret. She was sounding a lot more confident than she actually felt.

Tiger was staring straight ahead. He needed to keep his concentration focused.

'We wait.'

'For the Police to arrive? That's madness Tiger. You do realise that you are a wanted man?'

'Everybody wants Tiger.'

'You know what I mean.'

'The Police are not coming.'

'Of course they are, you just sent the driver to find one.'

Tiger turned his head slowly to look directly at Margaret and spoke slowly, 'the Police are not coming.'

'Daddy!' Margaret exclaimed. 'You've been talking to Daddy haven't you? And he's somehow managed to fix the Police!'

Tiger looked to the front again. He was in no mood to have this conversation with her. In fact he was not inclined to have any type of conversation with her.

The driver's door then opened and the large bulk belonging to Anthony 'Taff' Stone slid in behind the steering wheel.

'Afternoon Maggie,' stated Taff Stone, ignoring Tiger completely.

'What are you doing, you fool?' Replied Margaret, 'I've given you specific instructions and I don't recall 'joining me in a taxicab' was one of them.'

'Your instructions don't mean a thing Maggie.'

'But you're on my team!'

'No. No I'm not.'

'I've paid you to be on my team!'

'Banked it, cashed it, spent it.'

'For God's sake Stone you have no idea what's at stake here.'

Taff Stone turned his head for the first time and looked directly at her. 'You're a traitor Maggie. A rat. A rat that needs exterminating.'

'Don't be so stupid Stone, you have no idea what you are talking about. Tell him Tiger...'

Tiger said nothing and Taff Stone continued.

'After the Morocco fiasco last year you were seen meeting with someone you shouldn't have been meeting, Maggie. Very naughty. Very naughty indeed. Pictures were taken, notes were written and a file was opened on you because people way above your pay grade had an inkling that you never reported your meetings like a good girl should. Does the name 'Petricek Dvorak' ring any bells?'

Margaret said nothing for a whole minute. She was caught, and she knew it, but she would never admit it.

'It was one time, a very brief meeting with a person whose background I knew nothing about. I can't go around filing contact reports following every person I meet for the first time.'

'Margaret, Margaret, Margaret. It wasn't the first time you had met him, you met him during the Moroccan operation. He was your contact. You subsequently met him on seven separate occasions, none of which were brief and in fact, two of those meetings involved an overnight stay in the King Edward suite at the Sheraton Grand Hotel on Park Lane.'

'Utter tosh.'

'Pictures, Maggie. Surveillance footage, and the managers at Sheraton are on the books, Maggie, our books. They report to us and just so there is no mistake at all, just so we can tie up one massive loose end... so did Petricek Dvorak before he went rogue.'

Margaret Thornton attempted to leave the vehicle, she rattled the door handle but the cab security bolt was engaged and this could only be released by a switch on the driver's dashboard. She wasn't a screamer, well not outside a bedroom, and anyway there was nobody about to hear if she did cry out for help, in fact it was eerily quiet, a detail she'd only just noticed.

'You want to get out Maggie? That's not a problem, if you look at the Park entrance about...now... you'll see the subject of our little discussion.

Petricek Dvorak ambled into view towing his valise on wheels. He didn't glance at the taxicab parked twenty yards away, he just turned left into the Park and continued towards his meeting.

On the far side of the Park, Adrian spotted the spy dragging the valise immediately. He raised the cameras viewfinder to his eye and fired off a couple of framing shots to get the exposure settings correct and watched him pass three benches before he sat down on the graffiti bench. He looked to be really tired, he wasn't looking around, he didn't appear to be interested in his surroundings but Adrian knew he was a spy, probably a dangerous one and his weary, run down appearance was just an act. He'd met the man and a cold shiver ran up his spine just thinking about it.

Back in the taxi Margaret spotted Petricek and said nothing. What could she say? Tiger roughly grabbed her by the wrist and nodded to Taff Stone who released the door lock, he then opened his door and he dragged her out of the taxicab.

Miss Kelly was in a great mood, her Bonneville motorcycle had sailed through its Ministry Test with no faults at all. She didn't think there was going to be a problem but she always had a nagging doubt that something, somewhere, was going to fall off or stop working minutes before she presented her pride and joy to the examiner. But now, best of all, she had the rest of the afternoon free to ride her pride and joy.

Adrian continued watching Petricek through his viewfinder, he was sat motionless and impassive, then, a snatch of colour caught his eye and he looked to his left. Margaret Thornton was being escorted into the Park by Tiger and another big fat bloke that he'd never seen before. None of them were talking. Tiger steered Margaret into a seated position on the bench and then sat next to her squeezing her along until she was crushed between him and the cheap Macintosh covered bulk of the Czech spy. Taff Stone walked behind the bench and crouched down. He whispered in Margaret's ear.

'I'm not in possession of any recording devices Margaret, I am not wired up so do you have anything to say to your friend here?'

Margaret kept quiet, then winced as her hands were pulled roughly behind her back, presumably by Anthony Stone. Strong plastic straps were wrapped around her wrists.

Jesus Mother of Mary she was being handcuffed to the bench.

'You bastards! Let me go! What the hell are you doing? Tiger! Petricek! For God's sake stop this!'

Tiger was standing to the side of the bench looking straight ahead. Taff Stone stood up and patted Tiger on the shoulder. Their prisoner was secure. Tiger then bent down and gently rubbed the back of his hand down Margaret's cheek, wiping away the first of her teardrops, and whispered. 'Goodnight Sweetheart.'

Miss Kelly was sat comfortably astride her machine and was cruising along the City streets undecided as to what direction she would take to get into the countryside, after all, there was no rush and she had had all afternoon to make a decision. She spotted a 1968 Triumph T100S parked up a few yards from the entrance to the Arboretum Park, this was her all-time favourite bike. She loved her Bonneville and although it was 650cc she secretly coveted the T100S. It had a smaller engine, 500cc but she knew the 'T' stood for 'ton' the magical 100 miles per hour and she would've done absolutely anything to ride one.

Taff Stone and Tiger walked back towards the exit to the Park.

'The only reason I am not handcuffing you to that bench as well, Johnnie boy, is because I know for a fact that you love your Country and would never act in a traitorous fashion towards it.'

'The only reason you are not handcuffing me to bench old boy, is because you ain't big enough.' Tiger corrected him, adding 'and just to ensure that you didn't try anything on, I brought along a sniper as insurance. If I raise my right hand...like this...'

Stone automatically glanced behind him, and sure enough he caught a glint of optical glass from behind a tree some two hundred yards away. It could have been a photographer but that wouldn't have made sense and he certainly wasn't hanging about to see if it actually was a sniper. He grabbed Tiger's wrist, stopping him from raising it any higher.

'You sneaky bastard, Stripes.'

'It takes one to know one, Stone.'

Tiger turned left out of the Park, Taff Stone turned right, both men quite sure that they'd be meeting again in the future.

_____

Miss Kelly decided to stop, she wasn't sure why, some sort of womanly instinct perhaps? This was an instinct that had brought on many adventures for her in the past, so she listened to it and acted on it, bringing her machine to a halt and manoeuvring it next to the 500cc Triumph.

_____

Petricek Dvorak slid the valise from under the bench. He stood it on its little plastic wheels and unzipped it. Margaret Thornton just watched him, unable to move and paralysed with fear.

_____

Adrian had no idea what was going on, he kept taking photographs though, that was his brief and his only fear was that he would run out of film.

_____

Tiger walked back towards his bike. Another biker had pulled up their machine next to his. He watched with interest as the biker dismounted a rather nice Bonneville and began to remove their crash helmet. He stopped in his tracks once the helmet was fully off. The rider shook her mane of long black hair and casually placed her helmet on the ground and crouched down to take a closer interest in his bike.

~FIFTY~

Petricek Dvorak never said a word as he located the tiny arming switch behind one of the lead panels and flicked it on. The fireball ripped through the Park. The blast nearly knocked Adrian off his feet from over 80 yards away as he continued to take photographs. He knew, he absolutely knew that he had taken a perfect photo somewhere in the last six frames, but he also knew that he would never be getting the Pulitzer Prize. His perfect photograph would lay gathering dust in a secret file in a secret Government building before the day was out. Still, fifteen years wasn't that long a wait.

Dirt and debris, trees and shrubbery, the wooden bench and two humans, reduced instantly to their respective elements, rose in a mushroom cloud above the trees and houses of Derby City. Tiger instinctively ducked and opened his mouth to absorb the pressure wave he knew was coming. Tree branches and clods of earth rained down on him as he continued on his way to his bike and the girl with the long dark hair. Miss Kelly fell backwards onto her derriere as the sound of what must have been a terrific explosion punched her eardrums. She was sat on the pavement between two British built engineering wonders and slightly dazed. She looked up. A tall man with an easy smile was offering her his hand. She took the offered hand and was pulled effortlessly to her feet.

'Thank you. What the hell just happened?' She asked.

'Gas main I expect, are you okay?' He reached out and caught a battered fedora as it fluttered towards the ground.

'I'm fine.'

She watched as the man stuffed the hat under the front of his leather jacket before donning a battered looking helmet then throwing his leg over the 100 mile per hour Triumph.

'Er…I'm Miss Kelly,' she thrust out her right hand. She sounded flustered, perhaps a little desperate, but she wanted to know who this man was.

'I'm Tiger. I'm going for a ride over towards Buxton and then perhaps grab something to eat at The Cat and Fiddle. Do you fancy a ride out there?'

'I do,' she said, pulling on her helmet. 'I definitely do and I love your bike.'

'Everybody loves a Tiger,' said Tiger, turning on the ignition.

FORT WILLIAM

SCOTLAND

1975

~FIFTY ONE~

Six years after the horrific deaths of Margaret Thornton and Petricek Dvorak in The Arboretum Park in Derby City, Sir Andrew Thornton, former head of the Secret Intelligence Service, commonly known as MI6, had died. Before he took most of his terrible secrets to his grave, he had implemented two surprise moves. Firstly he had bequeathed a large sum of money to Arthur and Miranda Horseferry, a Kensington couple who had never heard of Sir Andrew let alone met him.

This was money gained by the sale of a town house on Midland Road in Derby City. Sir Andrew had instructed his Solicitors that he wanted nothing to do with the property, the fixtures and fittings or indeed any personal property that may be found within the walls of his traitorous daughter's former home.

There was little information attached to the donated sum, just a note in a neat copperplate hand writing, to explain that he was sorry for their loss, causing much puzzlement to Arthur and Miranda, who believed that their only daughter had died in a terrible accident at Derby Railway Station.

Secondly, and most bizarrely, the late head of MI6 had left behind directives in which he had unequivocally proposed that in the event of his death he wanted Anthony Stone, formerly of 22 Special Air Service, to be considered for the post of Chief.

~FIFTY TWO~

Tiger was hunched down next to his Triumph Trident T160V, his latest machine. He'd had a bit of trouble with the fuel flow on his last ride out, causing the engine to misfire, and had thought that perhaps the fault was one of the 27mm Amal Concentric carburettors, maybe a sticking needle valve. This turned out to be the case, and after two hours on the bench in his simple home workshop he was tightening up the last of the bolts to secure the carb in place before firing it up for a test run.

'Dinner's ready!' Miss Kelly popped her head around the door jamb and stood watching Tiger fettle his motorcycle.

'Five minutes sweetheart, I'm nearly done.'

'And don't think you're bringing those filthy hands into my kitchen either...'

Tiger sprang from his crouched position and embraced Miss Kelly, planting his hands on her posterior leaving two perfectly defined greasy hand prints on the rear of her white tennis shorts.

'Get off me you horrible man,' she shrieked, unsure herself if she was actually angry, or quite pleased that she had found herself being embraced by the love of her life.

Tiger kissed her forehead and released her. She smiled and turned towards the house.

'I'll get myself cleaned up now, but you may want to consider putting some laundry on, those shorts really are mucky.'

Miss Kelly stopped in her tracks and looked seductively over her shoulder. She slowly pulled her grease stained shorts to her knees and with a couple of shimmies she stepped out of them before bending over, her eyes never leaving Tigers amused gaze.

Tiger pounced again.

'Noooo!' Miss Kelly squealed in delight and started running. It took Tiger a dozen paces and he was on her, pulling her onto the freshly cut lawn where they rolled in a heap.

They giggled and embraced. A long smouldering kiss passed between their lips, and Tiger sighed deeply, 'I love you babe.'

'I love you too, Tiger.'

'Everybody loves a Tiger,' laughed Tiger as he got to his feet holding out his hand to pull Miss Kelly from the grass.

'We have a lovely life, Tiger. Tell me it will last for ever.'

Tiger never responded. His mood had changed abruptly. He stroked his chin leaving a smudge of oil across his jaw, and turned to wash up before dinner

~FIFTY THREE~

Miss Kelly pushed her empty plate away from her and leaned back in her chair. Tiger was getting stuck into second helpings. Cottage Pie was without doubt, his 4th or perhaps 5th favourite meal of all time. His half-drunk glass of Double Diamond bitter was slowly getting warmer. The evenings were unbearably hot, and his appetite didn't stretch to warm beer.

'You've got something on your mind, Tiger. Are you going to share?'

Tiger slowly placed his fork onto his plate, dabbed at his mouth with a fresh linen napkin, noting with a wry grin that it contained a blotch of what suspiciously looked like Castrol GTX. He looked up at Miss Kelly and said simply.

'Funeral.'

'It's tomorrow, darling, we agreed we would go. It's only 24 hours. The Hotel is booked The Firm is sending a car, Gruff is flying back from whatever sneaky stuff he is supposed to be doing in that terrible war in Angola, Adrian is getting a train down from Derby and Polly next door will keep an eye on the house for us. That all seems pretty straightforward.'

'Not Thorny's funeral.' Tiger still used the derogatory but kindly meant nickname for the now deceased Sir Andrew Thornton.

'Not Sir Andrew's? Then whose?'

'My funeral.'

'What? Exclaimed Miss Kelly suddenly very alarmed. 'What on earth do you mean 'Your funeral'?'

Tiger excused himself from the table and walked to his study to the side of the hallway and returned moments later. He sat back down and slid a brown envelope across the table towards an uncomfortable looking Miss Kelly.

She paused, looked at Tiger who nodded briefly, and she picked up the envelope. It was an official looking thing. It had the letters HMSO stamped in bold type on the face. It was addressed to Tiger at his place of work, which technically was also his home. She tentatively opened it and pulled out a single sheet of single paper.

It looked like a telegram.

Ignoring the headers and the General Post Office garbled language at the start of such things, her eyes scanned the text of the message.

TIGER JOHNNIE-STOP-P TO I- MY PROMOTION-STOP-
YOUR PRESENCE REQ'D SOONEST-STOP-DTG 08001707-
STONE-STOP.

Miss Kelly read it again and thought she had the gist of it
but had a couple of questions.

'What does P to I mean?' She glanced up and was shocked
to see Tiger's expression, she had never seen him angry
but there was now a barely hidden fury stretched across
his face.

'Pleased to Inform.'

'And DTG?'

'Date Time Group.'

'And Stone, is that Anthony Stone, that grease ball of a
man who grabbed my bottom at the Mayfair Hotel
Summer Ball a couple of years ago?'

'The very same grease ball, Miss Kelly, although now he is
head of MI6 and he's requesting my presence next
Saturday at eight in the morning.' He waggled his fingers
beside his head mimicking quote marks when he said the
word 'requesting.'

'Dear God, that's outrageous! What is this country coming to when they put a man like that in charge of our Country's deepest secrets?' Miss Kelly was genuinely appalled at the thought and quickly added. 'But what's that got to do with what you said about your funeral?'

'We have a history. I beat him once and now I am as good as dead. When Thorny was alive I had a modicum of protection, but now...' He threw his arms up in despair.

'What? I still don't understand, Tiger, talk to me. Please, I'm so worried now.'

Tiger directed her into the kitchen, opened the fridge selected a bottle of Chianti wine from the well-stocked rack, picked up a corkscrew from a drawer and asked Miss Kelly to grab a couple of glasses from the cupboard. Suitably armed with the drinking materials they headed into the garden where they sat under the welcome shade of a young Silver Birch tree.

And Tiger started talking.

~FIFTY FOUR~

St Martin-in-the-Fields Church was tucked away in the Northern corner of Trafalgar Square in London. Internationally recognised as a neo-classical Georgian building, it actually dates back as a church to the year 1222 during the reign of Henry III.

Adrian was aware of some of those facts, but wasn't thinking about them at this precise moment. He looked uncomfortable dressed in a grey lounge suit, it was the only suit he owned and he used it exclusively for weddings as his principal business was that of a professional photographer. The suit itself wasn't uncomfortable, in fact it fitted his ample frame very well and he looked rather smart. It was that every other person in attendance that morning was wearing black.

Gruff Wetherspoon had managed to fly 3000 miles from a war zone and even he had managed to find a black suit to wear on this occasion. Tiger, Miss Kelly, Gruff and Adrian stood as a foursome a respectable distance from the main mourners, most of whom looked as if it wouldn't be that long before they joined Sir Andrew.

'Good trip mate?' Asked Tiger.

'Yes.' From Gruff.

'No. I couldn't sleep.' From Adrian.

Miss Kelly giggled. She really liked Adrian and promised herself that if Adrian couldn't get a girlfriend then she would get one for him. There were problems though. He didn't have a driving licence, he couldn't cook. Whoa! Hold that thought. He couldn't even make a decent cup of tea, let alone cook, and he moaned about pretty much everything. But she would find someone somewhere.

'What do you mean 'no' old friend?' Asked Tiger, 'It was only a train ride down from Derby, What could possibly go wrong? Gruff's flown in from a bloody Angolan war zone and he's not complaining!'

'Gruff could probably strap himself to the wing of the damned aircraft and still get a good kip,' answered Adrian.

'I did,' Gruff replied.

'You did what? Get a good kip?'

'No. I strapped myself to the wing of the aircraft...'

'Stop it Gruff,' exclaimed Miss Kelly. 'You're teasing him.'

Adrian looked closely at Gruff, leaned towards him and whispered.

'You did, didn't you?'

Gruff laughed and didn't reply. What could he say? Adrian was a decent sort, bloody good photographer but he had the oddest sense of perspective. And his tea really was crap.

'Right, I suppose we should be getting in.' Tiger had noticed the main group were now slowly filtering into the side door of the famous church.

'The quicker this is over with, the better I'll like it mate.' Gruff had turned to Tiger, letting Miss Kelly and Adrian walk slightly ahead.

'I hear what you're saying Gruff. I feel very uneasy. Have you seen Taff Stone yet?'

'Nope.'

'He wouldn't miss this surely?'

'He's a first class bastard, mate, so he's probably up in his new office arranging our demise right now.'

'You got the telegram as well then?'

'I did. Mine came over the diplomatic wire at our embassy in Luanda. Are you meeting him at zero eight hundred on Saturday?'

'Aye mate. We'll talk later down the boozer, let's get this over with.'

Adrian and Miss Kelly were waiting just inside the door.

'Tiger.' Miss Kelly whispered.

'What?'

'Just before you came in, someone, I don't know who, it was all hurried a big crush of people squeezing past us, passed me a note. Here, it's got your name on it.'

Tiger quickly unfolded the note and read it.

'Meet me in the crypt before the service. I have something you need.'

Tiger passed the note to Gruff who scanned it and handed it back with a raised eyebrow.

'Are you going down?'

'I have to really.'

'Okay mate. I'll watch your back. Let's go.'

Tiger turned to Miss Kelly.

'Wait here sweetheart, I'm popping downstairs to the crypt with Gruff. I won't be long.

'Then I'm coming down as well.' She had that determined look on her face that quite positively said, 'don't argue with me.'

Tiger shrugged. What could go wrong? It was a Church for Christ's sake, suddenly realising that he'd had made a little pun. He turned to Gruff intending to repeat what he had said in his head but Gruff was already at the small door leading to the underground crypt.

~FIFTY FIVE~

It wasn't wholly dark as they descended the old stone steps, worn smooth with hundreds of years of constant use, but it wasn't exactly Blackpool Illuminations either. Miss Kelly kept her hand on Tiger's shoulder as they descended. Gruff was in the vanguard, up front where he played best.

'You okay? Tiger turned his head slightly and whispered to Miss Kelly two steps above and behind him.

'I'm fine. Look where you're going Tiger and why are we whispering? It's a room full of dead people.'

Tiger smiled in the gloom. The only light source appeared to be coming from electric lamps yellowed with age positioned in the ceiling at regular intervals. He could hear Gruff ahead of him and then he caught up as Gruff stopped after the last step into the crypt itself.

The light was only a little better here. The room was about thirty feet long and the same wide. A sign pinned to the wall to Tiger's right explained that brass rubbings were allowed but wax must be purchased from the curator.

As soon as Tiger stepped into the room he noticed that there was some sort of restoration work underway, but no sign of any workmen. A large plastic dustsheet was hanging from a small scaffold to the right and a temporary wooden workbench was situated in the middle of the room displaying a selection of tools that a stonemason might use.

To his left, more plastic sheeting, and the vague shapes behind them, suggested statues or people in coffins. He counted three large supporting arched columns running along the centre.

It was a strange place for a meeting of any sort and unless the writer of the note had some novel idea regarding brass rubbing it seemed like a futile visit.

They walked further into the room.

'TIGER!'

Miss Kelly's scream boomed across the small space, and continued to reverberate as she lunged forward and tackled him to the floor.

The breath was forced from Tiger's lungs as he landed awkwardly, temporarily winded and completely unaware for a second as to what had just happened. He heard a dull thud and then...

Complete silence.

He peered back at where Miss Kelly had been standing and saw her prostrate body. Something didn't look right. He got to his knees and crawled towards her, then recoiled in horror.

Her head had been crushed under a large granite block that looked to be in the shape of an animal, a bear perhaps. It had obviously come from the ceiling or one of the supporting columns.

'Gruff. Gruff!' Tiger yelled. His friend was at his side in an instant.

'Oh my God no,' stated a shocked Gruff, 'no no no no, not Miss Kelly.'

A pool of dark slowly coagulating blood had started to seep out from under the granite bear and weave its way slowly across the marble floor trying to find the path of least resistance.

'Step away Tiger,' ordered Gruff. Don't touch anything, just step away. This is a crime scene now.'

'Crime scene?' Spluttered Tiger, 'what are you talking about? How can this be a...'

He didn't finish his sentence. Gruff was pointing into the gloom. He followed Gruff's fingers as they traced an invisible line from the granite block towards the ceiling. No. Wait. It wasn't an invisible line at all, Gruff was tracing along a very fine line of thread.

'It's fishing line mate! Miss Kelly has been murdered, and I think you were the target. She saved your life.

'My God. Who would want...' Once again he failed to reach the end of his sentence as it slowly dawned on him, the cold, hard realisation of what had just happened.

'We've got to go, man. C'mon. Now.' He tugged at Tiger's shoulder as he still knelt next the dead body of Miss Kelly.

'Wait a sec.' Tiger fished in his pocket and produced a small box.'

'We haven't got time to dick about mate. Let's go...'

He watched in silence as Tiger produced a gold ring from the box and pushed it gently onto the third finger of his girlfriend's left hand.

'Now we go,' growled Tiger.   Raw steel in his voice.

~FIFTY SIX~

Tiger and Gruff retraced their steps and re-entered the church from the rear, nobody appeared to have noticed their absence including Adrian, who was busy singing along to some sort of burial service Cantata, in Latin. Tiger made his way outside through the back door, whilst Gruff went to retrieve their photographic friend.

They all met up again beside the convoy of black executive cars waiting at the rear of the Church, the respective drivers standing in small groups chatting and keeping a beady eye out for their Principals whilst having a crafty fag.

The thick dust on the knees of Tiger's trousers and the back of his Jacket, although odd, would give no clues to the most keen of observers that he had just left a horror chamber.

Yet they were being watched and he was a very keen observer. An observer with high powered binoculars and a reel of fishing line in his jacket pocket.

Gruff located their driver and all three men piled into the rear of his car. None of them spoke as the driver whisked them away from the Church and Trafalgar Square, heading for Paddington Green, the location of the capital's High Security Police Station.

~FIFTY SEVEN~

'So where is this note then?'

Detective Sergeant Phillip Adams didn't appear to believe Tiger who was sat opposite him in interview room number three on the ground floor of Paddington Green Police Station. He tended not to believe anybody anymore. Twenty five years of being lied to in various Police interview rooms around the London Metropolitan district had established that personal position.

He'd been interviewing Tiger for over an hour, and so far his story hadn't changed. If he was a liar, he was a very good one.

'I must have dropped it.'

'That's convenient. Where?'

'If I knew where, I'd probably still have it.'

'Who is the man you came in with?'

'I came in with two men, who are you referring to?'

'The one with the office on the fourth floor.'

'Why don't you pop up and ask him?'

'His door is always locked.'

'That's convenient.'

'What do you do for a job, son?' DS Adams was old enough to call most people 'son,' and he usually spat the word out, using it in a derogatory way, well, certainly not a fatherly one.

'My job is irrelevant to your enquiries.'

'Really? I think I'll be the judge of that. What's your job?'

'Dolphin Trainer.'

The gnarly old detective raised an eyebrow. He'd heard some of some pretty odd occupations before, but this was a new one.

'Right then mister Dolphin Trainer, let's start at the beginning again.'

'Am I under arrest?'

'No, not at present you are here giving a voluntary interview, as I explained earlier.'

'So I can leave at any time?'

'Yes you can.'

Tiger stood up pushing back the hard plastic chair causing it to grate along the concrete floor.

'Well I'll bid you good day then, Sergeant.'

DS Adams sighed and loosened his tie. He'd already worked a ten hour shift and there was an overtime moratorium in place. As of ten minutes ago he wasn't even being paid. He changed tack, softened his tone and said.

'Sit down son. We are trying to get to the bottom of this messy business. Look at it from my point of view. You stroll in here with some sneaky beaky operator working from the fourth floor, claiming that your girlfriend has been murdered, you were there when it happened, there were about eighty other people in the vicinity including I may add, some very senior Police Officers. You then leave the scene without speaking to any of them. It's all a bit odd, don't you see? Because if that did indeed happen, then you, by cooperating with us, can help us catch her killer.'

'I have already explained to you Sergeant that I can catch the killer, maybe with the help of the man on the fourth floor, maybe not. I don't need your help in doing that. What I do need help with, is getting some protection for the immediate future for me and my friends, because one of those eighty men at the Church is most probably the murderer and I was the intended target. I have every reason to suspect that whoever is responsible for Miss Kelly's death is not about to think, 'Oh, wrong person, let's leave it at that then.' Now, I am presuming that you're an experienced Detective on the Murder Squad, so you will know there is not a cat in hells chance of you ever being in a position to even speak to any of those eighty people, let alone interview and arrest one of them.'

Detective Sergeant Adams was the most experienced member of the murder Squad and he pondered Tiger's speech for a full minute, watching the second hand tick along on the Home Office approved clock hanging from the wall, before replying.

'Do not leave the Country, we know where you live, that has been verified. Do not contact any of the people that were at the Church. Do not conduct any sort of enquiries as I am pretty sure that Dolphin Trainers are not qualified for that type of work. We will be in touch with you.'

'So I get no protection and you want me to sit at home listening to Radio Four all day and do nothing?'

'Other Radio stations are available. You are free to go.'

~FIFTY EIGHT~

Gruff arranged for a car to take Adrian back to Derby, dropping Tiger off at his home in Lincolnshire. The journey from London was uneventful. Tiger arrived home four hours later and said a miserable cheerio to his old friend, declining Adrian's offer of staying for a few days.

He walked slowly up the short drive to his front door and fished in his pocket for his key.

'Cooeee. Cooee.' Polly Richardson, the old lady next door popped her head over the boundary fence.

'I see you're back Tiger, did you have a nice time?'

'It was a funeral Polly.'

'Oh. Yes, of course how could I forget...Is Miss Kelly with you?'

Polly noticed that he looked quite perplexed at the simple question and assumed he was tired after spending time down there 'in that there London.' She shrugged her frail shoulders when Tiger appeared to ignore her completely as he entered his property.

Once his front door had sealed him from the outside world, Tiger switched off the alarm system that was making a soft beeping noise and leaned back on the door tossing his house keys into a small bowl on the table in the hall and listened.

He heard nothing. Complete silence where there should have been laughter. Calmness where there should have been an element of activity. Stillness when there should have been movement. It was so unnatural, it scared him.

And Tiger wasn't scared of anything.

He made a mental note to apologise to Polly for his rude behaviour and bring her up to speed with developments a bit later on. Polly was okay, she could be a bit nosey and he suspected that she was in charge of the village gossip circle, but she was a decent old stick and he was bang out of order by ignoring her. Yes, he would apologise, maybe take her some flowers...

Moving into the spacious living room, he dumped his overnight bag on the sofa and headed for the drinks cabinet in the kitchen, pulling out a bottle of Jack Daniels and a chunky whisky glass. After placing them on the wooden table he sat down and spent a short time looking at the familiar shaped bottle, intent on having just the one drink. He unscrewed the bottle top and poured himself a generous measure of the amber liquid and realised that the whisky tumbler he'd chosen from the rack, was the one that Miss Kelly had brought back from Lynchburg, Tennessee the previous year, as his birthday present.

The 'best-selling bourbon in the world' remained untouched in the glass as his tears streamed unashamedly in rivers down both cheeks.

~FIFTY NINE~

By eleven o'clock the following morning Tiger was ready for a hot brew. He was some 130 miles from home in North Yorkshire at the A1 café at Scotch Corner.

Earlier he'd been to the local florist and purchased a large bunch of assorted cut flowers for Polly, his neighbour and apologised for his behaviour the previous day. She was now fully aware of the Miss Kelly situation and had promised to look after his property once more during his latest short absence. She fully understood why he would want to get away but didn't ask where he was going and Tiger never mentioned his destination either. He politely declined the offer of a cup of tea and had fired up his Triumph Trident and headed North.

His motorcycle was in fine fettle and running perfectly. As he'd set off he had a brief recollection of the repairs he'd made to the carburettors and it seemed so long ago, but it was in fact less than forty eight hours since he'd had them in bits on his workshop bench.

The hot cup of tea in the friendly little café at Scotch Corner was followed by a Chelsea bun and a quick perusal of his map book. His destination was 380 miles from Lincoln and he traced the roads with the tip of a teaspoon and memorised the route. Getting past Glasgow was the next leg, he had no real desire to meet any City folk, then join the A82 trunk road and keep heading North West into the highlands.

Fort William lay in the shadow of Scotland's highest mountain, Ben Nevis, and by default at over 4400 feet above sea level was the highest peak in the British Isles. The town itself was actually the second largest in Scotland after Inverness. However whenever Tiger had visited it was always quiet and although he didn't know exactly what he was looking for, or even if he'd find it, it was a nice enough place to start.

He fired up his beloved Trident once more and continued North, on a mission to calm his tortured soul and to dig deep into his personal reserves to find some answers.

~SIXTY~

When night falls in the Lincolnshire Wolds it falls extremely quickly, turning the picturesque countryside, the swooping hills and rolling pastures into ink-drenched blackness that's surprising for, and can be dangerous to, the many walkers who follow the Anglo Saxon and Viking pathways that crisscross its length and breadth.

But it's perfect for the type of man that uses high powered binoculars and carries fishing line in his pockets.

He'd parked his motor car some four miles away in the town of Louth, hoisted a black canvas rucksack onto his back and headed on foot towards Tiger's distant property. He didn't need light and he didn't need a map, his research had been thorough and he was well practised at this type of thing. He was two hundred yards from Tiger's boundary fence when he first stopped. He knelt down at the side of a large wild rhododendron bush and changed into black coveralls and black rubber soled boots, he smudged camouflage cream across the pointed features of his face. He could easily blend into the night.

He was the night.

His next stop was at fifty yards distance. He stood in complete silence for a full thirty minutes without taking his eyes from the back of Tiger's home. He moved to his right and jumped softly over a small dyke landing quietly on the edge of a freshly ploughed field and began to circle the property stopping every five yards or so to listen.

The farmhouse was in complete darkness, but the small cottage next door had a dull electric lamp burning in a back room splashing some light into an otherwise blue-black evening. He avoided looking directly at it, in order to keep his night vision at optimum performance.

After three hours of constant observation and moving ever nearer he was now convinced that nobody was at home. He had glanced through a small window into the hallway and seen the red light on the master box of the alarm system. It was armed. Tiger would not have been in the property with a live alarm system.

He moved stealthily towards the stables to the side of the house, he was in no hurry and he knew that one of those out-sheds was where Tiger garaged his motorcycle. He lay flat on his belt buckle and pulled the wooden door open half an inch; peering through the slight gap, he saw that too was empty. He sniffed at the air around the garage door, no smell of hot oil or exhaust gas. His quarry was long gone.

The cottage next door was always going to be a plan B. It was now time for plan B.

Polly Richardson had lived in the cottage for seventy years. She was born at the small hospital in Horncastle ten miles distant, where her mother had died during her birth. She was raised by her father, who had never remarried and worked on the farm as a tractor driver until he died when Polly was fourteen years old. The Carter family owned the farm and took Polly in as a house maid. She could clean and cook and was generally a pleasant little girl to have around the farm house. Polly loved it. She got to stay in the cottage with an aging Aunt Alice who had come up from Peterborough to look after her niece when her brother had passed away, and could ride some of the smaller horses after her chores and learnt to drive a tractor and feed chickens and help with the harvest in the summer.

The man dressed in black slid a large sharp blade under the sash window to a darkened room at the front of the cottage, easing the heavy wooden frame upwards. It made a slight squeal, but not loud enough to worry him as he climbed into the darkened room.

He stood for a minute or two and once again listened intently to the sounds of the property. He knew that every house had its own little peculiar noises. Most people wouldn't have heard anything but the man in black heard it all. A slight groan as a gust of wind bounced off a gable, a tiny splash as a leaky tap dispensed a drop of water into a tin sink.

And he sniffed the air. Stale chocolate biscuits. Cheap perfume.

The door in front of him was not close fitting, a trickle of light leaked under the door from the adjoining room. He heard the soft breathing of a female, and the almost indistinguishable sound of the same female humming a long forgotten country song.

He took three soft paces towards the door and slowly lowered the heavy brass handle to silently release the lock.

He then yanked the door open, stepping quickly into the occupied room.

~SIXTY ONE~

Tiger checked into the Flint Hotel on Fort William High Street. It would only be for the one night as wanted to rent out one of the small Croft cottages to the North of the town. His late arrival in Fort William had scuppered that idea for tonight. The 'Flint' had secure parking to the rear and the staff seemed pleasant enough, so he was happy with that although he had no plans to start making new friends.

After a refreshing shower, he emptied his motorcycle pannier and changed into a pair of blue jeans, his favourite hiking boots and a loose fitting white tee shirt before throwing his black leather jacket on and going downstairs with an intention to explore the local area.

Apart from a couple of middle aged ladies sat drinking tea, who glanced up at him as he passed through reception, nobody gave him a second look. He pushed the front door open and stepped onto a busy street.

As he walked past the pubs and restaurants he noted that nearly every establishment had something to do with the Cameron family, obviously the local clan name. He had never spotted that before. He had been to the town a few times in the past, sailing on Loch Linnhe, and taking part in the Six Day International Motorcycle trials as an official observer. He also remembered that two Victoria Cross recipients had come from the town.

The highest and most prestigious award for gallantry in the face of the enemy that can be awarded to British and Commonwealth forces, and here in Fort William there were two such recipients. One went to a Colonel John Wood during the Persian war of 1856 and the other to a Colonel Hugh Cochrane for his brave actions a couple of years later during the Indian mutiny in 1858.

He wasn't sure if anybody else from the town had ever made the big time.

As he passed number 98 on the High Street he heard the unmistakable sound of bagpipes from within the premises. He looked up and found himself outside the famous McTavish's Kitchen Restaurant. He peered through the window and saw that the place was packed to the rafters with diners.

A portly looking piper wearing a kilt, presumably a Cameron weave he thought, was blowing furiously into the bag whilst his chubby fingers danced up and down the chanter as he followed a waiter to a seated young couple who were holding hands across the table, gazing lovingly into each other's eyes and eagerly awaiting their meal.

Tiger sighed. He felt an immense wave of sadness overpower him and decided that he'd return to his room and get an early night.

~SIXTY TWO~

Polly Richardson placed her knitting to one side, stood up, and made her way to the small drinks cabinet by the living room door. She fancied another sherry.

Just a small one.

She paused after picking up the bottle. She'd heard a faint squeak from the front room window. She knew all the sounds that her house made. She'd lived in it her whole life.

Then, from the corner of her eye, she noticed the big brass door handle start to move down, very slowly.

A figure dressed from head to toe in black carrying a large knife leapt into her living room and before the intruder could get their bearings, she gave it to him.

With a hockey stick.

'SMACK.'

One blow, a full roundhouse swing, accurately aimed to the frontal lobe area of the head and the figure in black crumpled to the floor unconscious.

Lincolnshire Constabulary was never top of the league tables for prompt assistance, the County was massive and the recent cuts had taken their toll on response times. However, following a recent spate of burglaries in the Louth area, the Divisional Commander had stepped up to the plate and was, for now anyway, trying very hard to provide a proper service.

'You were lucky we were in the area Miss Richardson,' Constable Stevens the local Rural Beat Officer stated, as he placed the prostrate intruder in handcuffs before searching him.

'You mean that man was lucky.' She retorted pointing a bony finger at the person who had dared to interrupt her evening.

'Well that's odd. He has no identification on him at all. I certainly don't recognise him. Do you?'

'No. Why would I? He looks foreign.'

The conversation was stopped short as the ambulance crew arrived. The lead medic had a chat and exchanged notes with Constable Stevens whilst her partner knelt down and checked the intruder's vital signs.

'Checked for sharps, Constable?'

'Yes Duck, all clear.'

'Thank you.' The young medic then paused in her work and looked up at Polly.

'Hockey stick?'

'Yup.'

'Nice.'

~SIXTY THREE~

Anthony Stone was making an International call from a red phone box on Charlton Street in central London. He definitely had to be away from his spacious office on the eighteenth floor of Century House on Westminster Bridge Road in order to make this particular call. You could never tell who was listening.

Well you could. The building was bloody chocka block with damned spies.

Stone shouted into the phone. 'Stefan, are we heading in the right direction?'

The voice on the other end of the line was speaking English but with a heavy Eastern European accent. The connection was awful. It always was.

'Hello. Hello? This is Stefan... Yes... We have our best man on the case... It will be all over by tomorrow.'

'I don't want any cock ups this time. Make sure it's done.'

'Cock ups? What does that...'

The phone line had been disconnected.

Despite the assurances he'd just heard on the phone, the temporary head of the Secret Intelligence Service was still decidedly worried. Tiger bloody Johnnie was becoming a pain. How the devil had he managed to survive the trap in the crypt at Leicester Square? And the girl? How did that happen? He actually had no feelings whatsoever about the girl that had been crushed, she was collateral damage, nothing more, but it was a massive deviation from his plan.

He decided that he'd spent enough time in the office for one day and he rather fancied a large Irish whiskey. Jameson should do it, and he knew exactly where he could get one without the hassle and inconvenience of anybody knowing what his business was.

His mood brightened considerably.

~SIXTY FOUR~

The burglary report submitted by Police Constable Stevens the previous evening had been doing the rounds. Generally speaking such a report would lay on file for a few days before a uniformed patrol Sergeant gave it a cursory glance and rubber stamped it upstairs to C.I.D. The Criminal Investigation Department.

On this occasion, owing to the latest initiative laid down by the Divisional Superintendent, all burglary reports from the Louth area were despatched to his office immediately after they were typed up. His office would do more than glance, as was the usual practice. There would be no 'rubber stamping.'

The eight page report had visited the in-trays of no fewer than two Officers of Inspector rank and one rather ambitious Detective Chief Inspector. He was the one that had seen another report regarding a black rucksack that had been found by a dog walker under a wild rhododendron bush, not two hundred yards from a recent crime scene.

He was the one that had notionally connected the rucksack and its contents, a pair of 10x40 Zeiss high powered binoculars, a hire car receipt and a used spool of fishing line, to the aggravated burglary at a certain Miss Polly Richardson's residence.

By chance, that morning, he'd happened upon a colleague who had been a recruit at Police Training College at the same time. Sharing a pot of nasty tasting tea in the canteen, they'd spent twenty minutes chatting about the woes of the job and where their respective careers had taken them so far. The Detective's colleague had opted for Traffic division some three years earlier and was struggling to get a promotion to inspector rank, despite flying through the examinations.

Of more importance to the keen DCI was the fact he'd learned that a Ford Cortina motor vehicle had been found unattended in the small square in Louth town centre. It was a hire car from the Hertz car rental outlet at Heathrow airport and enquiries were ongoing as to the whereabouts of the driver. The DCI had a pretty good idea where the driver was at that precise moment but he didn't share that information.

Sat back in his spartan office he gathered his thoughts and his paperwork. He had a Hertz rental car with a missing driver. The registration number of that hired Cortina matched the receipt in the rucksack in the property store.

He had the binoculars, which had been bagged and tagged and whisked off to SOCO, the Scenes of Crimes department for finger print testing, along with a large knife found on the floor at the scene at Miss Richardson's addresss. And he had 200 yards or so of Dyneema 200lb breaking strain ultra-strong polyethylene fibre.

He also had an unidentified male at Lincoln City General Hospital.

If these pieces were not connected, he'd stop pushing for promotion to Detective Superintendent and join the Girl Guides. He wouldn't bother informing the Divisional Superintendent with his findings just yet. It's not as if they could actually charge anybody with anything.

Not whilst the main suspect was in an induced coma.

~SIXTY FIVE~

Tiger had woken from a fitful sleep and was up at the crack of dawn. He'd breakfasted on kippers and poached eggs with toasted home-made bread and was in the process of securing his overnight bag onto the back of his motorcycle. The weather had turned and was truly miserable. Wispy clouds scudded across the slate grey sky and the wind was whipping up the tops of the waves in the Loch. He donned his leaky waterproof over-suit - it was obvious to everyone that rain was galloping towards them - he threw his leg over his Triumph Trident and stabbed the electric start with his right thumb. This was his first ever machine with an electric start, a brand new concept on British motorcycles and along with the changing of the gear lever to the left hand side and the rear brake pedal to the right. I t would catch him out from time to time. His early morning journey would take him eight miles to the North east, along the A 82 to the small village of Spean Bridge in the parish of Kilmonivaig.

Tiger powered his machine skilfully towards his objective, the Dunlop TT100 tyres squealing under the pressure of his cornering ability. He tried to force a smile that wouldn't come and so concentrated on the road ahead. He usually loved this type of road, big sweeping bends with positive camber and small hedgerows blurring past him as he accelerated out of them. But not this morning.

It had started to rain as he pulled up at the Commando Memorial. He remained seated on his motorcycle with the engine switched off. The hot twin down pipes of the machine's exhaust ticked as they cooled, and hissed when instantly evaporating raindrops struck.

Tiger removed his crash helmet and placed it in his lap. The rain was coming down harder now, plastering his already unruly mop of hair to his face. He looked up unblinking at the seventeen foot tall memorial to the British Commandos who had given up their lives in defence of their Country during World War Two.

He didn't have to actually read the inscription placed under the feet of the three bronze heroes, and the driving rain coming down from the heavens in squall type quantities made it difficult to read. He'd seen it many times before and the words would be forever etched into his memory.

'UNITED WE CONQUER'

This puts it into perspective, thought Tiger. Those men lost hundreds of their comrades, their best mates. They suffered hardships that didn't bear thinking about and they still went unstinting about their business.

Tiger stayed in the lee of the impressive monument to the fallen for thirty minutes, ignoring the elements that howled around him, seemingly oblivious to the cold and the wet. It didn't matter to him. His miseries, his privations, were leaking from his body and being replaced with a cold, hard, icy steel resolve.

He replaced his sodden helmet squarely and firmly back on his head, fired up his motorcycle and headed back along the rain-lashed road towards Fort William at a much steadier pace.

The worst of the weather had eased as he approached the town. He stopped at a red traffic light, the twin cylinders of his Triumph giving out a distinctive rumble, the sound of true British engineering. A car pulled up alongside him as he waited.

Tiger glanced across at the driver - a young man with a combative glint in his eye, revving his car engine. A Ford Capri with a sporty red paint job. He kept his eye on Tiger as he did so. Tiger nodded slightly, looked back at the road ahead and gunned the powerful motorcycle engine beneath him, the traffic lights were still on red as Tiger momentarily released his clutch before hauling it back in and grabbed a handful of front brake as his machine lurched forward six inches and stopped.

The driver of the Capri was not looking where he should have been looking. He released his clutch at the same moment and hammered down on the accelerator. His vehicle roared into the junction.

'BANG'

A blue Ford Cortina coming from the right, legitimately driving through a green light, mashed into the side of the Capri. Broken glass tinkled onto the wet road like precious stones and bits of red and blue bodywork crumpled under the weight of forces that they were not designed to take.

Tiger's traffic signal silently turned to amber and then green and he carefully negotiated his way around what was probably once a nice chrome bumper lying in the middle of the road and continued back to his hotel with a smile wrapped right around his face.

Knowing that traffic enforcement Officers were going to be otherwise occupied for the next thirty minutes at least, he parked his motorcycle on no-parking double yellow lines to the front of the Flint Hotel and stowed his waterproof gear. He walked into the reception foyer with a spring in his step, and nodded at the two middle aged ladies who had been in the exact same positions the previous evening.

'Morning ladies.'

Slightly taken aback at such a cheery salute, neither of them could offer an immediate reply to the handsome figure in wet Levi jeans as he strolled past them heading for the check-out desk, although one of them was kind enough to blush.

'Room seven check out please.'

The young man at the polished counter was half hidden by piles of tourist brochures.

'Yes of course Sir.'

The transactions complete, Tiger turned on his heel and aimed for the exit.

'It's a bit miserable out there young man,' ventured the non-blushing lady. You be careful on that big motorbike.'

'Miserable?' Tiger had questioned as he opened the door to a howling blast of wind that was accompanied with crisp packets from the street and salt water spray from the troubled seawater Loch.

'Nonsense ladies, it's a cracking day. Good morning!'

Tiger was back.

~SIXTY SIX~

Gruff was concerned for his friend. Tiger wasn't picking up his home phone and things were moving quickly. He was also frustrated. Tiger needed the information that Gruff was collating and not able to pass on. Decisions, important decisions, had to be made.

Detective Sergeant Phillip Adams was becoming a right royal pain in the arse. Gruff couldn't enter Paddington Green Police Station without the duty desk Sergeant stopping him and handing him yet another hand written note written by the detective.

They'd started off friendly enough, a simple greeting followed by a polite request to have a quiet chat, but now, ten notes later, they'd reached threatening levels of impudence. The polite stuff had stopped at around the third note. The quiet chat had turned into a formal interview by the seventh and escalated into formal disciplinary action by the ninth. Gruff needed help, as well as another office and if Tiger wasn't making himself available to both these simple needs then he'd find somebody else who could, and he had just such a person in mind. Charlie Soper.

He sat, idly reading the latest aggressive communication that the Detective Sergeant had shoved under his door, put it down and made a telephone call. The call was answered promptly, a meeting was arranged. Gruff packed up his files, placed them into an attaché case and walked towards his office door throwing the latest crumpled ball of Metropolitan Police stationery over his shoulder where it landed in the waste paper basket, on top of ten other similarly crumpled balls.

~SIXTY SEVEN~

Tiger stopped outside a neat bungalow about two miles to the North of the town. Some considerable effort had been made to make the front garden look tidy and the walls to the building had been recently whitewashed.

The large sign at the front of the property informed the reader that some holiday crofts were still available and that Mrs Cameron was the lady to speak to. Tiger knocked on the front door and waited patiently before being admitted. The paperwork only took twenty minutes and Mrs Cameron had handed Tiger a front door key attached to a large wooden fish with the number '2' burnt into it.

'It will float if you drop it in water.' Mrs Cameron had helpfully told him.

'I can't see me having the need for that,' Tiger had countered.

'That's what all my guests say. But do you want to know how many actually do get dropped in water?'

'Not really if I'm honest.'

'Three. Three a year. Incredible isn't it?'

Armed with his floating fish key fob and directions to Croft number two, Tiger exchanged pleasantries with the mad old bat and went in search of the accommodation he'd just paid to rent for a fortnight.

It turned out to be a very short ride, less than four hundred yards and was absolutely ideal for Tiger's purpose.

Looking out over the northern tip of Loch Linnhe, it was typical of the type of property that a local fisherman and his family would have occupied thirty or forty years earlier. A simple weatherproof dwelling heated by a single peat burning fire, and access to fresh water from a little spring well at the bottom of the small back garden.

His nearest neighbour was some one hundred and fifty yards away but Tiger didn't yet know if the property was occupied or not. That information would come later. He was forced to bend down in order to enter the low threshold porch where he fiddled with the small house key attached to the oversized fob. It was a painful exercise, and water or no water the blasted fish fob would be going.

Once inside, Tiger poked his head around the first door jamb and scanned the living room. It was sparsely furnished but gave an appearance of comfort. He moved down the narrow hallway and checked out two small bedrooms, both with twin beds, and a small but functional bathroom.

The kitchen was bigger than he was expecting and adjoined the living room. It was very well appointed with up to date appliances and a quick check of the drawers and cupboards revealed a quantity of new looking cutlery and crockery. The fridge was open and not plugged into the wall socket next to it.

A couple of sheets of printed paper sat on one of the work surfaces. They turned out to be the simple rules and regulations for visitors to the property. Before picking them up for a read, Tiger made a bet with himself, a bet of £5, that one of the rules involved not removing the door key from the large fish fob.

A quick scan, third item on the list of do's and don'ts... and there it was...he'd won his bet with himself.

'Five quid up on day one! I'll put that towards some provisions,' he laughed to himself as he plugged the fridge in to the nearest power socket, closed the door and went back outside to his motorcycle.

Leaving the front door unlocked he rode back into Fort William to find a supermarket and a hardware store.

There was stuff he needed to buy, and he wasn't on holiday.

~SIXTY EIGHT~

Gruff was at the scene of Miss Kelly's murder under the guise of one of his many pseudonyms. He had chosen 'Mike Jackson' as nod to a British Army Captain he had served with during a stint with The Intelligence Corps, and whom he respected highly. The Reverend Peter Johns was in attendance. He was covering the holiday absence of the regular Vicar, The Reverend Austen Williams.

'What a terrible business, just awful and in the House of God!'

'Indeed it is awful Reverend, tragic.'

'My thoughts and prayers go out to her family and loved ones at this tortuous time, you said you know the family?'

'No, sorry Reverend I don't know the family, this is official business as I explained over tea upstairs. I just needed to ask some questions, see the scene and get a feel for it.'

'Well the Police have already been crawling about the place taking photographs and asking questions so I don't know what I can tell you.'

'I am sure the Police have done a thorough job. This is just a follow up. Did the Police take anything away?'

'No, not that I know of. I thought you were the Police, wouldn't you know that?'

'Follow up team. Different department, Reverend.'

'Oh. I see.' Which he clearly didn't.

The questioning continued.

'I see there are security cameras dotted around, were they switched on at the time in question?'

'The masonry works management team put in a request to have them fitted. It has nothing to do with the Church. Apparently there have been some thefts of tools...'

'I understand why CCTV cameras are fitted Reverend, I need to know if they were switched on at the material time, and if they were, what's happened to the recording tapes? You told me that you don't think that the Police took anything away.'

'The Police did look at some video footage in the office upstairs but decided that the lighting was so poor down here, that they were worse than useless and didn't need them.'

'I'll need to bag them up and take them.'

'I'm not sure that...'

'You'll get a receipt for them, Reverend. Now tell me about these animals at the top of the central support arch.'

'Ah, yes, well, that's Austen Williams' little project. He...'

'Austen Williams?'

'Er, yes. The regular Vicar. He's been officiating here since 1956 and has great plans for the crypt. He is a great scholar is Reverend Williams. He knows the Bible so well he can...'

'I am sure he is a fine man who loves his work, but please, tell me about the animals.'

'Well there are over thirty animals that get a specific mention in the Bible. Ants, bees, camels, leopards, wolves, locusts of course, whales, unicorns, bears...'

'Whoa! Hold it there Reverend. Did you say unicorns?'

'Unicorns. Yes.'

'The mythical beast type unicorn?'

'I know of no other.'

'In the Bible?'

'Oh yes. Unicorns get mentioned nine times in the King James Bible. Numbers, Job, Psalms and of course Deuteronomy...'

'Deuteronomy. Of course. Would that be Chapter 33 Verse 17?'

'I really cannot tell you Chapter and Verse but I assure you that they do get a mention.'

'I think you'll find I'm correct Reverend. So these biblical type animals are being carved by stone masons and placed up in the vaults and arches like gargoyles?'

'Yes, that's pretty much it.'

'Thank you for your help, it's been most interesting. I suggest we now retire to your office upstairs and take possession of that useless video recording.'

'I'll get a receipt right?'

'Yes Reverend, you'll get a receipt.'

~SIXTY NINE~

Tiger spent the rest of his morning ferrying food and other provisions from the town to the holiday Croft. His motorcycle could only handle so much weight and half a dozen trips were needed.

The fridge was now packed and fully operational and it actually sounded quite excited, judging by the noises it was making. If the drinks cabinet was slightly miffed at being used purely for the purposes of holding a lone bottle of Jack Daniels, it didn't say anything. It just sat in the corner of the living room looking as wooden as the day it was built.

Tiger had located a surprisingly large utility room connected to the kitchen. He presumed that it was for the storage of pedal cycles and the paraphernalia generally associated with holiday activities. Once he'd realised it was there, and empty, well, he utilised it.

Stepping from the shower he used a big fluffy white towel to dry his toned upper body and laughed out loud when he realised that he'd been in Scotland less than fifteen hours, and had spent five hours of that time soaking wet.

Once dry, he donned a pair of olive drab lightweight trousers and matching running vest, pulled on his hiking boots and laced them up tight. He stuffed a waterproof kagoul and his wallet into a bum bag, strapped it around his waist and headed outside. He locked the front door this time, with a fob-less key. He'd taken a risk by breaking the house rules, disconnected the big floating wooden fish and stuffed into the cutlery drawer.

Tiger was a risk taker.

He jogged towards the choppy waters of Loch Linnhe and found a track that loosely followed the shoreline. Although his boots were not designed for running he was perfectly comfortable in them and picked up the pace. An hour later he reckoned that he'd covered eight miles and felt good. Running had never been his favourite pastime. Downhill skiing was his thing, but he found that once he got used to the idea and actually got going it was an excellent feeling.

A doctor he had once dated – the medical sort - had him hooked when she explained that having endorphins rushing around his body was like taking a legal drug. The peptides activate the body's opiate receptors and cause an analgesic effect.

Well, that was an eye opener. Tiger understood well and truly how to punish his body. He had marched, swum and crawled thousands of miles in the pursuit of, and sometimes the evasion of, an enemy. It was always hard work and no fun at all. But he'd never realised that exercise could actually be fun, and good for him.

He sat down on a nearby rock and took ten minutes to get his breath back. The view across the Loch wasn't spectacular but it held a certain je ne sais quoi and Tiger approved. He'd not met another human being during his run and wasn't expecting to meet anybody on his way back, so he was surprised to see another runner approaching from the direction of Fort William. As Tiger stood, the distant runner stopped abruptly and appeared to be staring directly at him. There was about two hundred yards between them. Tiger noted that it was a bearded man about the same physical size as himself and dressed in a grey tracksuit. As the man turned and trotted off back the way he had come, Tiger could see that he was wearing a small black rucksack riding high on his back.

The hackles along the back of his neck twitched but didn't reach full danger mode. He decided that he'd head back anyway and if he caught up with the fellow, he'd find out a bit more about him. He set off at his usual eight miles an hour pace.

~SEVENTY~

Anthony Stone had been waiting outside the red phone box on Charlton Road for one minute and thirty two seconds. A man was inside the box making a phone call and the head of M16 could clearly see, and hear, that the man had been drinking.

'On Bayswater Close you say? Opposite the Coach and Horses pub you say?'

Stone obviously could only hear one side of this conversation, but he had heard enough to know that his own call was far more important, it always was and certainly didn't involve a hooker who advertised her services in a filthy phone box.

'That's a bit steep 'darlin. Can we negotiate? I only 'wanna blow.' His words were slurred.

A Pause.

'Wadda 'ya mean no? It's all open to negotiation, you're all slags at the end of the day...'

The phone box door was pulled open and the hapless man found himself being dragged backwards from the phone box by collar of his jacket. A woman's voice continued speaking as the receiver started swinging loosely from the phone.

'Oi Oi, what's your game?' The man protested.

Stone didn't say a word as he continued to drag the man another six feet before unceremoniously dumping him on the ground before stepping over him and entering the phone box. He grabbed at the dangling receiver and shouted into the mouthpiece.

'Try negotiating you fucker. It makes for better business,' and ended the call by pressing the cradle on top of the phone.

The previous caller had brushed off the street dirt from his clothing and approached the closed phone box door. Stone had started dialling an international number and never missed a digit as, without turning around, he pushed back hard on the door with the highly polished, double soled leather brogue covering his right foot.

The door caught the man full in the face, breaking his nose, sending a spray of bright red blood high into the air as he toppled backwards howling like a baby.

'What's the situation?' He spat into the phone as soon as it was picked up at the other end of the line.

'We are unsure as to what has gone wrong.'

'Can you say that again? I can't hear you properly.'

The line crackled and popped as usual, making conversation difficult and Stone had to press the dirty earpiece hard up against his ear to hear better. The man outside with a broken nose wasn't helping the situation, he was wailing like a banshee. 'Police! Police! I've been assaulted!'

Stone told the man he was trying to speak with to 'hang on.' He opened the phone box door and dragged the bleeding man back into the box and sat him on the floor under the phone. The man began roaring again and was quickly silenced as Stone kneed him hard in the face causing bits of cartilage to join the blood streaming from his nose. For good measure he raised his right leg and squashed the man under his heel, stuffing him into a corner of the confined space.

His attention then turned back to his call.

'Now then. What the fuck is going on?'

'There has been a problem.'

'What sort of problem?'

'We cannot contact our man.'

'You promised that he was your best man.'

'He was…Is…We don't know what has happened.'

'I am stopping payments to you as of now.'

'But…'

'No 'buts' you cretin. I'll do the bloody job myself.'

Stone slammed the receiver down, cracking the cradle, and gave the unfortunate man on the floor a sharp dig in the ribs with a right shoe before leaving the phone box.

'Shit,' Stone hissed under his breath.

He stood outside the box for another twenty seconds pondering this latest situation before reopening the phone box door.

'Shit,' he hissed again and gave the now unconscious man a further toe punt to the ribs before storming off.

He wasn't in the best of moods.

~SEVENTY ONE~

Tiger had taken another shower and had changed into a fresh white tee shirt and blue jeans. He remained barefoot as he sat in the kitchen. Despite the inclement weather outside, the Croft was surprisingly warm within. With a glass of Jack Daniels in his hand he was studying an Ordnance Survey map of the local area that he'd spread out on the table, held down by various condiments along its edges to stop it curling.

Using the very tip of a blade of grass, he was tracing the contour lines from Ben Nevis over to the East down its Western slopes towards Fort William. If he'd used his finger he'd have blocked at least 300 yards of ground. Old habits die hard.

His attention was interrupted by a soft knocking on the front door of the Croft.

Instantly alert, his immediate thought was who knew he was here? The mad old bat Mrs Cameron. That was all. It must be her. Perhaps he'd forgotten to sign something earlier as the signing over of the Croft did all seem a bit quick.

He stood and walked to the living room and paused. Shit, the bloody key fob. He back pedalled to the kitchen, opened the cutlery drawer and grabbed the floating wooden fish. He paused again in the hallway and reattached the door key to the infernal fob and opened the front door.

'Sorry to disturb.'

It wasn't Mrs Cameron. It was a lady of about thirty years, standing 5' 6' tall. Quite pretty in a classical way and casually dressed in a white polo neck top and black jeans. She had a very nice figure, short brown hair and green eyes.

Tiger noticed these things.

'Good evening Miss.'

'Well it's 'Mrs' actually,' the lady announced holding up her left hand for his inspection.

Shit. Tiger usually noticed these things.

'So, what can I do for you, Mrs..?'

'Brown. Anita Brown. I'm staying at the Croft next door.' She pointed needlessly to the Croft that Tiger had noticed on his arrival.

Tiger smiled. Mrs Brown noticed it.

'With my husband,' she quickly added.

'That's nice, so how can I help?'

'Well we were wondering, that's my husband Andrew and I were wondering, whether you'd like to pop over for a drink? Do the neighbourly thing and all that. That is if you're not too busy or anything.'

Tiger was trying to place her accent. Educated certainly. Local certainly not. Southern England, Home Counties but not the commuter belt, possibly edge of Hampshire...

'Slough.'

'Slough?'

'I'm from Slough. You looked as if you were trying to place my accent. I play that game all the time.'

Tiger was stunned. Slough? Jeez...He was getting old, and old meant slow.

'So?'

'So what?'

'Do you fancy a drink with us?'

'Er, yes. That'll be nice, I'll just chuck on some boots and a jacket and I'll come over.'

'I see you have still got that stupid floating fish attached to your door key.'

Tiger held up the pathetic looking bit of wood and forced a weak smile.

'I think it's in the rules.'

'I took ours off straight away. I don't play by the rules. C'mon get your kit on, it's freezing stood out here.'

Tiger went back inside and sorted out his boots and jacket, grabbed a bottle of wine from the rack and returned to the front door. He looked down at the wooden fish, and with a shrug he once again removed it from its key.

'She doesn't play by the rules.' Tiger ran that thought through his mind a couple of times, as the little dark haired, green eyed rule breaker escorted him along the dimly lit path towards the neighbouring Croft.

~SEVENTY TWO~

Tiger had introduced himself to his host-to-be during the short walk between the two little properties and as Mrs Anita Brown opened the front door to her rented Croft she turned to look Tiger in the eye and put a finger to her lips.

'Shhhh, come in Tiger, and please be quiet. Andrew is asleep...'

'Say what?'

'I'm joking silly, c'mon in.'

Tiger entered the Croft. It was a carbon copy of his own, same hallway, same furniture same everything, except...There was a man sat on the sofa, a bearded man, a man that Tiger had seen out running not four hours earlier.

Running man stood up as Tiger entered the living room and stretched out his arm, an open hand offered peace and greeting by way of a handshake. Tiger gripped the running man's hand, and although it was a firm shake there was no attempt to show a hand of strength from either man.

'Andrew Brown.'

'Tiger.'

'Tiger? Really?'

'Really.'

'Welcome, er, Tiger. Grab a seat. Anita darling, would you do the honours with Tiger's wine? Tiger there was no need to bring a bottle, we have plenty of booze here, don't we babe?'

'We do honey. Here Tiger let me take your jacket with that bottle.' She leaned closer...

'And your shirt...'

'What? My shirt?'

'I'm teasing Tiger, relax, and grab a pew.'

Tiger wasn't sure if Anita had been joking or not, he wasn't used to this level of banter from a girl and he definitely didn't subscribe to open love, threesomes, swingers and those lady-boy chaps that frequented the clubs and bars of The Haymarket back in London.

'So what do you do?' Asked Andrew as Tiger planted himself in a chair next to the fully stocked, but as yet, unlit fire.

'I'm a dolphin trainer.' It seemed to work with a cantankerous Metropolitan Police detective so Tiger decided to play on it here as well.

'Dolphin trainer? Mmmm.' Andrew turned his head and shouted over his shoulder. 'Darling, Tiger here says he's a dolphin trainer.'

Anita poked her head around the door jamb from the kitchen.

'A what? Did you say dolphin trainer?'

'Yes darling. A Tiger training dolphins.' He laughed at his own little joke.

'Well that's nice honey,' and Anita returned to the kitchen to do whatever it was that she was doing. Which was far too long, Tiger really could do with a drink right now. He'd left a large Jack Daniels back at his place.

'No, seriously Tiger.'

'I am serious. I am here to look at the possibility of relocating a school of dolphins from Miami in Florida to Loch Linnhe over there.' Tiger pointed in the general direction of the Loch.

'Why?'

'Tourism.'

'That's mad.'

'I know, its borderline mental but I'm still getting paid. Do you run?'

Andrew Brown didn't bat an eyelid at the abrupt question.

'No.'

'I didn't see you up on the Northern shoreline earlier today then?'

'Afraid not. I was in town all day today. Where were we today darling?' He called once again to his wife.

'We were in town all day.' Anita called back.

Tiger knew that he was lying and Andrew Brown, if in fact that was his name, knew that Tiger knew.

It was going to be a long night.

~SEVENTY THREE~

Gruff Wetherspoon and Charlie Soper had driven up to Lincoln in Charlie's motor vehicle. Charlie was an extremely capable driver, slicing the Range Rover 4X4 through the North London traffic and Northwards on the A1, the big V8 motor purring whilst the surrounding vehicles appeared to be roaring. The 110 mile journey had taken them less than 2 ½ hours. Tiger's property was in darkness, Gruff instinctively knew that Tiger was not at home and guided Charlie to park the Rover outside the neighbouring cottage of Polly Richardson.

'There's somebody in the cottage at least.' Noted Charlie. 'I just saw the curtains twitch, we're being watched.'

'We'll be fine,' said Gruff exiting the vehicle. 'I told you earlier this is Polly's place she's a friend of Tiger's. Harmless old thing.'

'I'll wait in the car, I've got some calls to make. Be careful Gruff.' Then reaching behind and dragged a heavy looking attaché case from the back seats, dumping it on the now vacant passenger seat.

Charlie opened the case. A full-duplex briefcase telephone, working on the Zero G radio telephone network, and although it was cumbersome and had its limitations it was still way ahead of its time and some aspects of it were still classified as secret.

'Nice. Where do you get this stuff?' Asked an impressed Gruff.

'Just be careful,' Charlie grunted.

Polly Richardson heard the knock on her front door that she was fully expecting. She'd heard a big motor vehicle pull up outside and had snatched a quick peek through the front room curtains. A green Range Rover, two occupants, one was a man she had seen before but couldn't quite place where.

A heavy fire poker rested casually against her little hall table, looking somewhat incongruous against the setting of lace doilies and a fresh white linen table cover. Her hockey stick had been taken away by the Police. 'Just routine.' Constable Stevens had told her. Well, routine or not, how could she sit and concentrate on her knitting without some sort of weapon close to hand?

She cautiously opened the door a fraction, her right hand hovering over the three foot rod of forged iron.

There was definitely someone in, thought Gruff, he could hear the sound of quiet movement behind the front door. Then it opened slowly allowing him to see the house owner glaring defiantly at him over a pair of reading glasses.

'Polly, how are you? Gruff Wetherspoon, friend of Tigers, I do believe we have met before.'

There was a moment's pause before Polly's face broke into a smile of recognition.

'Of course, of course young man, I thought I recognised you, please come in. Come in.'

Gruff entered the cottage and followed Polly through the hallway. It was hard to miss the black poker leaning against a pretty little table with its fresh white linen cover.

Once in the kitchen, Polly put the kettle on. Gruff smiled to himself, there was a song there somewhere...

'Isn't your friend joining us? 'Polly asked, as she busied herself with a packet of chocolate biscuits, spreading them onto a delicate bone china plate.

'Not for the moment Polly.'

'Ah well, tea for two then. I'll be Mum.'

Over tea and biscuits, Polly chatted and Gruff listened. She certainly had a tale to tell and Gruff's estimation of her grew with each sentence, but at the final analysis, she had no idea where Tiger was, and as such was an intelligence dead end.

Thirty minutes later, back in the Range Rover, Gruff briefed Charlie on the conversation he'd had over tea and biscuits with Polly Richardson.

'Never underestimate the will of a strong woman.' Charlie didn't seem all that impressed with Polly's recent bout of heroism.

'She's a tough old bird, I'll give her that and she had a poker ready for action at her front door, it must be bloody awful living on your own out in the sticks.'

'Don't feel sorry for her Gruff. If you took her away from here and planted her in a City, she'd never venture out, too many people. She'd just wither away and die, it happens all the time. You do know that some of the loneliest people in a city are living in tower blocks, surrounded by dozens of neighbours and they die alone?'

'That's true enough and a sad indictment of today's society. I hope it improves in the future.'

They both remained silent for a minute, staring through the big windscreen at nothing in particular. Charlie spoke first.

'So, where are we headed Gruff?'

'Lincoln City. The Police headquarters on West Parade, I know the way.'

Charlie gunned the engine and they slowly pulled away. Polly Richardson watched them through a chink in the curtains for a moment and returned to her knitting patterns, humming a long forgotten country tune.

~SEVENTY FOUR~

Tiger wasn't feeling comfortable. The chair he was sat on was pleasant enough and the wine he was drinking was refreshing and palatable. The trouble was in the shape of the lean, bearded man sat opposite him. Tiger wasn't particularly worried about his personal safety, Andrew Brown was far too comfortable in posture, Tiger could take him out in a heartbeat, it was as if he knew what the immediate future held, and was totally relaxed about it.

Tiger decided to take the bull by the horns and throw in a provocative question, stir things up a bit, as the last two hours of idle chit chat had produced nothing, other than double entendres from Anita and blatant lying from Andrew.

'Have you ever served?'

'What? As a waiter?'

'As in military service. You do have a certain military look about you.'

Andrew Brown paused and took a sip of his drink.

'What sort of look would that be?'

Tiger had noticed a subtle change of demeanour in Anita, she was now listening intently although still pretending to sit and play-act as the flirty wife.

'Oh I don't know, it's something you can't put a finger on, a set of mannerisms I suppose. You look young enough and fit enough...'

'Have you served?' Andrew threw the question right back at him.

'Aye, I've served.'

'Which mob?'

'Mob.' That word, right there, convinced Tiger that Andrew Brown had done time in the Armed Forces.

It was the small things.

'I was a steely eyed killer.'

'So... Catering Corps then?'

Both men looked at each other for about ten seconds, weighing each other up before they both stared laughing at some sort of private joke, which of course it was and pretty much the oldest gag in the Army inventory. Andrew Brown leaned forward in his seat and reached out his arm, his open hand palm upwards. It was an invitation to shake hands.

Another handshake? Tiger took up the invitation and he too leant forward and gripped the man's hand. This time it was a firmer grip and held for just a bit longer than was absolutely necessary.

'Int Corps.'

'Now there's an oxymoron.'

Andrew threw back his head and laughed again.

'Too damn right it is. Ha! Friendly Fire.'

'Liquid Gas.'

'Hells Angel.'

'Found Missing.'

Anita looked slightly puzzled and interrupted the two giggling men.

'Oxymoron?'

'You or me?' Tiger asked looking at Brown.

'I've got this,' stated Andrew turning to Anita. Oxymoron darling is when two words …'

'Don't patronise me Steve,' Anita retorted coldly. 'I know what an oxymoron is. I just don't get the context.'

'Ooops, well pardon my French. I mentioned 'Int Corps.' That's 'Intelligence Corps' and as anybody who has ever served knows full well, Military and Intelligence make up a classic oxymoron.

'Thank you. Do carry on with your fun.' Anita stood up and stormed into the kitchen.

Tiger had noted during this heated tête-à-tête that Anita had referred to Andrew as 'Steve' thus underpinning his belief that all was not as it seems. 'Steve' appeared not to have noticed the slip and Tiger decided to keep it under his hat.

It was the small things.

'Bloody women, can't live with 'em can't live without 'em.' The man calling himself Andrew sat back in his chair and let out a long sigh and asked.

'So, are you out or still serving?'

'I've been a 'civvie for two years now. You?'

'Out for over twelve.'

'Okay, but Chef? Really?'

'No.'

Both men laughed again and clinked wine glasses.

For Tiger the ice had been broken, he felt a bit warmer towards his new found brother-in-arms but there was still the issue of his real name. It could have been quite innocent of course. The man may be on a holiday break with his mistress. Andrew Brown, John Smith, cheating men used the most common of names, it happened all the time. The question for Tiger though, was is it worth questioning?

~SEVENTY FIVE~

Gruff waited patiently in the foyer of the Police Station in Lincoln City. The hard bench he was sitting on was not conducive to a long wait and the smell of cleaning bleach mingled with the sweaty odour of fear, panic and desperation permeated the walls of the small room.

The front desk constable had been shown some identification, and then had disappeared into the depths of the building to locate the detective in charge of the recent burglary at the Richardson dwelling in Louth.

No Police Station anywhere would be worth its salt, if it hadn't got the ubiquitous posters up on the walls, and Lincoln City Central was no exception.

CAN YOU HELP?

WANTED!

MISSING!

The 'big three' right there. Right where they should be. Gruff could have been anywhere in the English speaking world.

A door to the side of the foyer opened and a young man dressed in a sharp suit stood in the frame.

'You have information about a burglary?'

'I'm up from London.' Gruff stood up and rubbed his backside, trying unsuccessfully to get some circulation going again.

'Can I see some I.D.?'

Gruff hooked out an official looking card wrapped in laminate and held it up to the suited man.

'Jackson?'

'That's what is says on the card.'

'Follow me.'

Gruff did as he was bid and followed the man along a brightly lit corridor and up two flights of stairs. Every door that they passed was closed and bereft of any information as to what lay behind them.

'Here we go, in here.'

Gruff entered a large office space. There were about twenty desks neatly organised in pairs, all of them overflowing with paperwork. The lights were a bit dimmer in here but he could easily see half a dozen men scattered around, poring over files and talking quietly into telephones. Nobody looked up. There were no women.

This was the male preserve of Lincoln Criminal Investigation Department.

The suited man walked through the room and a couple of men acknowledged his presence.

'Evening Guv.'

'Guv. Can I have a word later?'

The suited man was obviously in charge and nodded to his men as he passed.

Gruff was invited into a small office at the far end of the room and offered a chair, a soft one that he gratefully accepted.

'So Mr Jackson, what have you got?' The senior detective sat himself down behind his desk. There was no nameplate.

'I'm at a slight disadvantage here in that you know my name and position but I don't know yours.'

'Does it matter? You're in a Police Station and you're here voluntarily.'

'It matters quite a lot. I need to talk to the person in charge of what is a delicate matter, a matter that reaches out to people in pay grades well over the heads of us both. It will undoubtedly be of international concern. So, a starting point involving a common courtesy would be for you to tell me, exactly who you are.'

The detective was not used to being spoken to on such terms, he paused for thought. He did have an interesting case, he did have knowledge that it might be far reaching and as of this moment he had failed to let his superiors know of his actions to date. Should he really be talking to the rather scruffy individual sitting opposite him? He made a decision.

'I really fail to see...'

Gruff stood up. He was tired, his backside was killing him and the bloke on the other side of the desk was acting like a first class prick.

'Correct. You are failing to see. I'll be back in the morning to speak to somebody with some manners, somebody more senior. The Divisional Superintendent would be a good starting point. Would you be so kind as to show me out or should I make my own way?

The detective stood up and brushed past Gruff.

'Constable Hobart!'

A man looked up from his work.

'Yes Guv?'

'Do me a favour and escort Mr Jackson here back down to reception.'

'Yes Guv.'

'And bring me a tea from the canteen on the way back.'

~SEVENTY SIX~

The clock on the wall of the Brown's Croft showed 11 o'clock. It was time for Tiger to go. He stood and stretched.

'Time I was off folks. Thanks for the drink.'

Anita came out from the kitchen a large glass of wine in her hand. She'd obviously preferred to spend the last twenty minutes drinking on her own.

'Goodnight Tiger.' There was a slight slur to her voice. 'Shall I walk you home?'

'I think I'm good Anita, but thanks.'

The man calling himself Andrew patted Tiger on the arm as he headed for the door.

'Welcome any time Chef.'

Tiger laughed and accepted the joke. Anita handed him his jacket and squeezed past him as they entered the hall. She reached for the front door and stopped turning instead to place both arms around his waist and give him a squeeze.

'See you tomorrow Tiger?'

'I expect so. I'll be about most of the day.'

'Tell you what, I can pop over and make your breakfast...How do you like your eggs?'

'In a cake. Goodnight Anita.'

Tiger stepped out into the wild Scottish night.

~SEVENTY SEVEN~

Gruff had booked accommodation at a local hotel chain. He'd checked in with Charlie. Separate rooms. One night. Cash. He preferred the anonymity of such places where nobody bothered you. Businessmen mostly, who were far too wrapped up in their own little worlds, worrying about that day's meeting, fretting about a similar meeting they'd be having in the morning.

He'd be having a meeting himself in the morning, but that certainly wasn't worrying him one little bit and he was a bit closer to finding Tiger. Charlie was a Godsend. When people wanted to go off-grid, Charlie Soper was certainly the person who could flush them out and get them back on-line.

Tiger had a lot on his mind. He honestly didn't think the Andrew/Steve character was a threat, his inbuilt radar for danger never bleeped during his short stay at their Croft. He wanted to know why he was lying. He couldn't quite grasp why Anita, if that in fact was her name, would be flirting with him if she was on a 'dirty weekend' with her lover. That didn't make sense either. It was all a bit odd. He downed the Jack Daniels that had been sitting patiently on the kitchen table in one gulp.

He'd sleep on it.

Steve Brown was in deep thought. Should he trust the man called Tiger? He'd had the man's motorcycle registration number checked out, and it had come back clean. No red flags. He was definitely ex-military, of that there was no doubt. Servicemen had a knack for weeding out the Walter Mitty characters that drifted in and out of military circles.

He should be asking the advice of his colleague Anna, but that would now have to wait until the morning. She was a first class operator, but had gone to bed worse for wear.

He found a blanket from a cupboard in the utility room, rearranged the cushions on the sofa as he lay down, pulled the blanket up to his chin and tried to sleep.

The fingers of an unconscious man lying in a bed on a secure ward at Lincoln General Hospital started to twitch. Audrey Collins, the Woman Police Constable who had been assigned to keep an eye on him, put down her trashy romantic novel and picked up the phone.

Detective Chief Inspector Edward Cousins sat behind his desk at Lincoln City Police Headquarters looking at an untouched mug of cold brown liquid that the canteen staff upstairs laughingly called tea, and wondered if he had just made a career-changing mistake.

~SEVENTY EIGHT~

'Yes Sir... Yes Sir... It's here on my desk Sir... Right away Sir.'

Detective Chief Inspector Edward Cousins slowly replaced the phone handset back in its cradle. He'd been summoned to the top floor. The Divisional Superintendent's office no less and the 'Super wanted the Richardson burglary file, the file that definitely shouldn't be sat on the desk in front of him, and he wanted it, and him, now.

He had the time it took to negotiate two flights of stairs and a short corridor in which to come up with some sort of plausible explanation as to why he had failed to carry out a superior's direct order.

Awkward.

As he approached his superior officer's door on the top floor he stopped, rubbed each of his toecaps on the back of his trouser legs and straightened his tie. He then knocked three times on the now ominous looking door and opened it.

'Good morning Sir...'

He couldn't help but notice that there was another person in the room. Good grief it was that scruffy bloke from last night, what was his name? Jackson? That was it, Jackson from the 'Met.

'Come in Edward sit down, I believe you have already met Mr Jackson from the Foreign Office.'

Foreign Office? What? Jackson hadn't mentioned that at their short meeting last night. Bugger.

'Er yes Sir. But I thought...'

'No Edward, you didn't think, that's why you are here. Mr Jackson and I have had a rather interesting chat this morning and it's only right and proper that you now join us. Is that the Richardson file?' He stretched out his arm to take the file.

'Er, yes it is Sir.'

The Divisional Superintendent opened the file and scanned through a couple of pages, making a couple of grunting noises before closing it and handing it to Gruff who placed it in his attaché case.

Detective Chief Inspector Edward Cousins was aghast! This was his file, his case and it'd just been handed over to Jackson, who'd made no attempt to read it and was obviously going to take it away!

'Sir. There is classified infor...'

'Edward. Did you get my memo?

'Memo Sir?'

'Yes, Edward. Memo. The one where I outlined the procedures that were to be carried out by my officers relating to any burglaries in the Louth area. That memo.'

`Cousins could see the traps that lay ahead and had no way of avoiding them. If on the one hand he denied seeing the memo, it would be at minimum, incompetence and at worst stating a falsehood to a superior Officer.

On the other hand if he admitted he'd seen the memo, he'd be in breach of the 'Super's direct orders regarding the new initiative on local crime.

He had to make a choice, pick the trap that would cause him the least pain.

He said nothing.

Gruff stood up and stretched out his arm. The Superintendent grasped his hand and shook it, his right thumb applying slight pressure to Gruff's knuckle. Gruff squeezed back.

Freemasons.

Brothers.

'Thank you for popping by Mr Jackson, if there is anything else we can help you with, anything at all, you know where we are.' He released Gruff's hand.

'Thank you, Derek. You have been a great help. I'll be sure to let the Minister know.'

Gruff walked down the corridor towards the stairs and the exit. Behind him came the muffled sounds of an angry man shouting.

~SEVENTY NINE~

It was a beautiful morning. The sun was still low in the sky to the east scattering floods of orange and amber among the heather, the long decreasing shadow of Ben Nevis was leaving behind a streak of warmth on the ground with every passing minute. Tiger breathed in the fresh air, filing his lungs and headed for his motorcycle. He noticed the sheet of white paper tucked under his saddle strap long before he arrived. It was a simple hand printed message.

CAFÉ CAMERON 10.00.

Block capitals and unsigned. Tiger removed the note folded it and tucked it into the inside pocket of his leather jacket. The last time he was passed a note somebody had died.

He stabbed the electric start button with his right thumb and the big twin cylinder Triumph instantly fired into life. Throwing his right leg over the saddle he adjusted his helmet strap, engaged first gear and slowly pulled away. His original plan was to go for a long ride, the roads in the Highlands were fantastic and the weather was certainly on his side this morning plus a good ride out always cleared his head. After a good night's sleep he was still no further forward in figuring out what his neighbours, the Browns, were up to and he'd decided that after his breakfast of Porridge Oats and toast he'd use the ride to work on it.

That was before the note.

Now it was after the note and his plans had changed. He headed into Fort William.

~EIGHTY~

Gruff and Charlie Soper were sat in the corner of a transport café on the outskirts of Lincoln. Big burly men wearing yellow fluorescent vests, some streaked with oil. Hard functioning men, who worked the road networks delivering goods across the country, were tucking heartily into huge plates of fried food. Friendly banter was bouncing backwards and forwards, it was obvious that some of the men knew each other and those that didn't joined in anyway. It was boisterous and cheerful and none of the drivers gave the two people in the corner a second glance.

'He's in Scotland, Gruff.'

'Okay… And how did we reach that conclusion?'

'He stopped for fuel at Markham Moor…'

'Markham Moor…The A1…There are two fuel stops there. One North. One South.'

'He went North.'

'He could've then headed back South, he does stuff like that.'

'His next stop was Scotch Corner.'

'Oh. Right, and then what?

'He had a mug of tea and a Chelsea bun.'

'Jesus Charlie, where do you get this stuff? I meant where did he go after that?

'I'm still working on it. He is North of Glasgow on the west side of the highlands. He stopped for fuel at Inverbeg. Loch Lomond. That's on the A82 Trunk road for the West coast.'

'Right. Lets go. I'll drive. You work the phones and do your magic.'

Charlie pushed the Range Rover keys across the table and shrugged.

'You're the paymaster.'

~EIGHTY ONE~

Anthony Stone had called his own meeting. He'd chosen a private room at The Holiday Inn at Heathrow Airport. So many people busying themselves no one gave a damn about anybody else, so it was a perfect point of contact for six dodgy characters in sharp suits.

Stone entered the room and noted with a grunt that five men were already seated around a conference table. Each had an official looking, unopened brown file in front of them. He wasted no time. He sat down and opened the meeting, he didn't refer to notes, and there would be no pencils and paper used here. There would be no minutes taken.

'Thank you for coming at short notice, Gentlemen. I'm going to keep this short and to the point. I have called this meeting with Black Team C. It would be…' He pronounced the last letter as 'See' before being interrupted.

'Charlie Sir. It's pronounced Black team Charlie, it's the phonetic alphabet.'

'What's your name?'

'Operational name?'

'No, real name.'

'Doyle, Sir. Dave.'

'Well Mr Doyle Sir Dave, this is my operation and this is my team and I'll call it what I fucking want. Mr Doyle Sir Dave you are excused.'

'Excuse me?'

'Get your fucking arse off that chair, leave my fucking meeting and generally just fuck off.'

Dave Doyle looked around the room at the other four impassive faces. Nobody would catch his eye. He stood up and walked around the table opened the door and left the meeting.

'Has anybody else got anything to say? Good I thought not. Moving on. It would be good if we introduced ourselves. From now on I am known as Mr Norwich.' He pointed with an open chopping palm to the man on his right.

'You start.'

'Yarmouth. Explosives.'

The men continued around the table.

'Caister. Communications.'

'Cromer. Medic.'

'Sheringham. Driver.'

Each man had cross over training within their group, each man was adaptable and understood the basics of each other's crafts, but they were primarily concerned with their own skill set.

'Good, 'continued Stone. 'In front of you is a file concerning your mission. There is a time frame attached to that mission. You have three days. Each of you will be paid £50,000 this afternoon. If your mission is successful you will receive a further £50,000 in three days' time. Urgency is of the greatest importance. Do I make myself clear?'

Four heads nodded in unison.

'Yarmouth is in command and he speaks for me. If he even hints or suggests something, then take that as a direct order from me. Clear?'

Four heads nodded in unison.

'Yarmouth. That Doyle wanker, what's his speciality? Did we need him?'

'Surveillance, Mr Norwich. As to whether we need him, until I read the brief I can't answer that.'

'There is no need for a surveillance specialist on this trip Mr Yarmouth you all know the basics. You a now have under your command a killing team. There will be no need for advanced surveillance.'

'Roger that, Mr Norwich.'

'My last point. The last team that attempted this mission got fucked over. I have a top tip for you all. Do not get fucked over. Mr Caister, pass me Mr Doyle's file. Any questions? No? Good. This meeting has ended.'

~EIGHTY TWO~

Tiger had parked his Triumph down a side street, walked a short way up the High Street and found a bench. It was situated about 150 yards from the Café Cameron, on the other side of the road and he had a clear view of the entrance. He couldn't see the back, and although he presumed that there would be a tradesman door or fire escape to the rear, he was on his own and this position would have to suffice.

It was 9.30 a.m. Thirty minutes early for the unusual breakfast meeting. Good tradecraft.

Old habits die hard.

The café wasn't particularly busy and those that he had seen enter, had left after fifteen minutes or so. Ten minutes to go.

He then became aware that he'd been joined on the bench. Slightly annoyed and unwilling to take his continuous gaze from his target door, he sneaked a fleeting glance at his new neighbour.

Andrew Brown!

'Morning Tiger. Busy?'

'Good morning Andrew. Fancy bumping into you here.' Tiger's emotions reeled. Was this a coincidence? Was Brown following him? This was a critical point in time for watching the damned café and he could really do without an interruption.

'It's a beautiful morning and it's a free country.'

Tiger didn't answer and turned his attention back to the café door.

'I'm parched Tiger, fancy a brew?'

'Er, I'm sort of busy Andrew, later perhaps?'

'There's a café about 150 yards away. Other side of the road to your right. Not sure if you can see it…The breakfast crowd have usually gone by now and I know they put fresh coffee on at Ten o'clock…'

Andrew Brown stood up, checked his watch and without another word crossed the High Street and walked towards the Café Cameron seemingly without a care in the world.

'Buggeration,' thought Tiger. 'I've been had. He too stood up and after a couple of seconds stretching his stiff legs followed the mysterious Brown towards the café.

The arrived at the front door together. Brown held the door open and a bell tinkled softly from somewhere within. The place was empty and not encouraging, to Tiger's mind, for what he had in store, although the smell of freshly baked bread and strong coffee was very tempting.

They both sat at a table with their backs to the wall. Both had a view of the door and the café serving counter. Tiger reached into his leather jacket and produced the note left on his motorcycle.

'Is this yours?'

'I do believe it's yours Tiger. But if you mean, did I write it, yes I did.'

There was no sign of any service. Tiger had some questions for Brown and a cup of strong coffee would have helped.

'I have some questions, Andrew. It's all about credentials.'

'So do I, Tiger. You first.'

'Right. Let's stop beating about the bush around. What mob were you in?'

'17th 21st Lancers and 14 Int.

The 17/21 Lancers were an old and well-respected Cavalry regiment. Their motto was 'Death or Glory.' 14 Int referred to No 14 Intelligence Company. A shady organisation that carried out top secret and extremely high risk surveillance operations in the provinces of Northern Ireland. It was technically an offence under the Official Secrets Act to even admit that it existed, let alone be a member.

The men continued the verbal jousting.

'You?'

'Grenadier Guards and 22 SAS.'

'Where was your Headquarters across the water?'

'Lisburn, although my team were parked in Flax Street Mill in Belfast.

'Who was your Commanding Officer at 22?

'Colonel Brigstock.'

'I know him. He works for us now.'

Tiger raised an eyebrow and looked directly at Brown. He wasn't lying. He continued.

'Where did you do your basic course for 14 Int?'

'Staffordshire.'

'Who was your chief Instructor at Hereford?'

'Taff Stone.'

The fast flowing question and answer session stopped right there.

~EIGHTY THREE~

Gruff and Charlie had spent the whole morning driving steadily North along the A82. Charlie had been busy on the phone collating information, but the Zero G telephone signal was getting weaker and weaker the further they moved from Glasgow. At the junction with the A85 they pulled over. It was barren landscape and the signal had been lost completely, so they now had to call upon their shared experience and nous as technology had abandoned them at a place called Crianlarich.

'We need to make a decision here.' Gruff swept his eyes over the Scottish countryside. The purple and brown heather stretched for mile after mile towards the grey flint escarpments of some distant mountain range that he probably couldn't pronounce. Charlie had the map folded to the correct area and was scrutinising it intently.

'Okay. We have two choices so that's not so bad. We go west on the A85 and that takes us forty miles to the coast, a place called Oban. Or continue north to a place called Fort William.'

Gruff was thinking, he knew, he just knew that he could get inside his friend's head if he had a trigger, a little mental leg up. Why the hell had his friend just pulled up sticks and buggered off? He obviously had a plan. Tiger wasn't one for impetuous action. Some of his antics may, to the casual observer looked damned reckless, but there was always a plan.

'Where can he go from Oban?'

'Ferry to the Isle of Mull and from there he could lose himself in any number of Islands.'

'He's not out to lose himself. He just wants to lose us. He'll have a plan. How far is Fort William?'

'Fifty miles give or take.'

'So about an hour or so to each?'

'Yes.'

'If I recall, Glencoe is north on the A82. Loch Levan. I spent some there with Tiger…Wait a 'mo…Let me think…Fort William…Fort William…'

Charlie gazed out of the passenger window and glanced up, the big grey clouds had been scudding overhead for some time and now, inevitably, it started to rain. Big fat raindrops crashed onto the windscreen as Gruff absently nudged the windscreen wiper control arm.

The rhythm was quite hypnotic, a full sweep of the screen then a pause followed by a small squeak. Full sweep of the screen, pause, small squeak. Sweep. Pause. Squeak.

A full two minutes later and Charlie thought he might be going into some sort of tantric trance, but she wouldn't interrupt Gruff's train of thought.

Sweep. Pause Squeak.

'Yes. I have it. Glencoe. We'll go north to Glencoe, you can ask around, but I reckon it's Fort William.'

'How did you reach that conclusion?'

Gruff pressed down the clutch and engaged first gear. He looked to his left at Charlie who returned his stare with an eyebrow raised in question.

'Three Commandos on a plinth.'

'Spean Bridge?'

'Yup.'

'I agree. Good call. Let's go.'

~EIGHTY FOUR~

Normal service appeared to have resumed in the Café Cameron. It was doubtful that either man had ran out of questions, but for now anyway, an unspoken truce had been declared, so Tiger took the opportunity and was getting stuck into buttered toast and strong coffee. He looked up at Brown.

'So it's Steve, not Andrew,' Tiger asked, in between mouthfuls of the delicious home-made hot buttered bread.

Brown examined Tiger over his large mug of sweet tea, his furrowed brow giving away his worry for the first time that morning.

'Okay, how did you deduce that?'

'Anita let it slip last night. I presume that isn't her real name either?'

'It's the small things right?'

'Aye, it's always the small things.'

'You never let on that you knew.'

'Would you have?'

'Nope.'

'Touché. So what's her real name?'

'Do you fancy her?'

'Nope. Too clingy for me. What's her name?'

'Anna. She fancies you.'

'Everybody loves Tiger.'

Steve Brown smiled, took another sip of his tea and said nothing for a minute.

'She's a good operator, Tiger.'

'She drinks too much. Loose lips...'

Both men laughed and finished the sentence together.

'Sink ships!'

There were a few more minutes of quiet contemplation whilst both men finished up their light breakfast. Tiger broke the silence.

'Soooo, Steve. Nitty gritty time. What are you doing up here?'

'I'm an instructor and I'm in the middle of an exercise.'

'But you have the time off to sit in your Croft drinking wine and have covert meetings in a café? I could do with a job like that.'

'One of the students got injured yesterday. We have a couple of days down time.'

'Who do you work for?'

Steve Brown paused briefly and eyed Tiger carefully again before speaking.

'I don't know why, but I trust you Tiger. I work for the Government. A department with no name. It's a black ops budget with no oversight. I, we, don't exist, although obviously we do and we answer directly to the second in command of the Security Service. The Deputy Chief of MI6.

'That's how you know Taff Stone?'

'I've known Taff Stone for a couple of years. He's dangerous.'

'So you also knew the late Sir Andrew Thornton?

'Yes of course I knew of him, but as head he didn't know about me. Us.'

'Are you telling me that the Chief Spy, the head of our Country's security, doesn't know about your department? Tiger looked sceptically at Brown.

'That's what I'm saying yes. It's a security issue that came about when Sir Andrew got the job. It was thought that he may be going rogue on the Nation, nothing actually occurred that I know of, but he was speaking to people that he shouldn't have been speaking to, not off the record anyway and it was getting awkward, there were no balances in place and somebody needed to keep things in check. As a result the Deputy Chief was approached by the Home Secretary and the Foreign Secretary and tasked with sorting out the mess. That's why the Deputy Chief will never become Chief. It's the rules.'

'Jesus, Brown, that's outrageous. Is that why Stone was promised the job? The old man knowing that his deputy wasn't allowed to take it?'

'I don't know Tiger, maybe. It's a dirty job but it keeps me in work. I'm not interested in the politics of it all, it's just a job.'

'So, Taff Stone is now in charge and he has no idea what his second in command is up to?'

'Pretty much. Yep.'

'I understand that Taff Stone was highly recommended for the top job by Sir Andrew, yet I know for a fact that he hated the man.'

'He was recommended yes, and as I said, Sir Andrew was nothing but trouble, he had fingers in pies he shouldn't have been touching and this is all a big joke as far as his legacy is concerned.'

'Bloody hell! What a mess.'

'In three days, no, two days now, there is a secret meeting of the S.O.C. The Security Oversight Committee, they are going to vote on whether our mutual friend Taff Stone is a fit and proper person to carry on with the job.'

'And you know this? How?'

'This exercise I'm conducting is all about preparing for the worst. I am reporting directly to the Foreign Secretary. If the vote goes the wrong way...'

'You kill Stone...'

'I dIdn't say that Tiger.'

'No. Your eyebrows did. It's the small things.'

~EIGHTY FIVE~

The man now known as 'Yarmouth' had assembled his crew at a hotel on the outskirts of Lincoln. Each man had been briefed with a specific task following the initial meeting with Anthony Brown.

'Right, gents. What have we got? Kick us off, Caister.'

'I have visited the Targe'ts home address, there was nobody at home and it appears as if he's not in any hurry to get back. I made an approach under pretext to the Target's neighbour, some frail old biddy, she had no idea where the Target is or when he's coming home. The home is a wash-out, it would be pointless putting it under observation.'

'Cheers. Good work. Even negative stuff is a positive. It's all about intelligence gathering. Cromer?'

'I've been researching the Target's background. Frequently visited places, UK based holidays, local pubs, to see if I could get the locals talking, but nothing of interest to report other than he prefers going to Scotland rather than holidaying in England.'

'Scotland? Interesting. He does have a Scots background, his Mother's from Glasgow. Good work Cromer. Sheringham?

'Vehicles for me. Contacts at the Driver and Vehicle Licensing Agency in Swansea have faxed me his current registered vehicle list. He has only the one that's legally registered for the road. A Triumph Trident T160V motorcycle which I suspect he is currently riding. There is another vehicle registered to his Lincolnshire address, an RS 1600cc Ford Escort, registered but that vehicle's unfit for the road, probably a project build and its whereabouts is unknown. It's definitely not parked in one of the garages at his home address. Caister will agree with me there.

Caister nodded his head in agreement, he'd quietly, physically checked every stable, garage and out-house at the property.

'So Gents, we don't have much, that's pretty clear, but what we do have is two days. So, phones. Tonight we work the phones. He's on a distinctive motorcycle, he's a distinctive bloke. Someone, somewhere, has seen him. Garage attendants, shop keepers, pubs and cafeterias. Start with a 10 mile radius of Louth and work out. Sheringham, what's the maximum mileage his Triumph will do on a full tank of petrol?

'I don't know if he has the three gallon or the four gallon fuel tank. If we go with the three gallon he can get thirty five miles to the gallon if he's riding hard and fifty to the gallon if he's riding like my Grandma. So if we call it forty miles average and he does have the small tank he'll get one hundred and twenty miles.'

'Then that's what we'll use as a guide. Ten mile radius to start, then move out to one hundred and twenty mile increments. Sheringham, fuel stops and garages. Cromer, do the

boozers and accommodation. Caister, you're on cafeterias and other short stop places. Are we all good?'

All three men stated that they were, and stood up to go.

'Before you go lads. I've had an extra snippet from our paymaster Norwich that there may be a mole in the Target's garden. I'll know more tomorrow. No sleep. No booze. Work the phones, we'll reconvene at breakfast.'

~EIGHTY SIX~

Gruff was now convinced that Tiger was in the Fort William area. Charlie had asked the pertinent questions around the small friendly town of Glencoe that sat idly on the shores of the picturesque Loch Levan. A lone rider had stopped for fuel and had made a couple of phone calls. The questioned individuals held no suspicion when they informed Charlie that he was riding a very nice looking modern Triumph motorcycle. The first hotel they came to on Fort William High Street was the 'Flint.' Charlie parked the Range Rover whilst Gruff entered the hotel lobby to enquire about rooms. He noticed two middle aged ladies drinking tea at a small table in the foyer and nodded to them as he passed.

'Good morning Ladies.'

'Oooh, another handsome Englishman!' One of them exclaimed.

'He hasn't got a motorbike though has he?' Stated her friend.

Gruff paused and turning to the two observant tea drinkers gave his best smile.

'This English biker chap, would he by any chance be a short stocky man with glasses?'

'Oh no. He was tall, very good looking and I don't think he wore glasses.'

'Is he a resident?'

'He was, but unfortunately he left yesterday, just as we were getting to know him.'

'Have you any idea where he went?'

'He left on his motorbike but he didn't go far. We saw him going into Miss Cameron's Café this morning.'

'Cameron's Café?'

'It's about two hundred yards along the High Street. Go left out of the door. She bakes her own bread as well.'

Gruff thanked the ladies and walked directly to the front desk. He plucked a couple of random tourist brochures from the massive stack and pretended to read one. At that point he became aware that someone, presumably the receptionist, was crouched down behind the desk and whispering into a telephone. He couldn't hear any part of the conversation and headed back to the High Street once again thanking his unsuspecting informants as he passed.

Back at the Range Rover Charlie was once more on the car phone. Gruff motioned for the window to be lowered as he approached. Charlie powered down the black glass.

'He's here Charlie. He's bloody here!'

'He's not Gruff. He checked out of the Flint Hotel yesterday morning…'

'You got that from the phone?'

'I did.'

'Well that's very clever as I keep on telling you Charlie. Now if you want to impress me even more, answer me this. Where was Tiger having breakfast this morning?'

'I haven't got that far yet.'

'No? Well I have. Do you fancy a brew and some home-made bread?'

~EIGHTY SEVEN~

Tiger and Brown walked back out into the rare sunshine that had decided to visit Fort William that morning. Tiger headed for his motorcycle and Brown strolled off in the opposite direction. They'd agreed to meet again later in the day. They still had a lot to talk about.

Gruff and Charlie were walking towards Cameron Cafeteria when Gruff grabbed Charlie's arm.

'Back to the car Charlie.'

'Change of plan?'

'There's always a change of plan. You know that. I've just seen Tiger, he's about two hundred yards walking with his crash helmet, C'mon were going to follow him. Look bloody lively or we'll lose him.'

They both turned and raced back towards the Flint Hotel car park. Gruff had unlocked the driver's door, jumped in behind the steering wheel and started the engine in seconds. Charlie wasn't far behind scrambling onto the passenger seat, barely having time to close the door before Gruff had the vehicle in gear and was rolling forward.

A glimpse of Tiger passing in front of them heralded good fortune - he could easily have gone in the opposite direction - Gruff eased the big Range Rover into the light traffic stream some five or six cars behind Tigers Triumph and began to follow. As vehicles between Gruff and Tiger turned off or pulled over, it forced Gruff to hold back a bit further and allow other vehicles to pull out in front of him, careful that he didn't allow a bus or a lorry to jump in and completely obscure his view ahead. Following another vehicle was really easy, unless you didn't want to be noticed, it then it became extremely difficult.

'Why don't we just catch up and let him know that we're here?' Asked Charlie.

'He doesn't want us to join in with whatever plans he has, Charlie. If I catch him up I guarantee he'll lose us within thirty seconds and that'll be that. We'll never see him again.'

'Okay. So what are we doing?'

'Fair question and well presented. We are going to 'house' him, see where he's staying, that makes it so much more difficult for him to do a runner.'

'You make it sound like he really doesn't want to see us.'

'He's my best friend, Charlie, and I'm sure that whatever he has planned, he's doing so because he doesn't want to get me into trouble.'

'Or killed.'

'Indeed, Charlie. Or killed.'

Tiger rode steadily back to his rented Croft and parked outside. Switching off the engine, he patted the fuel tank and apologised to his motorcycle.

'Sorry old girl, I know you wanted to go for a blast today. We'll try and find time to do it later. I Promise.' The Triumph didn't reply. It was probably in a bit off a huff. He dismounted from the machine and began removing his crash helmet as he walked the few yards to the front door of the Croft.

Although he tended to keep his keys in the same pocket, they sometimes mysteriously ended up in another one, like a really annoying magic trick. He patted all his pockets searching for his door key thinking that if he had a big key fob this minor task would have been much easier...

He looked over to the neighbouring Croft one hundred and fifty yards away. Anna Brown was stood at her entrance waving. He waved an arm in greeting and entered his own.

Two hundred yards distant, Gruff had stopped the Range Rover and watched Tiger enter a small Croft. He was pretty sure that he had used a key to gain entry and therefore was not visiting and he was confident that Tiger had no idea that he'd been followed.

~EIGHTY EIGHT~

Tiger was a bit concerned. He was fairly sure that he had been followed after leaving the town. It was only a twenty minute ride so he couldn't be 100% certain. There was time to try out some anti-surveillance manoeuvres, but part of him wanted to know who it could be. Shaking off his tail would have been straightforward as he had the speed and manoeuvrability to outpace a four wheeled vehicle, especially the big black Range Rover that he had seen, so he had decided to keep his enemy close, if in fact it was an enemy.

Once inside the Croft he carried out his usual checks to see if he'd had a nosy visitor in his absence. A hair with a lick of spit across a drawer and some lengths of cotton stretched across the hallway. His traps were still in place and once he'd satisfied himself that nobody had been rummaging around, he opened the front door a crack, sat down in the living room with a direct view to the door and waited.

Gruff turned to Charlie.

'I'm going in. I reckon it'll take five minutes before he accepts that we are here to help or he hoofs me out the door. You okay to hang on here?'

Charlie just nodded so Gruff got out of the vehicle and walked slowly towards Croft number two.

Tiger watched the shadow fall across the threshold. It was pointless closing the door, there was no peephole or any other method to see who came knocking. The shadow knocked sharply on the door. Tiger tensed his shoulder muscles and was ready to launch himself into attack mode.

'Tiger! It's me, Gruff, I'm coming in,' Gruff pushed gently on the door and it opened easily. His eyes slowly adjusted to the dark interior of a hallway. A small table sat against the wall with some keys and a large wooden fish next to a bowl.

'Tiger! I'm coming in...'

'Turn around and go away. Close the door behind you.' Tiger replied.

Gruff ignored his friend and stepped through the hallway and into a sparsely furnished living room. Tiger was sat on an armchair watching him. He wasn't smiling in greeting. Gruff plonked himself down on the chair opposite and eyed his best friend. He looked fit and healthy, there were no bags under his eyes, he was obviously sleeping well and there was no smell of alcohol. He definitely wasn't here to drown his sorrows.

'So you found me?'

'Well technically Charlie found you, I just tagged on.'

'Charlie?'

'Charlie Soper.'

'Charlie Soper?'

'An operator I use from time to time, an absolute whizz kid on computers and phones. Just grabs information and soaks it up. Can get information out of anybody. It's called Social Engineering or some such thing.'

'And where is this Charlie Soper now?'

'In the car outside.'

'Black Range Rover?'

'You saw us pull up?'

'I saw you tailing me from Fort William.'

'Bugger. You are good.'

'Not really. You're rusty. Well as you're here you might as well get Charlie in here as well, I'll put a brew on and we can have a nice little tea party.'

Tiger stood and went into the kitchen. He still hadn't smiled or acknowledged Gruff as a friendly face. Gruff walked to the front door, leaned out and beckoned to Charlie to come over.

Gruff and Charlie were sat in the living room when Tiger re-entered with three mugs of tea on a tray. He stopped in his tracks and his jaw dropped slightly.

'Charlie Soper? He asked.

'That's what people call me,' retorted Charlie.

'Bloody hell. You're a girl!'

Charlie looked at Gruff.

'You're right Gruff. He is a trained observer.'

~EIGHTY EIGHT~

The man known as 'Yarmouth' was wolfing down hot buttered toast and luke-warm coffee as he addressed his crew over the crowded breakfast table. Most had already eaten a full fry up, but Yarmouth had overnighted down south in London and had only just returned to the Lincoln Hotel. The traffic on the A1 heading back north was horrendous and as a result he was running late.

'Who's first? Caister?'

Caister put down his cup of tea and shrugged his shoulders.

'Sorry Yarmouth. I was up all night and couldn't find anything. I was on the short stops and they all close at night.'

'I had high hopes for you Caister, what, you being in charge of communication and all. Never mind. What about you Cromer?'

'Got a bit lucky and found out that out that our Target stopped at a cafeteria in Scotch Corner, but the proprietor couldn't, or wouldn't tell me when.'

'Okay. Sheringham?'

Sheringham leaned back and smiled. He was the specialist driver and if the Target was on wheels, two or four, then Sheringham fancied himself as the man to catch him.

'He stopped for fuel at Markham Moor, that's on the A1 Northbound side. Three hours later he stopped again, at Scotch Corner, again Northbound on the A1.' He glanced across at his comrade and threw him a breadcrumb of support. 'That ties in with what Cromer knows.'

Cromer acknowledged this with a nod. He didn't particularly like Sheringham, he was far too big for his boots but he was a damned good driver, he'd grudgingly give him that credit, and it would now appear that he is a pretty good operator.

'This is what I need to hear, Gents. So he's gone north. Sheringham, when did you find this out?

'About twenty one hundred last night...'

'...And you didn't think to share this with the others who may have been searching other points of the compass?'

Sheringham picked up his tea and tried to hide behind it. He said nothing.

'Gentlemen. We are a team. We will act as a team and we share information as soon as it gets in. That what teams do. Any more acts of selfishness will be noted, reported and duly punished. Are you all clear?' He was talking to the whole table but glaring at Sheringham as he spoke.

They all nodded.

'Anything else you wish to share, Sheringham?'

'He stopped for fuel in Glencoe yesterday.'

'Jesus Chris,t Sheringham...I'll be having a little chat with you later. Right, our Target is in Scotland. Let's pack up and ship out.'

The breakfast meeting ended. All four men stood up, three headed for their separate rooms to pack, Yarmouth walked into the reception area to settle the bill.

Black team Charlie were heading north.

~EIGHTY NINE~

Tiger had dragged some camping chairs out into the Scottish sunshine. You had to grab rare moments like this whenever you could. Gruff and Charlie were sat next to each other, facing Tiger, in what could have been described as a formal interview in an informal setting.

'So how long have you been looking for me?'

Charlie looked at Gruff who took the lead.

'A few days.'

'Was it difficult?'

'Not really but Charlie is very bloody good.'

'I'm sure, however my point is, if you can track me then others can as well, and that's a worry.'

'I have a question Tiger. What are you doing up here? Why didn't you let me know? It's obvious that you are planning something, is it revenge? Is it Stone?'

'That's four questions, Gruff.'

'Stop being so bloody stubborn. We're your friends. Talk to me.'

'It's complicated.'

'Bollocks.'

Tiger sat back in the uncomfortable canvas chair, tilted his head back and looked up to the clear blue sky above. Two or three minutes passed without an interruption. Gruff took out a battered tobacco tin and made a roll up cigarette. He'd tried giving up a couple of times over the years without success, but he had managed to cut down and now only smoked occasionally. He had only just put the Zippo lighter flame to the tip when Tiger grunted.

'Those things will kill you one day.'

'I feel like killing you today.'

Tiger looked back down and slid forward on his seat. He'd come to a decision. He glared at Gruff who glared back so he switched his gaze imperceptibly over to Charlie and smiled. She smiled back.

'Okay. I owe you an apology and an explanation.' With no reaction coming from either of his listeners he continued.

'I am convinced that Stone killed Miss Kelly. He arranged it, ordered it, paid for it to happen or did it. But, and it's a big but, I cannot prove any of that. I know her death was an accident and that I was the intended target. I don't know why he'd want to kill me now because he's had hundreds of opportunities in the past and hasn't bothered. Or, if he has bothered, then I've missed it and, as I don't miss much, it hasn't happened.'

He realised that he hadn't taken a breath and he was starting to ramble. He took a deep breath and continued in a more measured tone.

'I am going to lure him up here, to this Croft, interview him and then kill him and anyone else who comes with him. Everything I do from the moment he gets here, and he will get here, will be hugely illegal. I could go to prison for a long time, so for starters I don't need any witnesses and more importantly to me, I don't need my friends as accomplices to criminal deeds of that magnitude.'

Charlie spoke for the first time in thirty minutes. She had a soft voice, no obvious accent and very gentle on the ear, but there was an undertone of menace. People who she chose to speak to often listened.

Very carefully.

'You will not have to interview him.'

'Who? Stone? Of course I do, I need to know the truth.'

'We have the truth.'

'Bloody hell, Gruff, does she always talk in riddles?'

'No idea Tiger, she doesn't speak to me much, but we do have a video tape taken from the St Martins Church Crypt in-house CCTV camera...'

'From the Police?'

'No, not from the Police, although they looked at it briefly. I, er, borrowed it from The Reverend Peter Johns. He was standing in as duty God Botherer while the other chap, er, vicar bloke was on holiday.'

Tiger was suddenly interested. His friend had been investigating, something he really should have been doing himself.

'What's on it?'

'Have you got a video recorder here?'

'Aye, it's in the living room under the television set, but I've no idea how to set it up.'

Both men turned to look at Charlie.

'Bloody men.' She sighed, as she got up and entered the Croft.

~NINETY~

Charlie had spent hours on the video footage cleaning up the extremely faint images that were to be seen ghosting about in the Crypt of St Martin-in-the-Fields Church, early in the morning on the day of Sir Andrew Thornton's funeral, and Miss Kelly's murder. The process she had used was from the United States, developed by NASA to enhance the grainy images taken by deep space cameras with particle and dust hammered lenses. The software was highly specialised, highly expensive and highly impossible to obtain. Gruff never asked for an explanation and Charlie had never offered one.

Tiger pointed to the television screen. His lips were so tight with rage he could hardly speak.

'Stone!' He exclaimed. 'Who's the other bloke?'

'We believe he's a Czechoslovakian hit man called Jan Ježek.'

'I know that name. Wasn't he mates with Petricek Dvorak'

'It's Czech for hedgehog.'

'Mmmm, hedgehog you say? Well I am going to squash that hedgehog. I'm going to tear...'

'He's already been squashed.'

'What? By you?'

'Nope. Polly Richardson.'

'Bloody hell. I need to sit down.' So he did.

Gruff and Charlie exchanged glances. Gruff mouthed the word 'file' and Charlie silently turned and left the room. Tiger continued to look at the moving display on the screen. There was no audio available but the pictures told their own story. Stone was obviously directing the proceedings. Ježek was stood on a set of small ladders and twisting something unseen around one of the animal gargoyles that surrounded the central support arch. Tiger now knew that this was fishing line. The gargoyle animal of choice was a bear. Ježek rocked and wiggled it carefully to its tipping point on the edge of a narrow support platform and readjusted the fishing line.

The Czech then cautiously stepped down from his perch and both men were seen crouching, their arms out of view of the camera lens before disappearing altogether. The tape stopped some three or four seconds later.

'Do you want to watch it again?'

'Nope. That's all I need to warrant killing the bastard. Now tell me about Polly.'

Charlie re-entered the Croft holding a manila file, the one from Lincoln Central Police Station and joined Tiger and Gruff at the kitchen table. Gruff started talking.

'Stone and Ježek laid the trip wire. The bear had been loosened, quite innocently, by the stonemasons who were working on the renovations. Stone wrote the note and passed it to Miss Kelly in a crush of people at the back door to the Crypt...'

Charlie interrupted him.

'Poor choice of words, Gruff.'

'What? Crypt?'

'No. Crush.'

'Sorry. Stone wrote the note, verified by QDE...'

This time it was Tiger who stopped the explanation.

'QDE?'

'Questioned Document Examination. It's a forensic science discipline.'

'Okay…Do I need to know who…'

Gruff glanced at Charlie who gave an almost imperceptible shake of her head.

'No you don't need to know. Its fact, that'll do mate. Moving on. Ježek hired a Ford Cortina from Hertz car rental at Heathrow Airport using the name and documentation of a certain Jan Kámen. Kámen is Czechoslovakian for Stone, by the way, and left it parked on the square at Louth when he went to visit you at home with murder on his mind.'

'And Polly?'

'We don't know. He certainly put your place under close observation because we have his rucksack that was found quite close. We reckon that on ascertaining that you were not in, he went for the soft option…'

'Get information from Polly.'

'Most probably, but as you know she is no fool and somehow got the better of him pretty soon after he broke in.'

'He broke in? He never knocked on the door?'

'Nope, he opened a locked window and climbed through…'

'Was he armed?'

'Large knife.'

'At night?'

'Yes.'

'Aggravated night time burglary. He'll get ten years for that…'

'He won't Tiger, that's the point. Polly got him first.'

This information slowly lit up Tiger's face, like the morning shadow steadily retreating behind Ben Nevis as the sun had rose that very morning.

'Buggeration! Hockey Stick?'

'Yup.'

'Hahahaha! Good old Polly.' This was the first time that Tiger had managed anything other than a bad-tempered demeanour since Gruff and Charlie's arrival.

'Anything else?'

'We have the forensic analysis reports from Ježek's rucksack. Binoculars, receipts, knife and fishing line all with his prints and DNA. We can tie Stone in with a Czechoslovakian hit man in the Crypt, we can...

Tiger looked ashen.

'Are you saying we should keep this legal? Go to court? We'd get laughed out, and that's if we ever got in.'

'Is it not worth a try? Look we are going to lose the Czech. His country is asking for his return, he was in a coma. Now he isn't. The WPC looking after him is on our books, she has called us. It's at the highest level right now. Diplomatic bunkum I know, but it could easily bring Stone down. Legal and Legit.'

'I don't want to bring him down Gruff, I want to drag him down, stamp on him and then...'

'KNOCK KNOCK.'

Somebody was rapping on the Croft door. Heavy hand. Authoritative.

Tiger was instantly alert. He put his left forefinger to his lips. Silence. He nodded at Gruff and pointed into the living room. Gruff knew exactly where he had to go, where he had to stand, they'd done this many times before.

~NINETY ONE~

Six seconds later, with the two men in position covering the door Charlie put her hand on the door handle and looked at Tiger. As soon as the door had been opened Tiger was counting on a three second pause whilst the visitor assessed an unexpected female on the threshold.

Three seconds was all he needed to rush over the top of Charlie and take control. Gruff would be right behind him making safe any secondary threat. It was of course an extremely rudimentary plan and if there were more than three people outside it would turn into a very dangerous bun fight.

Tiger looked at Gruff, got the thumbs up and nodded at Charlie.

Charlie took a deep breath, pressed down on the door handle and swung the door open. A large built man stood in front of her. She summed up the threat in two seconds.

He was casually dressed in black trousers and an open necked, white, freshly pressed shirt. Not armed - well, not actually holding a weapon. He had a handsome face and smelled faintly of Aramis aftershave. There was a shadow lurking behind him. He looked surprised.

On three seconds she ducked down to the floor and shouted.

'TWO!'

Tiger rushed the door diving over the crouched figure of Charlie. He sensed, rather than felt Gruff's presence right behind him. Good man.

Tiger was fast. The man at the door was not. Tiger's body mass hit the visitor full in the chest and the pair of them spilled into the front garden. Tiger's strength and momentum continued until the man collapsed onto the grass shocked and winded. He'd made no attempt to draw a weapon.

Gruff was just as fast. He'd side stepped the rushing Tiger and grabbed the visitor's companion around the waist, was stepping behind and in the process of taking a wrist and placing it in a gooseneck lock when he realised it was a woman. She screamed.

'TIGER!'

For a fraction of a second Tiger turned his attention to the sound of the scream before a realisation dawned on him. He shouted.

'STAND DOWN GRUFF.'

Steve Brown shook his head as he slowly removed the grass and leaves stuck to his face. He wasn't angry - he was smiling. He held out his arm.

'Interesting way to greet visitors, Tiger. How many Postmen have you knocked out today?'

Tiger held out his hand and firmly grabbed Brown's, helping him to his feet.

Gruff had released the struggling Anna who rewarded him with a stinging slap to the face. He didn't even flinch. He then turned to Tiger and raised an eyebrow.

'Friendlies I presume?'

'Aye, they are,' Tiger replied.

'Awkward.' Said Gruff, resisting the temptation to put his hand to his face and soothe his burning cheek.

339 Tigers Revenge

~NINETY TWO~

Anthony Stone had been in meetings all morning. He was in the Chair for most of them; the only exception was the last one, a rather difficult conference with the Home Secretary and his staff. He had, he felt, been treated as a naughty schoolboy at that one. He was titular head of the country's security, for God's sake, not some errant short trouser wearing miscreant who'd been caught having a smoke behind the bike sheds.

He'd received an interesting telephone call earlier in the morning, one he was expecting, on the private line in his office. This call had brightened his day and nothing was going to change that. Certainly not the man sat opposite him at a ridiculously large conference table somewhere in the depths of Whitehall.

He thought the man was a buffoon anyway, his policy regarding prison reform was a joke, a laughing stock. Hardened cons had asked, no, demanded - via the negotiating position of a fucking prison riot - to have access to education and gym equipment. Gym equipment? If Stone had been in charge, the squalid Victorian buildings would've been lucky to have a lick of paint every five years, and why should those scum be educated? Nonces and murderers the lot of 'em.

'The trouble is, Anthony,' the buffoon had droned on...' that we're not too sure about your pedigree. I fully understand why your predecessor, the late Sir Andrew would have chosen you, what with your military background and all, but, and please don't take this personally, we feel that there are more, er, politically correct individuals who would fit the bill in a more, er, appropriate manner.'

Stone replied.

'I am not, nor will I ever be a political animal. My remit is the security of our great nation, and I believe that I am the man qualified for that job. As for that namby pamby political correctness, it's just a buzz word, it means nothing, it's got no legs and when the press get bored of using it they'll move onto something else. Anyway, I am politically aware. I'm as astute as the next man...'

'Or woman,' interrupted one of the Home Secretary' senior aides. Stone just turned his head and glared at her.

The Home Secretary interrupted. 'If we could just get back on track please, my point is, Anthony, the people at number ten...'

'Oh those pricks...'

And that, pretty much ended the meeting.

~NINETY THREE~

Tiger had spent most of the next hour apologising to the man sat opposite him at his kitchen table. Brown, of course, was milking it.

'That was a dodgy way to deal with a potential enemy, Tiger.'

'Rubbish, Brown, and I'm not saying sorry again. I, we, felt threatened. I was, and now we are, in a difficult situation here, it's fluid, there are no rules, no lines and it's potentially life threatening so we used the cards we were dealt with. You'd have done it differently I suppose?'

Brown said nothing, he was a surveillance operator and although his background was that of a Special Forces nature, he was not an ex 'blade in a Sabre Squadron. Those lads were pure Alpha males.

Anna, however, was not so quick to forgive, and she'd hurt her hand slapping the man she now knew was called Gruff. The handsome man called Gruff. The handsome man who was oblivious to pain, called Gruff. She checked her thoughts momentarily, quite sure that she would return to them fairly soon. She looked him square in the eye.

'That hurt didn't it?'

'What did?'

'My slap.'

'You slapped me?'

'Well I didn't put all my effort into it obviously.'

'I thought you'd seen a wasp or a midge and was flapping it away.'

'That's crap Gruff, that hurt you.'

'Well it did a bit.'

'A bit?'

'I wanted to cry.'

The kitchen erupted into gales of laughter at Gruff's simple admission. Any lingering frostiness that had developed had been well and truly thawed. Anna then turned her attention to Charlie.

'So, you're Charlie.'

Charlie looked directly at Anna. Two pairs of green eyes locked. The hubbub of general conversation in the kitchen had vanished to Charlie's ears. She flicked at a wayward strand of hair that was threatening to spoil her vision and smiled.

'That's what they say Anna.'

'What do you say, Charlie?'

'I say we need to go for a walk, let these idiots chat, fight, talk guns, wave their willies about, whatever...'

Both women stood, eyes still locked neither wanting to break the moment. Tiger however had noticed the subtle change of atmosphere.

'Going out ladies?'

'If you must know, we're going for a chat, Tiger.'

'Well, be careful out there.'

'We're not going out.'

Tiger stroked his chin and smiled as the two operators headed for the bedroom.

~NINETY FOUR~

Black team Charlie had made a slight detour to the Army barracks at Catterick Garrison. Stone had arranged for a visit to the armoury and a bit of shooting range time, not that the men were rusty, far from it, they were all up to date with their firearm certificates but it was a quick and dirty way to obtain the firepower that may be required in the very near future.

Out on the 50 yard firing range Yarmouth assembled his men. The range had been cleared of any other military activity; for a start, the seemingly casual way in which the Black team operatives handled military hardware would have given a Range Safety Officer palpitations, but mainly because some things were meant to be said, and done in private.

'What have you got Cromer?'

'Mark 3 Browning Hi Power Pistol.'

'Maximum effective range?'

'Fifty yards.'

'Muzzle velocity?'

'One thousand one hundred feet per second.'

'Weight?'

'One of your English pounds, Yarmouth.'

'Caister?'

'SMG. Sterling Sub Machine gun Yarmouth.'

'How many rounds in the magazine?'

'Thirty four.'

'NATO designation?'

'L2A3.'

'Good. Sheringham, you have my favourite toy. You won't be using it today. I could only manage to get three of the buggers. They're like rocking horse shit at the moment, but tell me about it anyway.'

'This, Yarmouth, is a Claymore anti-personnel mine. Made in the United States. Designation M18A1. Twenty four ounces of C4 plastic explosive will blast seven hundred steel ball bearings at nearly four thousand feet per second over one hundred metres, with a ten percent chance of hitting a man. Fifty metres is the optimal range with a thirty percent chance of a kill. It's great for soft skin vehicles as well.'

Yarmouth nodded his agreement.

'It's vehicles I had in mind, Sheringham. But if somebody should get in the way…'

His men laughed, despite the fact that they'd all seen the carnage that such a weapon could cause.

'Right lads, the Claymore aside, why are we taking the SMG and the Browning pistol on this mission?'

'Ammunition.' They all chorused.

'Correct. They both use the standard NATO nine millimetre ball round. Cheap to manufacture and even cheaper for us to get hold of, in fact I have two thousand rounds in the back of the Land Rover and it didn't cost us a penny, and there's plenty more where that came from. So let's get on the firing point and start using it up.'

The team all laughed again. They were always happy when it came to guns.

And killing.

~NINETY FIVE~

Steve Brown had brought Gruff up to speed with regard to his military career and what he knew about the Anthony Stone situation. Tiger was in charge of the brews, busying himself with the teabag counting and kettle watching. The three men were not the type to swap war stories, so it had been brief and to the point. Gruff had listened, asked a couple of pertinent questions and excused himself, saying he wanted some fresh air, and had walked outside and over to Charlie's Range Rover. He fired up the telephone case, connected to the Zero G network and made a telephone call.

'So, Tiger. Do you actually have a plan? A real one, one with specific points of action and a realistic timeline?'

'I have an idea, Brown.'

'An idea? Wait let me guess...You make a call to Stone, er, you somehow trick him into coming up here to Scotland, and, er...You...You grab him, and, and, and... knock him about with a stick. Is that close?'

'Close? It's spot on Brown. Are you a mind reader?'

'It's idiotic, Tiger, and hardly worthy of an ex 22 man...'

'Follow me.' Tiger abruptly stood up and made for the utility store, 'what's that lot?' He had opened the door and pointed inside.

Brown squeezed past Tiger and poked his head round the door, and let out a low whistle.

'Jesus,Tiger. Been shopping I see.'

A dozen bags of fertiliser and canisters of various nitrates were neatly stacked against one of the walls. Against another was a small stack of 4inch piping all cut to about two feet in length. Brown recognised immediately what he was being shown.

A bomb factory.

'Okay Tiger, so you have some material, you now have a small team and you have the knowledge to do something with it all. I still haven't heard a plan though.'

'It's a work in progress.'

'Really? Well it's your turn to follow me.' Brown turned and walked down the hallway and out of the front door. Tiger followed, and as he turned and headed off towards Brown's Croft he noticed Gruff speaking animatedly on Charlie Soper's car phone.

Brown opened the front door to his Croft with a key. Tiger idly noted that his key didn't have a floating fish attached to it.

'In you come, Tiger.'

Tiger knew from his earlier evening visit that this Croft was pretty much identical to his own and wasn't surprised when Brown approached the utility room. What he hadn't reckoned on though was the sight that lay before him now.

On the floor of the room lay a green and brown rifle transit case with the digits L42A1 embossed on the hard plastic. Four canvas satchels labelled L2A2 and four Mark 3 Hi Power Browning pistols. Two ghillie suits were hanging from a peg like dead scarecrows. It was standard British Army equipment and had been for some time. Tiger was more than familiar with all of it.

'Nice, Brown, very nice. Sniper rifle, a dozen hand grenades and personal side arms. I presume there is ammo?

'Suitcase in the corner, Tiger. Five hundred rounds of seven point six two millimetre for the rifle and four magazines.' He opened the suitcase whilst he talked.

'Four hundred rounds of nine millimetre for the Brownings and they've got two magazines each.

Sitting in their respective green plastic cases, the dull lead bullet heads contrasted with the gleaming shine of their brass jackets. A deadly combination.

'Who made the ghillie suits?' Tiger was referring to the six foot long camouflage netting items that were hanging up, covered with strips of burlap and elastic loops that could hold small tree branches and other vegetation. Invented by Scottish gamekeepers as portable hides after the Second World War, many armies around the world had copied the idea for their snipers.

'A couple of the lads on my recent course.'

'Same course you obtained the firepower?'

Brown remained silent. Some questions shouldn't be asked. Tiger should have known better.

Tiger picked up one of the Browning pistols. He flicked off the safety catch with his right thumb and slowly drew back the top slide with his left hand about half an inch and peered inside past the working parts. He could see the black hole of the start of the barrel, the magazine wasn't fitted so he now knew that the weapon was unloaded and safe to handle. He let the top slide snick rearwards and click into place forcing the firing pin hammer to lock, and had a good look at the working parts and the state of the barrel. They were immaculate. He eased the top slide back into the forward position, inserted a long experienced finger into the magazine housing, located the magazine locking catch and squeezed the trigger allowing the cocked hammer to snap back into its resting position.

'The reason I'm asking, Brown, is these weapons still have the serial numbers clearly stamped into them. They're definitely British, so I presume that they were officially issued to somebody at some point and that somebody would presumably like them back?'

'At some point, yes, preferably without some sort of history attached to them as well.'

'Point taken...'

At this moment Gruff poked his into Brown's Croft and shouted.

'TIGER! BROWN! Look sharp. We've got company!'

~NINETY SIX~

The man known as 'Yarmouth' had left his men to finish up on the firing range, there were at least two thousand empty brass casings that needed picking up. This was often standard practice in the British Army - the Ministry of Defence accounted for such things - but it was an essential operational necessity for Black Team Charlie. Brass is fantastic for retaining fingerprints. Leaving fingerprints, well, not so good.

He'd ensconced himself in a corner of the Garrison Officers' Mess, nobody had asked him for identification, people rarely did if you looked and acted as if you belonged. He had made a couple of phone calls and was waiting for a reply, lazily leafing through a copy of that day's Daily Telegraph newspaper.

'Excuse me Sir.'

Yarmouth glanced up and looked at the young trooper who was currently carrying out his duties as a Mess Waiter. Fresh faced, no more than nineteen years old, and dressed in the ubiquitous uniform of Cavalry mess waiters everywhere. Highly polished black shoes, black dress trousers with a red stripe down the seam and an immaculately pressed white shirt open at the neck.

'Excuse me Sir. Will you be taking tiffin?'

Yarmouth blinked furiously as his brain tried to engage. Did he mean 'take tea' as in have a cup of tea, or 'take tea' as in a late afternoon light meal? He could have done with a hot brew as he was bloody parched, however he didn't fancy his chances at surviving another minute in the mess if he was forced to eat cucumber sandwiches with a group of legitimate Cavalry subalterns. Too many awkward questions, so he played it safe.

'No thanks, I won't be much longer.'

'As you wish Sir. Have you got time for a pot of tea before you go Sir?'

Yarmouth was on the point of panic. What was this? Tiffin? Wasn't tiffin some kind of posh tea? Shit, he was out of his depth, British Army Officers obviously had their own language, so he just blustered as if the waiter was annoying him, which he wasn't bluffing, the damned waiter was annoying the hell out of him.

'Well, as it happens, I do thank you. Milk and two. I'll pay cash.'

The waiter winced as he turned towards the kitchen. Milk and two? Cash? It wasn't the NAAFI canteen and he'd bet his next meagre pay packet that the man in the corner pretending to read the Telegraph didn't hold the Queens Commission and never had.

As he continued his perusal of the newspaper, Yarmouth had two thoughts, firstly he'd somehow managed to get a brew without acting like an idiot, and secondly he wanted that phone to ring really soon.

He needed to get up to speed on the big picture, get back with his team and head north. Surrounded as he was, by rich leather Chesterfield furniture, expensive carpet and priceless oil paintings depicting battles that would never be forgotten made him feel very uncomfortable. The fact that Stone had told him that he wouldn't be noticed in the Mess and it was the only place in the Garrison where he could sit by a telephone undisturbed wasn't really helping.

~NINETY SEVEN~

Brown had snapped a magazine onto one of the nine millimetre pistols and handed it to Tiger who weighed it in his hand for a second before nodding and jamming it into his waistband at the small of his back. Although there was now a magazine fitted to the weapon, it was completely safe. It wouldn't start getting dangerous until he snapped the top slide back again and let it go, forcing a round into the barrel.

Tiger then walked up the hall to the front door, poked his head out of Brown's Croft and looked towards his own. He couldn't see anything amiss. He couldn't see Gruff either but that was unsurprising, the man was probably snaking his way through the heather in order to set up a flanking manoeuvre should one be needed.

Old habits die hard.

'I'm walking up Steve. Moving now.'

Steve Brown was conscious of the fact that Tiger had called him by his Christian name for the first time. He didn't believe it was because of nervous tension, it was probably a sign that Tiger trusted him and now considered him a friend. Brown could live with that.

'I'm right behind you.'

Tiger walked slowly and deliberately towards his Croft. Still no sign of Gruff. He noticed that the front door was still open and a battered green Land Rover was parked next to his motorcycle. He patted the weapon in his waistband. Comfort in a one kilogramme package.

Voices could be heard from within the Croft. Women's voices? He had to get closer to make sure. He signalled for Steve Brown to circle the little building, check the rear, whilst he positioned himself next to the front door.

After the embarrassment earlier, acting too hastily when there was no actual threat, he was erring on the side of caution. The slightest movement of heather to his front caught his attention and Gruff slowly raised his head above the growth. Tiger raised his right thumb for a second and then reversed it, thumbs down – Enemy? Or Friendly? Gruff made no gesture in return. He didn't know. Tiger pointed to the Land Rover and pulled his right forefinger across his throat. Disable that vehicle. Gruff disappeared once more.

Brown had appeared at the door opposite Tiger. Both men were ready to enter. In the next seven seconds they could've caused mayhem. Both men had done time in the Killing House in Hereford, the hostage practice building where real live rounds were fired, as a highly trained team entered, sourced the cardboard bad guys, shot them, and rescued the real live friendlies. But for the moment they paused and they listened.

It was women's voices. Anna Brown could clearly be heard laughing. There was a chink of glass. A couple toasting? Tiger looked at Brown and whispered.

'My call?'

'Your call.'

'Friendlies. I'm going in.'

'I'll cover the door.'

'Moving now.'

Tiger slowly entered the hallway to the Croft. The voices were coming from the kitchen. Once he stepped into the living room he would be seen, it would be over, one way or another.

He stepped into the living room.

~NINETY EIGHT~

Alex Fontain had been an Officers Mess waiter for four months. He'd finished his basic Army training and a couple of courses after that, so he was just killing time until his Headquarters posting order came through, authorising his journey to Germany to join his Regiment. This was a common feature of Army life and he was quite enjoying his time in the Mess, and given that it was highly unlikely that he'd ever be a member, he was strangely protective of it.

He sought out his superior, Staff Sergeant Joe Keans, the Mess Manager, who was to be found in a cramped office behind the kitchen, with a chicken drumstick in one hand and a cup of strong black tea in the other. A linen napkin was tucked into his collar and spread across his ches, protecting his shirt and tie from spillages.

Trooper Fontain outlined his concerns to Staff Sergeant Keans.

'He's definitely not an officer, Staff, and he's definitely not a member of this mess.'

'Okay, Alex I believe you. But there are plenty of other people who can use the mess son.'

'I'm aware of that Staff, and they have to sign in, I've just checked the register, our man in the corner hasn't signed in. He hasn't signed anything. I'm not saying he's a wrong 'un, but after last week's security briefing and last month's bombing in Germany...Oh, and the bloke reeks of gunpowder...Well, I'm just being careful, Staff.'

'Okay Alex. Has he got an Irish accent?'

'I don't think so, Staff. He didn't say much, just ordered a brew and wanted to pay in cash.'

The experienced Mess Manager had a couple of options open to him. He would have to speak to the man of course. Identify him as that was part of his job. If he wasn't happy with the man's answers he could ask him to leave, again that came with the job. All sorts of people tried to gain entry into his mess, for the most part it was the troops having a dare, usually after drink had been taken, some sort of bragging rights and it always ended in tears.   Or in the Guardroom.

But young Trooper Fontain had, quite rightly, mentioned the security status of the Garrison. There was a definite threat of being bombed. And there was the gunpowder issue. The Irish Republican Army had killed dozens of soldiers already and they were getting better at it. He put down his chicken snack and his brew and reached for the phone.

'Hello. Guardroom. Sergeant Smith.'

'Smudge, its Joe Keans, Officers Mess.'

'Now then Joe, what's up?'

'We may have a problem in the Mess. I want to call 'Operation Whistler.'

'Op Whistler? Bloody hell Joe, are you sure? We're only on Bikini Amber.' The Regimental duty Sergeant was referring to the security state of the Garrison. He couldn't remember if there had ever been a Bikini Green, a totally safe environment and Bikini Red called for a camp lockdown, a doubling up of the guard and armed soldiers at the gates. Pretty much throughout the world the British Army was on Bikini State Amber.

'Not really mate, but we've got a visitor in the members lounge. He doesn't fit and he stinks of gunpowder.'

'Okay. Whistler's too high, that'd involve a thousand people, suppose I downgrade this to Operation Peacock?'

'Christ Joe, what's that when it's at home?'

'It's a baby Whistler, won't involve Garrison HQ in the initial stages and we'll stay on Bikini Amber.'

'Understood. You don't want the wheels to fall off, Smudge. Does it still involve a COT, an armed Crash Out Team turning up to remove my gunpowder guy?'

'Sure Joe. Say when.'

'When.'

~NINETY NINE ~

'There you are Tiger! We were wondering what you chaps were up to. Outside playing silly games or talking about motorcycles I suspect?' Tiger just mumbled something in agreement. He was getting a tad fed up with the whole situation he'd found himself in. He'd come to Fort William on his own, shrouded in a cloak of grief and with vengeance on his mind. He'd made some plans, loosely based ones he'd admit, but they were, in his mind, workable. On his own. What was it with rigorous planning anyway? Every General since Hannibal knew that a battle plan went to a ball of chalk as soon as contact was made with an enemy. Fact. He was now surrounded by people who obviously didn't have the same goals that he had. He was surrounded by people who were beginning to think that this was some sort of game, or even worse a holiday of some sort. He was surrounded by...Well, he was surrounded, and it didn't sit right with him.

Charlie Soper and Anna were sat at his kitchen table together with an opened bottle of wine and two glasses. A large pot of tea was sat in front of the third lady, a rather stern looking Mrs Cameron, the owner of the Crofts.

Shit! Mrs Cameron! Landlady! Key! Keyfob! These thought rushed through Tiger's head. Twenty seconds ago he was ready to kill people, now he worried about a bloody floating fish key fob. He reached behind him and as subtly as he could, un-tucked his shirt to hide the Browning pistol that was pushed into his trouser waistband.

All this nervous energy. He needed to sit down.

So he did.

'Hello Mrs Cameron, is there a problem or is this just a casual visit?'

'I'm just passing, Tiger. Thought I'd pop in and mind how you were.'

'Well, I'm fine thanks.'

Mrs Cameron might have been a bit mad in Tiger,s eyes, but she was an astute business woman and quite able to handle a bit of backchat, especially from one of her guests who was as attractive as this Tiger fellow. She continued on in her soft Scottish burr.

'I can see that, Tiger. You've got yourself quite a little clan gathering going on by the look of things. I did think you'd be on your own though when I took the booking. Ye ken?

'Aye Mrs Cameron, I hear what you're saying, and I am on my own, this is my friend, er, Charlie and, well you already know, er, um, Anita from the Croft next door, they're not stopping here, er long, er at all. They're not...'

Anna was holding up his door key, she'd somehow replaced the bloated fish key fob and was dangling it like bait in front of him, obviously amused with his tongue tied attempts at placating the inquisitive minded Mrs Cameron.

'We'll just finish our drinks, Tiger, and then we'll be off...' Anna was trying to rescue Tiger from further embarrassment.

Steven Brown then entered the lounge.

'Hello all.'

Mrs Cameron didn't bat an eyelid.

'Quite the wee party animal aren't we Tiger, for somebody that wanted to spend some time alone in quiet reflection...'

'Well aye, Mrs Cameron, I was having a quiet time, and I promise you that this is just a casual gathering of friends.'

'Well that's fine Tiger, as maybe, I wouldn't want to have to rearrange our contract, you can add more guests of course, but that'd mean a bigger rental charge, ye ken?'

'Aye, Mrs Cameron. I ken...'

Gruff then chose this moment to enter the lounge. His dishevelled hair and dirty face was in keeping with his crumpled clothing. Small twigs and clumps of heather clung to knee soiled trousers.

'Tiger mate, I'm just going to clean up if that's okay?'

Tiger sighed, looked at Mrs Cameron and trying to lighten the atmosphere said.

'I know Mrs Cameron. I know. It looks like a really bad play, the cast making ill-timed entrances from stage left when they...'

Mrs Cameron stood, her chair scraping along the stone flagged floor.

'Bad plays I can deal with Tiger. Shenanigans and Monkeyshines I can well do without. I'll remind ye that I run a respectable business Tiger and I'll accept no nonsense from ma guests, you'll no be bringing any of your weird English ways up here ye mind? I've heard all about them orgies and whatnot. Now, if ye don't mind I'll be taking my leave. I'll see myself out.'

As Mrs Cameron brushed past Gruff on her way to the front door he said.

'Mrs er, Mrs, is that your green Landrover parked up front?'

'Aye young man it is. Why're ye asking?'

Gruff looked over at Tiger, raised an eyebrow and mouthed 'Monkeyshines?' Tiger suppressed a grin and just nodded in the general direction of the outside world.

'I think you may need a hand getting her started.'

369 Tigers Revenge

~ONE HUNDRED~

Staff Sergeant Joe Keans confidently approached the man in the corner. Expertly balancing a silver salver containing a pot of tea and the other accoutrements required to make a soldier's proper brew he realised that Trooper Fontain was bang on the money. He could definitely smell the gunpowder residue from five paces away. The man appeared totally relaxed as he read the mess copy of the Daily Telegraph.

'Pot of tea Sir.' He leaned forward and placed the tray on a low table to the right of the gunpowder guy. The man looked up.

'Cheers. Thank you. How much is that?'

'It's free Sir. Officers from another mess do not pay for light refreshments Sir.'

'That's mighty kind of you. Thank you.'

'Can I enquire as to what Mess you actually belong to Sir? I couldn't see an entry in the visitor's book.'

'Well, actually, er, um… I am no longer serving, I am here as a guest you see.'

'I do see Sir, and who might your host be?'

Yarmouth really didn't want this conversation, he couldn't give his real name or the department he worked for, he didn't know any Officers in the Garrison, so he took a punt at name dropping and hoped that the waiter, manager, whatever he was, would then just fuck off. He leaned forward slightly, reaching for the teapot causing his jacket to fall open slightly.

'Anthony Stone at the F.O.'

'F.O. Sir?'

'Foreign Office. Give them a call, they'll vouch for me.'

'I'll do that Sir. In the meantime enjoy your tea.'

Staff Sergeant Joe Keans smiled at the man and turned to walk away, and almost as an afterthought turned around and said.

'Oh, sorry Sir, as a guest you probably won't be aware. We'll be having the fire alarm tested in about five minutes. It's fairly loud obviously and you may hear people scampering about, just ignore it, it's a weekly thing. Rules and regulations. I'm sure you know the drill.

'I'll try not to panic.'

'Right, Sir. Do enjoy your tea.'

The crafty old Staff Sergeant headed back to the kitchens and reported to the Duty Officer who had been notified by the Duty Sergeant at the Guardroom that Operation Peacock was now in play.

2nd Lieutenant Jeffery Satchel -Blythe had no idea what Operation Peacock was all about until he had read the relevant chapter in Garrison Standing Orders. This was a mighty thick tome that was available to all personnel on duty, and covered every eventuality that may occur at a military base at any time, ever. It was cross-referenced with The Army Act 1955 and Queens Regulations and wasn't considered bedtime reading. If an event, well, any event out of the ordinary occurred, then the duty Officer grabbed the book and had a jolly quick read.

'So, Staff. What have we got in there?'

'Male aged about thirty-five, casually dressed, sitting in the corner of the Members lounge Sir. He smells of gunpowder residue and he has a Browning nine mill in a shoulder holster under his left armpit. He isn't an Officer from this, or any other Mess and he's told me that he's a guest of somebody called Stone from the Foreign Office and frankly Sir, I am sure he shouldn't be here.'

'Which corner is he in?'

'Under the painting of Lord Raglan Sir.'

'Ah, Raglan. Terrific fellow. I did my finals thesis at the Academy on him. Did you know Staff that during the battle of...'

'Yes Sir, I know the story. The Guard Commander, Sergeant Smith has called for the COT Sir, Maybe we should get out of their way?'

'Indeed Staff. Yes. Indeed. Er...Where do we go?'

'Far away, Sir. I am now going to set off the fire alarm and the Crash Out Team will then probably abseil down from the roof and clatter through the windows or something equally mental and whilst they are doing that I'm going to join Sergeant Smith in the Guardroom. I'd advise you to follow me Sir.

'Er, Righto Staff. What a jolly jape...Although maybe I should go in front and you follow me?'

~ONE HUNDRED ONE~

Gruff re-entered the Croft, a bemused look on his face.

'Well Mrs what's-her-face didn't appear very happy, Tiger.'

'None of us are very happy Gruff...'

'I am.' Charlie Soper butted in as she raised her arm.

Tiger decided that that was the last straw. He'd had enough.

'There really isn't any need to raise your arm Charlie. You're not at bloody Kindergarten asking to go for a pee pee. This is not a holiday outing. I'm not dicking about up here in this midge-infested environment. I am being deadly bloody serious. We all need to sit around this table right now and have a proper chat, I'll tell you all what I'm about, and why I am here. If you can help, fine. If you want to goof about that's fine too, but please go away and do that somewhere else.'

Tiger's tone had changed the atmosphere completely. He really was fed up and even Gruff picked up on it.

'Tiger's right. We have interrupted his party without so much as a by-your-leave and we expect him to stop whatever he was planning. We, that is, Charlie and I came up here because he's a mate. A very good mate and we were worried for his welfare. I still am.' Gruff looked Tiger in the eye and continued. 'Well... We found him, he's okay, a bit grumpy but he's okay.' He then turned to Charlie. 'So are you ready to go home, Charlie?'

Charlie looked at Anna. Anna looked at Steve Brown who just shrugged.

'I'd like to stay up here a bit longer... Now that we're here.'

'Fine, we'll do just that then, but only because you've got the wheels. Let's get ourselves back to civilisation and book into The Flint Hotel. We'll stay a couple more days and leave Tiger to his own devices.'

Tiger stepped forward.

'I don't want you to go,Gruff.'

Tiger had been listening and watching the dynamics of the group he was with. He liked it, he had a team. A team of professionals, one of whom had saved his life. Twice.

Gruff replied instantly. 'Well, stop all this moody bollocks and speak to us, let's find out what you want and we'll help.'

Tiger sat down. 'I am going to kill Stone and anybody else he brings up here with him. I am prepared to go to prison to achieve that aim, and I want this done sooner rather than later. The killing that is...Not the prison bit.'

Steve Brown had also been studying the group dynamic as well and knew that Tiger was serious about his mission, and yet it was also obvious that he didn't want to involve his friends as that could mean a long spell in prison for them as well. He knew exactly the dilemma that Tiger found himself in. He coughed and raised his arm. Tiger scowled at him.

'Can I speak?'

It wasn't really a question that Brown had asked, he really was a statement kind of guy and therefore nobody answered him, so he continued.

'I actually do have a plan, and if it goes to, er, plan... Nobody goes to prison. I'm not going to go into detail as to why Anna and I are up here, not yet, but it is an odd coincidence that Tiger is here at the same time.

Tiger knows the basics and that's good enough for him so it should be good enough for everybody else.'

'You've told Tiger?'

'Not the detail Anna.'

'Bloody hell, Brown, if the Brigadier finds out that...'

'Brigstock? I've spoken to him this morning. He knows Tiger and he's rubber stamped my plan.'

'Bloody hell!' Exclaimed Tiger. 'Brigstock's now a Brigadier?'

'It's nominal Tiger, he came to us as a Colonel, but there was a space to be filled at that level and he fitted the bill. It's all Politics.'

'All the same, Brown, you could have consulted me. I'm on your team.'

'You are correct. Anna and I apologise. I was getting around to it, and then, well events got a bit silly.

Gruff was trying to take all this in. His plan was to lie low, pretend to leave and get stuck in at the last minute like the cavalry. There was no way he'd have left Tiger on his own. He wasn't sure about this Brown feller though, he hadn't been properly introduced, knew nothing about him whatsoever and although he and Tiger had obviously had a chat at some deep level it was still all a bit odd. He challenged Steve Brown.

'So, Brown. Are you some sort of James Bond? Got a licence to kill?'

'James Bond is a fictitious character Gruff, I'm very real.'

'You are skirting the question, Brown.'

Brown paused and looked at Tiger who nodded his head.

'Yes, I have a licence to kill. More importantly to you, or should I say to Tiger is the fact that I have a licence to kill Anthony Stone.'

'What? Anytime you like?'

'No, only in specific circumstances.'

'Specific circumstances!' Gruff laughed, this was idiotic. 'What specific circumstances allow you to kill the head of our Country's National Security?' He looked over at Tiger expecting some sort of reply. None was forthcoming.

'Tiger? Are you listening to this? Do you honestly trust this bloke? He's got to be mad.'

'Gruff. He's not mad, he is allowed to kill Stone and we'll know tomorrow if the er, conditions are right for that to happen.'

Brown looked at Gruff.

'Have you ever heard of 'White Watch' Gruff?

'Everybody on the Security circuit has heard of 'White Watch' Brown. It doesn't exist. It's a myth and I would know.'

'Really? Well you had better sit down Neil. Can I call you Neil? I know that nobody else does. You look surprised? So Neil. Neil Wetherspoon, the ex-Grenadier Guardsman and late trooper of G Squadron 22 SAS. Bodyguard and driver for the late Sir Andrew Thornton when he was head of the Russian 2nd Directorate desk at Century house. You're commonly known as Gruff though. Or do you prefer to be called Alan Thornberry? No? You're looking puzzled, so I'll remind you. Alan Thornberry represented Great Britain in the Olympics. Karate and Judo if I recall correctly. Which I do. That was you. Or what about Mike Jackson? Terrific moniker by the way, erstwhile member of a non-existent Metropolitan

Police department. So, which one of those characters would know for a fact that 'White Watch' is a Myth?

Gruff was totally taken aback. There weren't more than a handful of people in the world who knew this stuff. His PerSec, his Personal Security, was watertight. Had Tiger been talking? That was inconceivable, if true. He looked at Tiger and raised an eyebrow.

Tiger responded by raising his own eyebrow, grinning and mouthing the word 'Neil'?

'I need to get some fresh air.' Gruff stood up and, still looking utterly bewildered, walked towards the front door.

~ONE HUNDRED TWO~

As promised the fire alarm in the Mess went off. Yarmouth did indeed hear people running and some minor commotion in the ante-room next door, but he just smiled to himself, It's only a bloody drill people, happens every week. The noise was jarringly loud though, he'd admit that, he couldn't concentrate on the newspaper and glanced out of the window to his right. Uniformed soldiers were running across the manicured lawn of the Mess. Was that usual? For a fire drill?

BOOM!

The Members lounge of the Garrison Officers Mess seemed to explode. Yarmouth's ears were ringing. Impossibly bright lights penetrated his eyes causing his brain to overload into a jelly mash, causing utter disorientation.

BOOM!

He fell forward and tried to crawl. He couldn't. He tried to stand. Impossible. Somewhere part of his mush of a brain heard raised voices but he couldn't distinguish who was shouting or who they were shouting at. He couldn't breathe. Was it gas? He lay still and gagged for air, scared and semi-conscious as he lay on the expensive

Wilton pile carpet, utterly clueless as to where his rather nice cup of tea had gone.

CRASH!

The window next to his seat shattered into a thousand pieces, showering him with glass, two large shadows dived through the open space and launched themselves at the prostrate figure on the carpet. Yarmouth was by now unaware of this, he had passed into unconsciousness.

'CLEAR ONE.'

'CLEAR TWO.'

The shouting continued, despite the threat now being obviously a non-threat.

Train hard. Fight easy.

'WEAPON!'

'MADE SAFE.'

The two shadows breathing easily through the filtration system of their personal issue Mark 6 respirators picked up the limp body, one under each arm, and dragged him through the lounge, through the ante-room, across the hallway, down three concrete steps and dropped him on the front lawn.

Two other men stepped in, rolled him over and with practised ease, looped two lengths of plastic tie around his wrists making them secure.

A young woman wearing a beret with a badge depicting the distinctive Maltese cross on laurel leaves of the Queen Alexandra's Royal Army Nursing Corps pushed an oxygen mask over Yarmouth's face. She stepped back, stifling a cough as the latent CS Gas entered her lungs. She wasn't going to lose face though, not on this mini operation surrounded by the Alpha Males of the Crash Out team. Not a chance.

2nd Lieutenant Jeffery Satchel–Blythe strolled over to the edge of the front lawn and paused at the temporary red and white barrier tape that had been set up. He'd organised that bit, and was rather proud of it. Temporary barriers weren't mentioned in the Garrison Standing Orders, not relating to Operation Peacock anyway. He'd perhaps casually mention it to the Garrison Commander. Later. Over a brandy.

384 Tigers Revenge

~ONE HUNDRED THREE~

Three men sat in a green Land Rover some two hundred yards from the Garrison Officers Mess. They had just finished picking up the brass at the firing point on the fifty yard firing range. They were now supposed to be picking up the man they knew only as 'Yarmouth.'

There appeared to be some sort of exercise occurring on the front lawn and they really didn't want to rock up to the front door and ask for Yarmouth when there appeared to be some fifty heavily armed uniforms milling about.

'Jesus Christ, what are we watching?'

'Shut it, Sheringham. You're already on thin ice. I'm trying to think.'

'Who put you in charge, Caister?'

'I put me in charge. I'm communications. You're a bloody driver.'

'What's that supposed to mean?'

'I'll make it really simple, Sheringham. Are you behind the steering wheel?'

'Of course I bloody am.'

'Are you actually steering? Are we going anywhere? Are you actually driving?'

'No. Not yet, I don't know where we're going.'

'Exactly. You're not driving you're just sat there doing nothing. Stay doing nothing and let me bloody well think...'

Cromer leaned forwards from the rear seat.

'Can I ask a question? Isn't that Yarmouth those squaddies are dragging along the floor?'

All three men turned their collective attention back towards the Officers Mess.

'Jesus, Cromer, it bloody well is Yarmouth, he looks unconscious, and cuffed! What are we going to do?'

'Right,lads. Something's happened that is outside our control. We have to play this hand with the cards we've got.'

'What have we got, Caister?'

'We have the King, that's Yarmouth over there, unconscious and in cuffs. We have the Queen, we are after all on Sovereign property in the middle of a Military

Garrison and Yarmouth is currently being held by military personnel, but we also have an Ace.'

'An Ace?'

'Yes, Cromer, an Ace. We know, because of the above that he will be going to either a military hospital or the guardroom so he won't be going far, and both of those places are a piece of piss for us to take over.

'We're going to get him back?'

'How many rounds of ammo do we have left over back there, Cromer?'

Cromer lifted the lid to one of the storage bins next to the rear wheel arch and had a rough count of the left over ammunition.

'Looks to be about five hundred odd, Caister, all nine millimetre obviously.'

'So we're armed, we have enough ammo to start a small war, we have the element of surprise and best of all if we get Yarmouth back, it'll be chocolate cake and fucking medals all round.'

Although an ambulance was at the scene, it didn't appear to be needed. Two men manhandled Yarmouth into the back of a Land Rover and got in with him, a fourth got into the driver's seat and a few seconds later it accelerated out of view.

'Sheringham. Are you in gear?'

'No.'

'Well for fucks sake man, choose one, put the vehicle into it and follow that fucking Land Rover, you're supposed to be a fucking driver.'

Patience plainly wasn't a virtue in this little group, but Sheringham had no trouble following the Land Rover in front, it wasn't going very fast. There appeared to be a 10mph speed limit all over the Garrison and there were, of course green coloured Land Rovers everywhere for cover.

Sheringham talked as he drove, describing what points of interest he was passing, his speed, the speed of the vehicle he was following, his direction of travel, how many vehicles he had between him and the followed vehicle that were being used for cover. His two passengers never said a word. They all did it unconsciously anyway. The passing on of crucial information by radio to a following team in other vehicles was part and parcel of passing even the most basic surveillance course.

'I have the eyeball, left left left at the tee junction, speed ten, passing Aldergrove Avenue on the nearside, two for cover, approaching a crossroads...No change, speed ten, approaching a mini roundabout, not one, not two, off at three now on Saint George Way, one for cover...'

Caister gently interrupted the commentary flow coming from the driver's seat.

'We came in this way, so we're definitely heading for the Garrison exit. In that case two things can happen. Firstly he's being taken to the civilian Police, which I doubt. These boys like to keep things in house, or we're heading for the Guardroom. Wait...Wait, Yep! There it is up there on the left, slow it down Sheringham, we are going to pull over. Eyes on.'

The Land Rover holding Yarmouth drove up to the side of the Guardroom and stopped. The small tailgate was dropped and the same two soldiers, who had loaded Yarmouth, dismounted the vehicle. They didn't appear to be in any hurry, perhaps they were waiting for further orders.

Sheringham, Cromer and Caister could have done with some orders as well right at that minute, but they made do with two of them keeping an eye on their target vehicle, whilst Caister loaded up half a dozen Browning magazines and after slamming one into each of the three weapons, handed one to each of his colleagues.

They were now armed, extremely dangerous and ready to eat chocolate cake.

~ONE HUNDRED FOUR~

Tiger gave Gruff a minute and then followed him out the door. He spotted him sat astride his Triumph Trident, it was an obvious choice if he wanted to sit down. Charlie's Range Rover would have been locked and there was no garden furniture to sit on.

Tiger was never happy when somebody sat on his pride and joy, there were exceptions, and Gruff was one of them though. He couldn't do any harm even if he had the keys. He probably wouldn't know how to start it. One of not many failings in his life was his complete inability to understand motorcycles.

'Want to go for a spin mate?'

Gruff looked up as Tiger approached.

'Sure, mate. Hop on the back.'

Tiger threw his leg over the saddle and located the rear pillion footrests with his boots, a bit of an awkward manoeuvre as he'd never sat on the back of his own bike before, and settled himself. He hunkered right up to Gruff's back, chucked an arm around his best mate's waist and squeezed.

'Steady on, Tiger. You're not turning into one of those queer chaps are you?'

Both men laughed, but Tiger removed his arm, as it did actually feel slightly odd.

'No mate, just making sure you don't fall off. Where are we headed?'

'I'm thinking of another planet mate.'

'That bad eh? Any one in particular?'

'Nope.'

'Well let's just pick one at random.'

'Okay. All aboard who's coming aboard. Last chance to see Uranus!'

Both men laughed again. Real laughter. It was like being two kids again and it was a long time since Tiger and Gruff had been kids, and since then there hadn't been much to laugh at. Two young men with fire in their hearts and a burning ambition to stop violent men in violent places from destroying all that they held sacred, had left two older men with scars and sleepless nights and a kind of hell in their souls.

'You know, what you said back then, in the Croft. You wouldn't just do a runner on me would you, Gruff?'

'What do you reckon, Tiger? Have you changed? Gone to the dark side?'

'I reckon, Gruff mate, that you'd have checked into the Flint Hotel, doubled back here as soon as possible and set up a nest in the heather about two hundred yards to the north. You'd have a backup observation post about a thousand yards away, certainly within sniper scope distance, maybe on one of the west facing escarpments of Ben Nevis. You'd then come charging in, if it looked like going tits up and take all the glory.'

'You mean like back in Aden?'

'I mean like back in Aden.'

'That did go tits up, you were surrounded.'

'I know.'

'You never thanked me.'

'I know.'

'Do I get a thank you today? Now? Is that what this little meeting is all about?'

'No, no and no. But I do have something of importance to tell you.'

'What's that?'

'You should change up a gear. The vibration in first is giving me a hard on!'

Both men laughed uproariously. They should have done this a long time ago.

~ONE HUNDRED FIVE~

Anthony Stone was seething.

When he arranged for a member of his team to be in a certain place at a certain time, it was an order. Not some sort of fucking polite request. He had key information to pass to a so-called trusted associate relating to the operation that was floundering somewhere between Billingsgate Market and the Scottish fucking border.

He didn't have a clue where Black Team Charlie were, he didn't have a clue what they were up to and he didn't have a clue what was going to happen to his position when the Security Oversight Committee voted on his worthiness for his current post. Sure, the meeting was secret and he wasn't supposed to know about it, but he was a spy and spies had mates who were also spies.

It was a spy thing.

I Spy with my little eye something beginning with 'F'.

Well, 'fuck all' was the answer to that, and that is why Anthony Stone was seething. The last instruction he'd given that idiot Yarmouth was to get his arse up to the armoury at Catterick Garrison, draw some suitable firepower, check that they were suitable on the ranges and then phone him from the Officers Mess when he was happy. Using a contact as a favour to get weapons, well favours like that do not come cheap. Favours like that often had a nasty habit of biting somebody on the arse and Stone was in no mood to have his arse bitten.

Okay, so he'd received a call from Yarmouth some two hours ago explaining that he was in Catterick, he was now armed, his crew was starting to work as a team, there were no problems to report and that he was heading for the Officers Mess. So far so good. Stone had told Yarmouth to sit tight and wait for further orders.

Stone was ready to give those orders now as crucial information had come to light and speed was the key here. Speed and some fucking communication.

But nobody was answering the phones at Catterick. His own contact up there was obviously bloody incompetent, or on drugs. Some sort of Garrison lock down. Involving peacocks?

The crucial piece of information he'd received related to the exact whereabouts of Tiger Johnnie, relayed to him during a very recent and rather interesting telephone call. A couple of grand in cash was a very small price to pay for material like that.

The only small crumb of comfort that kept him from beating his secretary to within an inch of her life, flying to Catterick and beating Yarmouth to within an inch of his life or leaving his office and punching the first person that smiled at him, was that Tiger bloody Johnnie wasn't so infallible after all and he definitely should be looking after his mates a bit better.

~ONE HUNDRED SIX~

'Wait, there's movement.'

Sheringham had noticed that another vehicle was parking next to the Land Rover containing Yarmouth. It looked like a Triumph Stag convertible. The two soldiers to the rear of the Landover visibly stiffened as it approached. A man stepped from the car and both men sprang to attention and saluted.

'An Officer,' said Cromer, still sitting in the back of the watching vehicle.

'No shit Sherlock,' retorted Caister. 'Did you pass the surveillance course?'

'Of course I did.'

'The question was rhetorical, Cromer.'

'Ree- what?'

'Shut up man, I'm thinking.'

The Officer was 2nd Lieutenant Jeffery Satchel - Blythe, the duty Officer, and he was now supervising the removal of a very shaken, but now conscious Yarmouth, from the Land Rover and into a side door of the Guardroom. Once the three men and Yarmouth had gained entry, the Land Rover driver reversed his vehicle from its space and headed back the way it had come. The three occupants of the watching Land Rover briefly ducked their heads as it crawled past them at the regulation speed of 10mph.

'How many men are in the Guardroom?' Asked Sheringham.

'Good question, and well presented. I don't know. Ask me one on sport,' replied a frustrated Caister.

'No need to be sarcastic.'

'It was a stupid question. How the fuckitty fuck am I supposed to know that?'

'I thought you were an ex squaddie?'

'You know nothing about me, as I know nothing about you. Other than you're a fuckwit.'

Cromer still had eyes on the situation whilst his comrades continued their petty bickering.

'Ladies…There's two coming out of the side door. They look like the same blokes that had Yarmouth.'

The two soldiers walked away from the guard room. They were on the pavement to the side of the road.

One of them was carrying something wrapped in black plastic. Caister made a decision.

'Shit. That'll be Yarmouth's weapon. They'll be taking it to the armoury, we cannot let that happen. Sheringham. Quick smart, follow those blokes and pull up next to them, engage them in conversation.

'What?'

'For Christ's sake man, do not let them get to the armoury, that weapon came from the armoury, it has a serial number on it and our bloody prints all over it, the brown stuff will hit the spinny thing when that Browning is checked in. We need to stop them. You pull up beside them, ask them where the Gym is or something, I don't care. Cromer, stay in the back. I'm going on foot in case they leave the road.

Caister opened the passenger door and hurried towards the two soldiers. Sheringham drove steadily. Sixty seconds later he pulled to the side of the road, a few yards past the soldiers and leaned across the passenger seat and slid the window open. He noticed Caister in the mirror, hanging back about twenty paces away, pretending to tighten his bootlace.

'Hello lads. Armoury is it? Hop in I'm going that way myself.'

The two soldiers looked at each other and shrugged. The older one said.

'Did Baggy send you?'

'Baggy?'

'Lieutenant Satchel -Blythe. Baggy. The Duty Officer.'

'I didn't catch his name, you mean the Rodney in the Triumph Stag. Same bloke?'

'That'll be him. Jumped up prick.'

'Yep, so are getting in or what?'

The younger soldier looked at his colleague.

'You might as well get a lift, Jack. I'll see you in the NAAFI in twenty minutes, it doesn't take two to hand in a bloody Browning anyway.'

The soldier called Jack opened the passenger door and stepped into the vehicle. No sooner had he closed the door and started to relax he felt something cold and hard touch the back of his head. He'd seen the movies and he knew exactly what it was.

'So, Jack, my old mate,' said Sheringham, 'I want you to keep perfectly still. I mean do not move an inch. Don't cough, don't speak, don't even try and smile. My colleague in the back is a bit twitchy and his finger is on the trigger of a nine millimetre semi-automatic Browning pistol. Do you know what one of them is? Don't answer, it's reetortical...Or something. Anyway...Of course you know what it is. Oh look! You seem to have one in a little plastic bag right there. Hand it to my twitchy friend behind you, there's a good little Jack.'

Jack slowly passed the package over his left shoulder and it was grabbed from his grasp. He kept looking to his front, making no attempt to look at the driver of the Land Rover. He didn't want to see him. He'd seen that movie as well.

Sheringham slid open his side window and gave Caister the thumbs up. We have a prisoner. We have what we believe to be Yarmouth's pistol. Caister returned the gesture and walked to the rear of the Land Rover, flicked the canvas cover out of his way, climbed over the tailgate and took control of the situation.

'Let's drive…' Sheringham put the vehicle into gear and pulled away from the kerb.   'What's your name soldier?'

'Please don't shoot me.'

'That's a fucking weird name. Shoot him Cromer…'

'Nooooo, don't shoot, it's Jack. Jack Cunningham.'

'Thank you, Jack Cunningham. That was easy, now for something a little easier. How many people are there in the Guardroom?'

'I don't know…'

'Cromer…'

'FOUR! There were four when I left. The Guard Commander, the duty Officer and two Regimental Policemen.'

'Are they armed?'

'No.'

'Okay, this is good. Now the vehicle is going to stop in a moment and I am going to get out and walk to your door. Do you understand?'

'Please don't shoot me...'

'Cromer...'

'Noooo. I mean yes. Yes I understand. Oh God.'

'Good. When I get to your door you are going to climb over the seat and get in the back with my colleague. Do you understand?'

'Yes.'

Sheringham stopped the Land Rover and Caister got out of the rear. Cromer tapped Jack on the side of the head with his pistol and he scrambled over the seat and into the rear. Cromer then told him to lay face down and put his hands behind his back. Jack complied and felt plastic tie cuffs cutting into his wrists as Caister resumed his position in the passenger seat.

'Drive back to the Guardroom mate. We're going straight in through the front door Sheringham. Me and you.'

'Sounds good to me.' Replied Sheringham as he drove towards the Guardroom.

The Triumph Stag was still to the side of the building, the red coloured sports car looking absurdly out of place in a military setting, but at least it sent a signal to Caister that an Officer was still in the building. Sheringham stopped in a vehicle search bay right outside the guardroom front entrance. He noted one man on duty at the red and white striped barrier pole about thirty yards away, the guard was looking out of the camp, not in. He left the engine running and turned to Caister.

'Are we good?'

'Yes we are. Cromer. You okay in the back?'

'I'm fine. Straight in and out mind, I can't see fuck all from back here.'

'Right, Sheringham, I've got the Officer, you just have to cover me, okay?'

Sheringham was already halfway out of the vehicle as he quickly nodded his head. Both men entered the front door after walking up three concrete steps with their pistols held tightly by their sides. Three strides and they were in. The place smelled of Brasso cleaning fluid and bleach. A customer desk ran three quarters of the way across the room with a hinged access hatch to the right. The hatch was open.

Three more strides and both men were in the inner sanctum. Caister had his pistol in front of him at arm's length and had marched directly at the Officer who had his back to him chatting to a Sergeant sitting at a table with a mug of tea in his hand. The Sergeant started to rise, a look of complete disbelief appearing across his face.

'Sir...Sir...'

'SIT BACK DOWN AND SHUT THE FUCK UP.'

2nd Lieutenant Jeffery Satchel –Blythe had turned and was now looking at a very angry looking man holding a pistol. He was stunned into inaction. The man took two steps towards him and jammed the pistol into his nose and kept pushing forcing him to take awkward little steps backwards.

'CELL KEYS. I WANT THEM. AND I WANT THEM NOW.'

Caister kept pushing the Officer backwards until he was stopped by the wall. Then he pushed a bit harder and blood spurted from the Officer's nose.

The Sergeant Guard Commander was being covered by Sheringham, there was no sign of anybody else. So where were the Regimental Policemen that Jack had spoken of? He asked the Guard Commander.

'You. Where are the cell keys and who else is in this building?'

'It's just us. The keys are in my desk drawer.'

'Well get them out of your fucking desk drawer, didn't my colleague ask clearly enough?'

The Guard commander was an experienced soldier, but he was faced with two determined men who had weapons he was very familiar with. He didn't know of course if they were loaded, but the magazines were fitted, and given that he had recently taken a similar weapon from the prisoner now in cell one, and that one was certainly loaded, he had decided that today was not the day he was going to get a medal. For being dead.

'I'm opening my drawer...here's the keys...'

'Keep the fucking keys you moron and take me to the man you arrested earlier from the Officers Mess.'

So now the Sergeant understood, A Jail Break. Well if that's all they wanted they were welcome. He stood slowly holding the keys out in front of him, and pointed to a door at the rear of the room.

'This way...'

Sheringham kept his weapon levelled at the Sergeant's back and followed him through the door.

'IF I HEAR ANY SOUND THAT I'M NOT HAPPY WITH, THIS FUCKER GETS IT IN THE FACE.'

Caister couldn't keep himself from shouting, he was really keyed up. He flicked his weapon towards the rear door and back to the Officer's face.

'BACK UP RODNEY, THROUGH THE DOOR AS WELL.'

Caister poked and jabbed the unfortunate and bloodied Satchel –Blythe all the way to the cell area. The Guard Commander had opened the door to cell one and stood back.

'Don't be fucking shy Sergeant, that's my mate in there get him out.'

The Sergeant entered the small cell and a few seconds later half carried, half dragged Yarmouth from the cell and leaned him against the wall. He didn't look well at all. His face was puffed up and he had two black eyes. Somebody had given him a good kicking by the look of it.

'BOTH OF YOU IN THE FUCKING CELL.'

The Orderly Officer scurried past the Sergeant into the cell whilst the Sergeant himself was rather more prosaic. He took one last good look at the men that had invaded his space before entering the cell and having it slammed behind him.

Grab him. Let's go. My lead.'

Caister led the way through the deserted Guardroom, down the steps and to the back of the waiting Land Rover.

'It's me Cromer, we've got him, and he's in a bad way, you'll need to hold him up.'

'No problems here... Get him in.'

Caister released the rear tailgate and Sheringham sat Yarmouth down on it. Cromer's strong arms appeared from under the canvas, hooked under his armpits and gently pulled him into the back of the vehicle. Caister slammed the gate shut and secured it before jumping into the passenger seat. Sheringham was already behind the wheel gunning the engine.

'Out the main gate, Sheringham. Nice and steady, they're looking for baddies getting in, not baddies getting out.'

Both men smiled.

They'd been in the Guardroom for eighty seconds.

~ONE HUNDRED SEVEN~

A shrill whistle stopped Tiger and Gruff's laughter. They both looked for the source and saw Steve Brown waving at them from the Croft.

'Down to Mother Earth with a bump,' stated Gruff.

'Aye mate, but it was great voyage, we'll do it again,' replied Tiger as he dismounted from the rear of his motorcycle and started walking towards his Croft.

Tiger entered the Croft, into a completely different atmosphere to the one he had left ten minutes earlier. Brown had spread Tiger's local map out on the kitchen table and was stood over it. Anna was busying herself making tea and toast. Charlie was sat in an armchair in the lounge with an attaché case on her knees fiddling with some sort of electronic device.

A hive of activity.

Tiger and Gruff sat at the kitchen table and waited for Brown, this was obviously his show, for the time being at least.

'We are looking at the worst case scenario here lads.' Brown stated. 'My plan involves the three of us and the two girls. I am going to assume that Stone will arrive at this Croft within twenty four hours and he will have a team of no less than four men with him.'

'Do we know who these men will be?' Gruff asked.

'No, however I have a good idea. Stone will have access to a wet squad called Team Black, hired killers, who, for the most part are from Eastern Europe although there are locals who'll take his coin. They're a last chance saloon outfit really.'

'You don't rate them then?'

'No I don't. Sure, they'll carry out orders and take a life, that's what they get paid to do, but they're not a proper team, they're dribs and drabs made up from whoever is available on the market and that's a major weak point.'

'How do they get around, transport wise?' Tiger butted in.

'They'll use whatever Stone can get for them. Stone has access to a helicopter, he uses it all the time but he cannot be seen mixing with these people so they won't be flying. He calls in favours and uses hire cars, trains and even military wheels for these people.'

'And weapons…?'

'Same. They cannot bring their own so they have to be sourced in the UK, and again that'll be done through Stone, probably using his Army contacts. More favours.'

'When will you get notified about the result of the Oversight Selection Committee?'

'Tomorrow morning. Before noon.'

'And what happens to you and Anna if they decide he should remain in office? Are you just going to bugger off? And if you do where does that leave us?'

Brown paused.

Anna then plonked a tray of hot buttered toast and mugs of steaming tea onto the map, looked at Brown and said.

'We stay here with you. Regardless.'

414 Tigers Revenge

~ONE HUNDRED EIGHT~

'Okay Caister, just what have you got in store for the squaddie in the back?' Black Team Charlie were approaching Scotch Corner, and Sheringham had decided to mention the elephant in the room or, rather, Jack, the hapless kidnap victim currently being used as a footstool by Cromer in the rear of the Land Rover.

'I'm more concerned about Yarmouth. How's Yarmouth doing back there, Cromer?'

'He's just the same as when you asked four minutes ago, Caister.'

'Shit. We're approaching Scotch Corner, maybe five minutes. Do you reckon Yarmouth can walk? We're going to stop at the café.'

'There was a mumbled conversation in the back of the Land Rover as it whined its way North on the A1.

'Yarmouth says he feels fine, and he says he needs to make a call, so yes, affirmative to the walking.'

The next five minutes were spent in silence. Caister felt that he was now in charge, and it was his plan that had freed Yarmouth, however he was mindful of the fact that it was actually Sheringham and his quick thinking that had got them back as a team again. Enticing a soldier into the vehicle and getting Yarmouth's weapon was a bloody masterstroke. Although he wasn't going to mention that to him any time soon.

Sheringham had spent most of the last hour with his eyes darting from the view ahead to his rear view mirrors, convinced that they were going to be followed and then stopped by some angry and heavily armed soldiers and he knew there was very little he could do about that. He was happy to shoot, kill and murder but there was no way he was going to get into a fire-fight with a platoon of trained soldiers

Cromer was getting more than a little pissed off. Caister had assumed some sort of command and he felt like the tea boy stuck in the back of the vehicle. Okay, he was supposed to be the team medic, but that didn't mean he could be trampled over by the two dick heads in the front.

Yarmouth appeared to be slowly coming to his senses, he understood that he was in the back of the team Land Rover, and he knew that Cromer, the team medic, was sat next to him keeping him from slumping over, but he had no idea where they were, which way they were heading and who the fuck was laying on the floor under his boots?

Sheringham pulled off the A1 and eased towards the café and filling station.

'Scotch Corner, lads. All out if you're having a brew. I'm going to fill up at the pump and I'll join you in the café in five minutes. Two sugars in mine, Caister.'

Sheringham pulled alongside the fuel pump and stopped. Caister got out of the front passenger seat and walked to the rear of the vehicle, released the tailgate and helped Yarmouth from the back. Cromer started to get out.

'Where are you going Cromer?' Asked Caister.

'I'm going for a brew.'

'Uh huh, I don't think so Cromer, who's going to look after soldier boy?'

'He's unconscious, Caister. I've spent the last sixty minutes kicking him in the head.'

'He's your responsibility, Cromer.'

'No way, Caister, I'm the medic, I'm looking after Yarmouth and if you're not happy with that, then, then... You baby sit the unconscious squaddie.'

Caister really didn't want to lose control of the situation but Cromer was technically the medic and Yarmouth probably did need looking after a lot more than an unconscious bloke, but he was gagging for a brew and there was no way he was going to let these lads sit and chat over recent events without him being there.

'Fine, get your arse in the café and look after Yarmouth whilst he makes his call but mark my words Cromer, if that squaddie is bluffing...'

Cromer guided Yarmouth across the potholed car park to the side of the café, and they entered a noisy smoke filled atmosphere. The greasy smell of all day breakfasts competed with the stench of cigarettes and sweat.

It certainly wasn't the Ritz, but the thought of hot tea in big chipped mugs outweighed the discomfort, and there was a working telephone in a booth at the far end of the café.   Perfect.

~ONE HUNDRED NINE~

Brown was still in charge of the show. Tiger had the rudimentary equipment, and that would certainly do the job, but Brown had the weapons, the radios, the legitimacy and more importantly a coherent plan. He was poring over the map once more.

'Anna is going to cover the overview from this point here. It's fairly close to one thousand yards away.' Brown was pointing to an escarpment on the craggy western slope of Ben Nevis.' He was using a toothpick as a pointer; a stubby finger covered too much ground. 'There's no chance of climbers or ramblers getting in the way but to be on the safe side she'll be in a ghillie suit. Anna? Are you still okay with the L42A1?

'The sniper rifle? Sure.'

'Anna? Sniper?' Gruff asked in astonishment. He had made an assumption that this was his job.

Anna looked Gruff square in the eye and said.

'It's my weapon and it's zeroed for me,' she was referring to the fact that she had been on the ranges with the rifle, and had adjusted and fine-tuned the sighting system to suit her eyesight. She continued. 'It was my personal weapon for a while and I have a wardrobe full of silver from competition shooting at Bisley.'

'You've fired at Bisley?'

'Best shot last two years.'

'What? Best woman?'

'Nope. The United Kingdom.'

'Really?'

'I'm bored with this conversation Gruff, go and pick on someone else. It's my weapon, I know how to use it and you'd better trust me on that. It's your arse I'm covering.'

Gruff looked suitably chastised and suppressed a cheeky grin behind his tea cup. Brown continued with the briefing.

'Anna will be call sign 'Eagles Nest.' Gruff. You're our cut off, you'll be in the second ghillie suit, tucked up in the heather, close quarters, no more than one hundred yards away from here. You're going to let Team Black get past you and into, or near to the Croft. I have a feeling that they will approach real slow, but if they get twitchy and back off they're all yours. Your call sign is 'Ground

Hog.' You'll have a Browning pistol with plenty of ammo and four grenades.'

'Roger that, Brown.'

'Charlie. How did the test go with those perimeter warning things?'

'I've got seven, Brown. Five are working, two are kaput. I've placed them three hundred yards away in a loose circle. With two missing there will be gaps.'

'Okay, liaise with Gruff, show him the weak points, he'll dig in there. Oh and Charlie, your call sign is 'Babbage,' as in the computer nerd.'

'Thanks for that, Brown.'

'Anytime, Charlie. Tiger is going to stay in his Croft. He'll be blind as to what is exactly happening on the ground so he needs updating on any movement. Communication is absolutely vital to our timings as is everybody staying at their respective posts. Tiger's call sign is 'Trident.' I'm going to monitor the radios and perimeter tracking devices with Charlie. We'll be in my Croft and my call sign is 'Zero.'

Brown then issued the weapons and gave everybody a radio and charger.

'These radios are not brilliant out here, but they have a working range of a mile so we should be okay. In sixty minutes we'll get ourselves in position and carry out a radio check, and then we'll rendezvous back at mine before last light and fine-tune things. It goes without saying that you must keep your weapons out of sight from passing civilians. Last, but not least, does anybody have any questions?'

'I have a couple of hundred Brown.'

'We all do, Gruff. Pick one.'

'Why is orange jam called marmalade?'

~ONE HUNDRED TEN~

'Yarmouth, mate, we need to speak to the boss, wossisname, er, Norwich, and you're the only one with his number.'

Yarmouth was sat at the table in the Scotch Corner café, with Caister and Cromer, his mug of tea untouched in front of him. He did not look at all well.

Caister had been trying to coax some information from him for the last fifteen minutes and was getting nowhere. Sheringham was in the toilets and had been there for some time, Caister wasn't concerned about him at all, his attention was focused on Yarmouth.

'C'mon mate, at least speak to me...'

'Oh one two two two...'

'Shit, Cromer have you got a pen? Say those numbers again Yarmouth, c'mon mate...'

'Oh one two two two...'

Yarmouth was trying hard to tell Caister the telephone number he required, but it wouldn't come out, his speech was slurred and he had started to dribble.

'Oh. One. Two. Two. Two...'

'Yes Yarmouth, I've got that what about the rest?'

'Oh. One. Two…'

'For FUCKS sake Yarmouth, I've got that, what about the rest?'

A couple of truck drivers looked up from their meal as Caister's impatience rose to aggressive crudity. He waved an apology in the general direction of the two men and continued in a lower tone.

'C'mon mate, you're nearly there only a couple more digits…'

'Four five five four.'

Caister was writing down the numbers as they slipped from Yarmouth's lips but he wasn't sure if he had said four or five. He put the mug of lukewarm tea to Yarmouth's lips but there was no response.

'Cromer, you're the fucking medic, can you do anything?'

'He needs a Doctor, not a medic, and he needs rest and possibly drugs, painkillers at the very least. What he doesn't need is cold tea and an interrogation by you in a fucking transport cafe.'

'We need to make contact with Norwich, you know what at arsehole he can be. He'll be going ape-shit right now. Guaran-fucking-teed.'

Cromer looked out of the window, there was nothing to see other than a muddy potholed car park, but it was more interesting than talking to Caister.

He didn't need any of this shit, he didn't sign up for arguing with his team, storming guardrooms and kidnapping soldiers. Kidnapping soldiers! If it wasn't so serious it'd be a fucking joke.

It was a mess and he wanted out. Fuck the job. Fuck the rest of the money, he had fifty grand sitting in his bank account, that'd see him and his missus okay for a bit.

'Fuck this for a game of soldiers, Caister.'

He scraped his chair on the lino floor as he stood up, and without another word he walked over to the lorry drivers' table.

~ONE HUNDRED ELEVEN~

2nd Lieutenant Jeffery Satchel - Blythe was nervous. He'd been released, together with Sergeant Smith, from the tiny cell in the Guardroom when the two Regimental Policemen had returned from a break. He was now stood at attention in the vast office of the Garrison Commander and his black Labrador.

The dog was lounging on a leather Chesterfield settee and watching him through doleful eyes. He'd seen them come and go. Promotions, medal ceremonies and death messages. He'd seen men stripped of rank and watched rockets fly up subordinate's arses. His master was known as a fair man, but he also carried a mighty metaphorical stick and was never afraid to use it. Brigadier Emmerson Goth-Palmer had over three thousand men and women under arms in his command, the second largest Garrison after Aldershot. He'd been a professional soldier for thirty four years and this was to be his last command. He glanced up briefly from the notes he'd been writing, notes for his memoirs, and looked at the sorry specimen of an Officer stood before him.

'So. 'Baggy. Got yourself locked up then?'

'Er, yes Sir, only for a short time though…'

'Length of time is not an issue here 'Baggy, it's the actual act of getting locked up that concerns us here, you understand?'

'Yes Sir. Completely.'

'You are the Orderly Officer of the day are you not?'

'Yes Sir I am.'

'Then why are you incorrectly dressed?'

'Excuse me Sir?'

'Incorrectly dressed man. Has a ten second spell in a cell affected your hearing?'

'It wasn't ten seconds Sir...'

'Where's your Sam Browne cross belt and sword? My Orderly Officers wear full uniform on duty Baggy.'

'It's in my room in the Mess Sir, I thought that...'

'Don't think Baggy. Please don't start thinking...It doesn't bear thinking about.'

'Sir...'

'I knew your Father Baggy. He was bloody useless as well. Did you know that he once lost an entire Tank Regiment?'

'Sir...I must...'

'A whole damn Regiment, Baggy. Fifty six Chieftain Main Battle Tanks swanning around Germany and the Commanding Officer had no idea where they were.'

'But Sir...'

'The man was a cretin Baggy, should have been cashiered for that alone, let alone any other of the moronic plans he came up with, and I am afraid that you are heading that way...without the tanks of course, nobody is trusting you with tanks are they Baggy?'

'Well Sir, I am...'

Before the wretched Jeffery Satchel-Blythe could frame any sort of answer, the Brigadiers dog, very loudly, broke wind.

'Did you say something Baggy?'

'No Sir, I just ....'

'Jesus Christ man, it smells in here. Is it you Baggy? Bringing cell smells into my office?'

'No Sir It's the...'

'Full report Baggy. On my desk at Oh Six Hundred. Bring it personally, and make sure you're properly dressed. There's a good chap.'

'Yes Sir, of course Sir.'

'Still here I see, Baggy. Anything else?'

'Er. No Sir.'

The Brigadier didn't wait to see if the junior Officer saluted before he left the office, he was stuck on chapter thirty-eight, and memoirs don't write themselves.

~ONE HUNRED TWELVE~

'All call signs this is Zero, radio check… Over.'

'Eagles Nest loud and clear… Over'

'Ground Hog. Loud and clear… Over.'

'Trident loud and clear… Over.'

'All call signs, this is Zero. I hear you all loud and clear, return to my position for briefing in figures six zero minutes… Zero out.'

An hour later Tiger and company were once again in his Croft. The kitchen table had been cleared and half a dozen warm plates were sitting next to two bottles of wine and a group of cold beers.

'Party?' Enquired Tiger.

'Pizza,' replied Brown, 'my treat and they should be here any minute.'

There was a loud knock on the front door.

'Excellent timing, Gruff would you do the honours please? They've been paid for, just say thank you for the delivery and please try and restrain the impulse to knock them unconscious.'

Gruff scowled and headed for the front door.

Over pizza and drinks, Brown outlined his plan in more detail. Anna would have an overview of the Crofts from her perch in the craggy lee of Ben Nevis and would give a running commentary if necessary. Gruff would dig a shallow hide one hundred yards from Tiger's Croft and, dressed in his heavily camouflaged ghillie suit, would act as a cut off.

Charlie had shown him the gaps that existed between her wireless controlled movement detectors, and following Gruff's advice she'd moved two of them and Gruff was now happy to cover the void. It was a key position.

Charlie was to act as the first point of any contact. She would sit in her vehicle with a set of binoculars somewhere south of Fort William. The A82 was realistically the only way into the town from the south and could easily be covered by one person.

She couldn't know for sure what vehicle, or vehicles, would be used by any enemy, but she'd call in anything vaguely military looking and vehicles with multiple male occupancy. Brown would do the vehicle number plate checks.

Tiger had mixed his lethal concoction of fertiliser, oxides and nitrates and carefully filled the short lengths of plastic pipes. These were placed in a narrow trench that he'd dug around the Croft and re-covered with earth. He'd figure out the fuse mechanism in the morning, so although the place was virtually mined, it was, for the moment anyway, perfectly safe.

Tiger had something tickling his mind and had been waiting for the right moment to quiz Gruff. He'd seen him making a telephone call earlier in the day, from the phone in Charlie Soper's vehicle and he'd appeared quite animated when making that call.

'I noticed you making a call earlier Gruff. Is everything okay?'

'Telephone call?'

'Aye, this afternoon, from Charlie's car.'

'I don't remember doing that, Tiger, and technically it's not a car.'

'Skirting the question, Gruff. But I did see you in Charlie's vehicle?'

'Er yes, I was probably looking for a file or something. Are you grilling me?'

'No mate, why would I do that? You looked slightly distressed, I was puzzled, that's all.'

'Well there's nothing to be puzzled about okay?'

'Aye mate. Okay.'

Tiger let it go, but Gruff was definitely on the phone that afternoon, and he was wondering why his mate was lying to him.

'Well I suppose an early night is called for, it could be a busy day tomorrow,' and with that statement Brown had effectively ended the evening.

'What's the sleeping arrangements?' Gruff asked, looking directly at Anna.

'Charlie and I have a room booked at the Flint Hotel,' said Anna. 'We don't really care what you boys are doing.'

'Fair play,' replied Gruff. 'But if you're going in Charlie's vehicle I'll need my sleeping bag out of the back before you go.'

'I'll get it Gruff.' Tiger said. 'I need a bit of fresh air before I turn in.'

Charlie tossed him her keys and Tiger left the Croft and walked briskly towards her Range Rover. Once he'd gained entry he leaned in the driver's side and located the car phone system and powered it up. He opened up the rear door and grabbed a military looking sleeping bag that he presumed was Gruff's, a second bag had flower decorations printed all over it.

Leaning once more into the front of the vehicle the phone had powered up to full strength and Tiger scrolled through the basic menu system.

Looking for the last number called.

Bingo! There, in the dim backlight of the phone menu, was a number he recognised.

Tiger powered down the phone and stowed it before locking the vehicle and heading back to the Croft. He threw the sleeping bag to Gruff, who said, 'Tiger mate...That's Charlie's sleeping bag.'

~ONE HUNDRED THIRTEEN~

Caister thought he had the numbers he needed to call Norwich. Armed with a small pile of ten pence pieces he was at the public phone in the cafeteria at Scotch Corner. He dialled the number that he had scribbled down following a disastrous conversation with the semi-conscious Yarmouth. The phone number was good. Somebody had picked up.

'Hello is that...'

'Miss Whiplash, here to please...'

'Dear God. No! I'm after Norwich...'

'We do French we do Greek, we do sub and dom...'

CLICK.

He replaced the receiver, juggled the numbers and tried again.

'Hello?'

'Hello?'

'I am looking for Norwich. '

'Where are you now?'

At last!

'Norwich! Thank God, I'm at the café at Scotch Corner, Yarmouth is…'

'Scotch Corner you say?'

'Yes, it's not going well. Yarmouth is…'

'You need to head south on the A1 for a couple of hours. Pick up the A17 and head East…'

'Eh? Is that an order? Is that where our target is?'

'Target? I thought you wanted directions to Norwich?'

'I thought you were Norwich?'

'No. I'm Chris.'

'Jesus Fucking Christ…'

'Not sure about the churches in the area but I'm presuming that there will be…'

CLICK.

Caister was so desperate, he would try every combination of the numbers scribbled on his pad if he had to.

'Hello, I'm looking for Norwich?'

'Who the fuck is this?'

'Er...Caister.'

'Where the fuck is Yarmouth?'

Caister was very, very tempted to give directions to the seaside town on the East Coast, but discretion being the better part of valour, and this bloke sounded like Norwich...

Only angrier.

'He's not well, Norwich.'

'What? What the fuck does that mean? Is he sick?'

'He's had a good kicking, Cromer says he needs a hospital.'

'Cromer? He's the fucking medic isn't he? Cant he just do his job and patch him up?'

'Cromer's gone.'

'Gone? Gone where?'

'He's jacked it in and hitched a lift with a lorry driver, I don't know where he is...' 'You fucking bunch of idiots. Give me a verbal report of what the fuck is actually happening. I daren't ask another question in case something even more cretinous spills out.'

Caister brought Norwich up to speed with events as best as he could without making himself look too bad. It was a difficult, one sided conversation with Norwich just ending a sigh with the word cretin at the highlights of their recent escapade.

'Okay. I'm up to speed. Where's Sheringham?'

'I don't know. I think he's in the building somewhere...'

'Right. Find him and...'

'Sorry Norwich, I never mentioned the soldier.'

'What. Fucking. Soldier?'

'The one in the back of the Land Rover. The one we kidnapped.'

'You fucking morons. As of now, you are off the case. Leave it. Fuck off. Go home, I don't care, but you'll be hearing from me again you fucking idiots.'

'What about...'

CLICK.

~ONE HUNDRED FOURTEEN~

The sun lowered itself into the Western landscape casting a red and orange ethereal glow in its wake, promising, to those who believed in such things, a glorious day to follow.

The owl community awakened and together with the bats, prepared themselves for the night's activity. The small furry hunter-gatherers of the corn fields and hedgerows came out to forage and scrabble for the first meal of the day.

Oblivious to all this activity around him, the man known as Sheringham continued to walk cross country in a generally southern heading, putting as much distance between himself and his old team as was humanly possible without the benefit of wheels and an engine. He'd had enough as well.

Independently, Caister wasn't too far behind, on a slightly different route, but again avoiding the main roads. He'd had Norwich slam the phone down on him in the café following his vulgar dismissal when he became aware of a rotating soft blue light that swept across the muddy car park and filtered through the café windows. The briefest of glances past the curtains had told him all he needed to know. That it was time to go.

Cromer had thanked Bill, his new best mate, the lorry driver, for going out of his way and dropping him fairly close to his house in Bedford. They promised to keep in touch.

The green Land Rover belonging to the erstwhile Black Team Charlie, had become the focus of attention of The North Yorkshire Constabulary. Not only had they discovered the unconscious form of a Private Soldier in plastic handcuffs in the rear, a cursory search had unveiled a quantity of ammunition and firearms as his bedmates.

Green Military Land Rovers containing firearms and soldiers in compromising positions should have been no surprise, but having run the number plate through PNC, the Police National Computer, and finding that the number was false, only fanned the embers of suspicion that were now growing.

Enquiries started naturally enough with the proprietor of the adjacent cafeteria, where the only thing out of place was a customer who looked at death's door, and was sat in front of two mugs of cold tea. So for want of something better to do, the drooling uncooperative man, with no identification on his person, was taken into custody. His companion was nowhere to be found.

The Policeman making the enquiries availed himself of two fresh mugs of tea and a couple of warm Barm cakes, 'on the house Officer,' and sat in the patrol car together with his partner, a comatose soldier and the unidentified male, to await the Force Firearm Team, the Duty Ambulance, Detectives from the Criminal Investigation Department, Military Police from Catterick Garrison, the Force helicopter and any other asset that the Duty Inspector at Police Headquarters could rustle up. It looked like there could be some overtime on this shift.

Tiger couldn't sleep. He was going along with a plan that wasn't his, devised by a man he'd only just met and involving his closest friend who was now lying to him. He couldn't shake off the slight feeling of impending doom.

Brown was busy on his SatPhone to his superiors and making notes, he had no concerns. He had a mission to carry out and now he had some unexpected help that would expedite that mission. He'd be having a good night's sleep.

Gruff was lying peacefully in his sleeping bag on Tiger's settee. It wasn't that comfortable but he'd certainly had worse nights and when Tiger had turned in, he'd helped himself to a large tumbler of Jack Daniels which he now cradled, and gathered his thoughts for the day ahead.

Anna and Charlie were fast asleep in a warm glow, wrapped in each other's arms after an acrobatic evening of sex approaching cosmic proportions.

Taff Stone had calmed down considerably, the steel nipple clamps currently being screwed into his sensitive flesh by a tall leggy blonde Lithuanian woman who went by the name of Carla, was helping, but at the back of his mind he knew he was on his own now, and in the morning he'd be throwing the last roll of the dice.

~ONE HUNDRED FIFTEEN~

Overnight, Taff Stone had ordered his private secretary to ensure that the Service helicopter was at his disposal for 0800hrs. A flight plan was to be arranged from its hangar at Royal Air Force Ruislip in West London to a private airstrip outside the town of Glencoe in Scotland. It was to be a three hour trip and he'd be travelling alone.

Tiger, Brown and Gruff were having breakfast in his Croft, they'd arranged for the girls to arrive an hour later. Brown looked at Tiger.

'Tiger, I received information about two hours ago that the Service helicopter has filed a flight plan for this morning.'

'Do we know who's on it Brown?'

'Not yet, but I know where it's going…'

'So do I,' interrupted Gruff.

Tiger and Brown both put down their coffee cups, looked at each other, then at Gruff. Tiger broke the silence.

'Really? And how would you know that mate?'

Gruff looked at Brown for a full ten seconds before he spoke.

'Please don't tell me it's going to Glencoe.'

'It's going to Glencoe.'

'Damn. I'm sorry Tiger.'

'Sorry for what, mate? And how did you know it was Glencoe?'

'The telephone call you mentioned yesterday?'

'Aye.'

'Well I did make a call. Adrian has been pestering me for three days about your whereabouts and I wasn't happy with his tone.'

'Adrian? Photographer Adrian? From Derby?'

'Yes mate, crap tea Adrian from Derby. He wasn't in the slightest bit interested in your welfare, he was just desperate to know where you were. Yesterday afternoon I called him and sort of told him.'

'So he now knows where I am? Well that's hardly a problem, he's a mate.'

'When I say, sort of, I mean I told him you were at a hotel in Glencoe. He couldn't wait to get off the phone mate. He never even asked how you were.'

'Whoa there Gruff, back up a minute.' This from Brown, who didn't have a clue what was going on. 'You told this Adrian chap, a photographer friend of Tiger's that you had found him and he was staying in Glencoe. Why? Why would you do that?'

'Before yesterday afternoon, as far as I am aware, not including the five of us here, nobody, but nobody knew where Tiger was. I was unhappy with Adrian's attitude and just planted a false lead. See where it went. If I'd received a call today from Adrian that he was on his way up north to see Tiger, I'd have let Tiger know and we'd sort it from there, but Adrian hasn't called…'

'Are you saying that Adrian has been in contact with Taff Stone?' Asked an incredulous Tiger.

'Why else would Stone's helicopter be flying to Glencoe?' Asked Gruff. 'It was a random Scottish town that we passed through on the way up here. I made it up on the spur of the moment during the call, so unless Stone has coincidently decided to use his company chopper to do a day's fishing… Then yes, Adrian is somehow on Stone's payroll.'

'I don't believe it. I can't believe it. Not Adrian. It must be a fluke of some sort...' Tiger tailed off as it slowly dawned on him, the reality of the situation unfolding over his porridge and coffee.

Adrian was a traitor.

Brown was straight to business.

'Right then, in the light of this information I'll call the girls. Charlie can drop Anna off at a suitable point on the mountain, she has everything she needs with her, and I'll get Charlie to drive to Glencoe. It's less than twenty miles from here. What hotel did you mention, Gruff?'

'The Glencoe Inn Hotel. I saw a sign on the way up. God knows why I remembered it.'

'Okay. I need to make some calls. I'll be back in ten minutes.' Brown then left the Croft and hurried to his own where his SatPhone was on charge.

'I'm really sorry, Tiger.'

'You've got nothing to be sorry for mate, your phone call and subsequent denial has bloody kept me awake all night, I suppose you can say sorry for that, but I still cannot believe that Adrian is in Stone's pocket, it really can't be true.'

'Will you believe it if Stone turns up at the Glencoe Inn Hotel?'

Tiger didn't answer. How could he? What could he possibly say?

Gruff was on washing up duties, whilst Tiger was figuring out a way to make a simple detonator and fuse system for his explosives when Brown returned.

'We have it sorted. I have arranged for Charlie to be behind the reception desk at the Glencoe Inn Hotel from 10.00hrs this morning. She'll be there if Stone shows up.'

'How on earth did you manage that?' Asked Gruff, 'that's really impressive work.'

Brown just smiled and tapped the side of his nose. Gruff gave him a playful two fingered salute. 'Fuck you.'

'Is that wise, Brown? Won't that be putting her in harm's way? Asked Tiger.

'How could it? Stone's never met Charlie, she'll just be a receptionist doing receptionist stuff.'

'Well what's the point of that? Asked Gruff.

'If and when Stone turns up, he'll need a meeting place for his crew and when he finds out that Tiger is no longer at the Glencoe Inn Hotel, he'll feel safe using that as a base....'

'What do you mean Tiger is no longer there? He never was there.'

'Stone doesn't know that does he? And he'll be asking the staff about Tiger, that's guaranteed, and who better to let him know where he is now?'

'One of us...'

'As an innocent receptionist...'

'Is she up for it, Brown? Asked Tiger, still concerned.

'Up for it, Tiger? It was her bloody idea.'

~ONE HUNDRED SIXTEEN~

After a monotonous flight from Ruislip, the Secret Service helicopter pilot brought the machine into wind and made an aircraft type landing at a private airstrip a couple of miles to the west of Glencoe. After a brief conversation with the pilot who told him that that this was a one way flight - apparently it was due a major overhaul that afternoon - Taff Stone removed his headset and clambered from the helicopter as the blades were still turning overhead. His black Volvo 262 hire car was waiting for him with the keys in the ignition. He threw an overnight bag into the boot and after ramping the driver's seat as far back as it would allow he was ready to go.

Graham, the owner of the Glencoe Inn Hotel, was fascinated with the part he thought he was about to play. Charlie had to explain that the best course of action for him was to stay the heck away from the front desk, the bar, the rooms and the other guests. In fact it would be a great time to take a few days off and take his wife somewhere nice.

He had scurried about the back rooms trying to find a white blouse and a black waistcoat that'd fit her, and an old name badge that she could pin to it.

'I'm sorry hen, I don't even know your name?'

'I'll be called whatever name appears on the badge you rustle up Graham.'

'I've got one with the name 'Sheila' on it somewhere. She left us about three months ago. I'll have a look in the office drawers if you're sure.'

'That'll be fine Graham.'

'You don't look like a Sheila.'

'My name actually is Sheila'

'Oh. Perhaps I could find another one…'

'Graham. Please, It's okay, there is no need to fuss.'

'I've never done this sort of thing before…'

'Well I have, Graham. You can just sit in the back office and let me deal with the guests. It'll be fine.'

Charlie was going to have enough on her plate in a couple of hours, she really didn't want Graham butting in and trying to act out whatever role he had in his head. She had no idea who had called him to arrange this deception or what they had said, but he'd obviously agreed and here she was, in a strange little hotel, as a receptionist.

Called Sheila.

Anna was making herself as comfortable as she could amongst the rocks and clumps of heather that were to be her home for the foreseeable future. Once her sniper rifle was in position she removed the rubber covers from the optical scope and made some small adjustments to the focus and had a look through it.

She scanned the view in front and below her, concentrating on the area around Tiger's Croft. Despite being one thousand yards away, she could see every detail perfectly clearly.

Her orders were just as perfectly clear. She wasn't to open fire unless one of her targets was in possession of a firearm and there was no doubt in her mind that it was going to be used to harm one of the team.

She picked up her radio and pressed the send pressle switch.

'Hello Zero...This is Eagles Nest...Radio check...Over.'

The call was picked up immediately.

'Hello Eagles Nest…This is Zero, I hear you loud and clear, are you now in position and have everything you need…Over.'

'Eagles Nest…Affirmative.'

'Zero…Excellent…Now we wait…Over.'

'Eagles Nest…Roger that.'

'Zero out.'

~ONE HUNDRED SEVENTEEN~

Tiger and Brown were sat across the kitchen table. Tiger was fiddling with short lengths of wiring, a hot soldering iron was resting next to some mini circuit boards and other electronic bits. Gruff was busy outside stuffing heather and grass into his ghillie suit, he was making it look easy but there was an immense amount of skill involved in not being seen.

Especially when your life depended on it.

Brown put his radio down, took a swig of his coffee and said.

'Right, Tiger, that's Anna all set to go and I expect I'll hear from Charlie within the hour to let me know that she's good.'

'I don't know how you do it, Brown. Most people would start flapping when things go wrong. Here we are in the middle of nowhere and all you do is make a couple of telephone calls and things are back on track, as Gruff says, it's pretty impressive.'

'It's not me Tiger, I'm just a small cog in a big wheel, it's a team thing and we are very practiced at it.'

'All the same, I've been in some pretty dicey situations, as has Gruff, and our team was as professional and motivated as you can get, but nothing ever moved as fast as I've seen you operate.'

'You're talking about war zones Tiger. Shitty wars in shitty countries with shitty communications and limited equipment. It only takes one individual to take their eye off the ball, failing to listen to a radio call, forgetting to pass on a message, not bothering to check daily codes and passwords...'

'Yeah yeah, I get the drift Brown, so what else can you tell me about White Watch?'

'Nothing Tiger.'

'It doesn't exist right?'

'Correct.'

An easy silence developed over the next twenty minutes, Tiger still absorbed in his electronics and Brown occupied himself with cleaning his Browning pistol.

'Tiger. Serious question?'

'Aye. Go ahead.'

'Gruff. Is he as switched on as I'm led to believe?'

'Switched on? In what way?'

'Militarily. Fieldcraft. Weapons. Surveillance.'

'He's an expert, Brown, probably the best out there, why are you asking?'

'I hadn't come across him before he appeared up here.'

'He knows how to keep his mouth shut and his eyes open, but I got the impression yesterday that you knew all about him.'

'Telephone calls. Teamwork.'

'Right, you had him checked out?'

'Checked out? I suppose it was that, however I prefer to call it research. Vetting.'

'Vetting? You're vetting my mate for a position in an organisation that doesn't exist?'

'I didn't say that Tiger, you just did.'

'Bloody hell Brown, you can be infuriating, you know that?'

'I do Tiger, I do. But you know how it works. Is he reliable?'

'Yes. Totally.'

'Is he a team player?'

'He can work independently but yes, he's a team player.'

'He seems to be a bit on the serious side.'

'We're in a serious situation here.'

Brown smiled.

'What? Do you want him to dress up as a clown?'

'No. It's just that...'

A shadow appeared in the doorway of the Croft and a small purple bush entered.

'Anybody putting the kettle on? I'm bloody parched.'

~ONE HUNDRED EIGHTEN~

Taff Stone drove the short distance along the A82 into Glencoe, he wasn't happy about the choice of car that his secretary had ordered, he'd be having words with her when he got back. Stern words. The car was very comfortable, much better than he'd thought it would be and probably top of the range for the make, but it wasn't British. He drove British cars not Belgian, or wherever the hell they made Volvos. The Glencoe Inn Hotel came up on his right hand side. The Glencoe Mountain Rescue Unit had a building directly opposite. The mountains ahead were covered in sunlight, the golden slopes and splashes of purple were truly fantastic, but the siting of the Rescue Unit made for sobering reflection.

So pretty and yet so dangerous, just how Stone liked his women.

He smiled at his own thoughts.

The traffic was light to non-existent as he drove slowly past. It was a modern double storey building with parking to the front, and a wide access road to the right, which led, presumably, to an overflow car park at the rear. The front car park had two cars in it. One was in a spot reserved for Staff, a newish looking black Range Rover with black tinted windows, the second, a green

Citroen of indeterminate age with a French number plate was badly parked next to it.

If Tiger was stopping here he wasn't in or his motorcycle was parked where he couldn't see it, maybe around the back. He'd have to drive in. He carried out a 'U' turn one hundred yards along the road and returned.

Turning left into the car park and following the side of the building to the rear, his assumption was correct, it was another bigger car park but it was empty. He reversed parked the big Volvo into a space and switched off the engine. Leaving his overnight bag in the boot, he walked to the front of the building and entered through a single glass panelled door into a bright and airy reception area. A young woman was behind the desk and looked up as he entered.

'Good Afternoon Sir.'

An English woman! Well that was a good start, at least he'd be able to understand her. She had a name badge informing anybody that cared to look that she was called Sheila. Damn. He hoped to God she wasn't bloody Australian...

'Good afternoon. I wondered if I could use the restaurant for a coffee? I've had a long drive.'

'Certainly Sir, If you'd like to take a seat I'll arrange that for you now. Will you need a room for tonight?'

'I'm not sure yet. I'll have a coffee, make a call and have a look at your rooms after that if it's okay?'

'Of course Sir, Restaurant is behind you, sit where you like and I'll prepare your coffee.'

Stone entered a small but pleasant dining room. Watercolour paintings depicting local highland scenes were tastefully hung around the room. Real linen tablecloths on the eight tables and proper looking cutlery set for a lunch menu. Stone was pleasantly surprised. If he wasn't in such a damned hurry he could be tempted to stay awhile. Spend a couple of nights here relaxing, he thought, show that Sheila from reception what a real Englishman could do in bed, yes, this could be very nice.

He walked around the room idly looking at the pictures when the receptionist entered with a tray.

'Where would you like to sit Sir?

Stone was tempted to tell her where he would really like to sit, but refrained. For now.

'By the window, there, if that's okay?'

'Not a problem Sir. If you need anything else I'll be at reception.' Charlie placed the tray on the appointed table and made to leave.

'There is one thing Miss, er, Sheila.'

'Yes Sir?'

'I was due to meet a friend of mine here a couple of days ago, but I got waylaid, I don't suppose he is still here is he?'

'What's the name Sir.'

'Johhnie Stripes, he sometimes calls himself Tiger.'

'The name rings a bell Sir, Stripes, but I have been off for a couple of days.'

'He'll be in the guest register won't he?

'If he did stay Sir, yes of course but I'm afraid I can't give out that sort of information Sir.'

Stone was unperturbed. It was the only answer he expected. He reached for his wallet and extracted a fresh twenty pound note and slid it slowly across the table. The receptionist didn't move, but her eyes told Stone a different story. Twenty pounds must have been close to a week's pay up here.

Another twenty pound note sealed the deal. The receptionist stepped forward and after a hurried look behind her, the money disappeared into her waistcoat pocket.

'I'll have a look for you now Sir.'

'Thank you Sheila. No rush, I'm not going anywhere, I'm just here to enjoy my coffee.'

Tiger was here, thought Stone as he sipped his fresh brew. And if he wasn't, he wouldn't be far away, he just knew it. He smiled again as he admired Sheila's cute little arse as she left the restaurant and headed for her workstation.

Forty measly quid. Everybody has a price.

~ONE HUNDRED NINETEEN~

Gruff had removed his ghillie suit, it was too hot to sit around in a kitchen and drink tea, and frankly he felt bloody foolish, it was gear designed for outdoors.

Brown placed his SatPhone down on the table. The call he had just received, as usual, was short and to the point.

'Gentlemen. Stone is currently drinking coffee in the restaurant of the Glencoe Inn Hotel. He's alone and arrived in a black Volvo, we haven't got the registration number yet, however that's a moot point as it's going to be a hire car.'

'Was that from Charlie?' Asked Tiger.

'Yep, and he's asking after you already.'

'Bloody hell. Glencoe is what? Twenty miles away? Certainly less than a thirty minute drive isn't it?'

'Correct, Tiger, but we'll have immediate notice when he leaves.'

'I'm wondering where his team is.' Gruff mused.

'That's certainly an issue Gruff,' replied Brown, who now, for the first time, appeared to be slightly concerned.

'He wouldn't come up here without a kill team would he? That'd be suicide.' Tiger muttered.

'Well, let's look at what we have here.' Brown was back on track. 'Tiger. You don't know for sure that Stone wants to kill you up here in Scotland do you?'

'He tried to kill me in London.'

'That's true, however your plan was to lure him here and kill him wasn't it? Stone has not contacted you directly and stated that you are a dead man walking has he?'

'No but...'

'He doesn't know what you know. He doesn't know that you know he's coming and he doesn't actually need a team, although I'll be very surprised if he hasn't put something together, the man's a coward and doesn't like getting his hands dirty, but the fact remains, he is capable of coming up here on his own and finding you and not necessarily to kill you.'

'He isn't here to buy me a tartan scarf or some shortbread biscuits…'

'I know that Tiger, but you're missing the point. You, we, are holding all the cards so whether he has a team or not is academic. We have planned for taking out any team that might show up, so if Stone turns up alone - more fool him.'

Brown's SatPhone began chirping again. He picked it up and held it to his ear and said 'Brown'. The call lasted less than twenty seconds and Brown never said another word. He put the phone back on the table, the short call obviously terminated.

'That was my boss.'

'The Foreign Secretary?'

'Yep. Stone's been turned down for the job as Director Secret Intelligence Service. He is to be placed under internal investigation with a view to sacking him completely. The vote was unanimous.'

'Where does that leave you and Anna then?' Asked Tiger.

'The call ended with the words 'Goodnight Sweetheart.' It was quite clearly spoken.'

'That's a bit familiar for a business call isn't it? Smiled Gruff.

'It's code Gruff.'

'I know it's a bloody code, and we know what it means. We have all had a sweetheart call.'

Brown picked up the radio.

'Eagles Nest…Eagles Nest…This is Zero…Over'

'Eagles Nest…Send…Over.'

'Zero…Tango One is now in the frame…Do you copy? Over.'

'Eagles Nest…Roger…Over.'

'Zero…We have the green light…Do you copy that? Over.'

There was a pause of ten seconds. Brown didn't push the call, he knew that Anna was gathering her thoughts.

'Eagles Nest...Roger that...Goodnight Sweetheart...Over.'

'Zero...Goodnight Sweetheart...Out.'

Brown placed the radio next to his SatPhone and stood up.

'It's time, gentlemen. No more questions? Good. Let's take up our positions.' He picked up his SatPhone and radio and strode from the kitchen and across the lounge. He paused at the front door, then turned around and said.

'Marmalade, Gruff. It was originally made in Portugal from a fruit called Quince. The Portuguese word for Quince is Marmelo, the preserve itself once made, was called Marmelada. Good luck Gents. I'll see you on the other side.'

The door closed behind Brown as Gruff struggled to get back into his ghillie suit. He looked at Tiger and said.

'I knew that.'

~ONE HUNDRED TWENTY~

Taff Stone had just finished his coffee when the receptionist Sheila returned.

'I've had a look in the guest register Sir and there was a guest called Stripes booked in. He stayed just the one night in a single room and paid in cash.'

'When was this?'

'Two nights ago Sir.'

Stone wanted to swear. Damn, he thought, he was so close and now…

'He left a note though Sir.'

'A note?'

'He was expecting some mail, a small package and has left some money and a forwarding address.'

'Where's this note?'

Charlie didn't reply, she just stared at him.

'Oh, I see…More money? Well you're not getting any more money, Oh no… Just show me the damn note.'

Stone started to rise from his chair and Charlie backed away two steps.

'Last chance Sheila. Show me the note.'

Charlie removed a folded piece of paper from an inside pocket of her waistcoat and dropped it onto the table. Stone sat back down and grabbed the note then unfolded it and started to read.

Would you be kind enough to forward any mail to me? I am expecting a parcel and it is of vital importance that I get it. I am leaving £5 to cover any further costs that may accrue. My address for the next two weeks is : Croft 2. Cameron Croft Lettings. Fort William. Many thanks for an enjoyable one night stay.

The note was signed off by Tiger Stripes. Stone couldn't believe his luck, Tiger was a bloody idiot and now he had him. Fort William wasn't that far away either.

'Thank you, Sheila. That was painless wasn't it? How far is Fort William from here?'

'About 16 miles North Sir, you need the A82, it's the next major town.'

'Then I shall take my leave. Thank you for the coffee, I'm sure you've earned enough today to take care of the bill.'

Stone stood up and straightened his jacket. In doing so Charlie caught a fleeting glimpse of a shoulder holster under his left armpit.

'Thank you Sir. Maybe we'll see you again?'

'Maybe, maybe not Sheila. Who knows what could happen in this wicked world.'

Charlie didn't reply. She watched Stone walk across the reception area and out of the front door. He turned left and she saw him through the restaurant window as he headed for the car park at the rear. Thirty seconds later she watched his Volvo leave the car park and turn left on the A82.

Picking up the phone in reception she called Brown at Fort William and reported in. She then got changed in the small staff room and went to find Graham.

'Well that's it Graham, we're all done here.' Charlie handed over the blouse, waistcoat and name badge.

'Thank you, umm…Sheila…Er…Crikey. That was quick. Is there anything else I can do?'

'You could pop this in the Glencoe Mountain Rescue tin.' She handed over two crumpled notes.

'But…But…There's forty pounds here Sheila…'

'I'm sure it's a great cause. Thanks again Graham you've been a real star.'

Charlie left Graham clutching the charity money and a look of confusion on his face as she left the building and got into her Range Rover.

Four miles North along the A82 she glanced down at the fuel gauge and noticed that the vehicle was about to go into reserve. She knew there was a filling station in the small village of Onich about a mile ahead.

She pulled into an empty forecourt next to a diesel pump and filled the fuel tank. After grabbing an apple from the fruit basket and a bottle of chilled Highland Spring water, she paid the cashier with a credit card and returned to her vehicle.

No sooner had she put her seatbelt on, she felt something ominously cold and hard poke into the back of her head.

A voice she recognised immediately sent a cold shiver of fear along her spine.

'Hello again, Sheila.'

~ONE HUNDRED TWENTY ONE~

Tiger had worked out a fuse and detonation system. He had reverse engineered one of Charlie's dud motion sensors and had recalibrated his automatic garage key fob to the same radio wavelength frequency. However, once he had assembled everything for a dry run, it became obvious that the 12v power output from the pack of batteries he'd purchased was not powerful enough. After some head scratching it occurred to him that his motorcycle had a twelve volt battery and, with the engine running, that voltage increased to a little over thirteen volts. He really didn't want to use his beloved Triumph as part of a bomb, but it seemed to be the only way.

Anna had followed Tiger through her magnified sight optics and watched as he pushed his motorcycle behind the Croft, removed the saddle and started fiddling with the battery. A minute earlier she'd seen Gruff walk from the Croft and place himself in his hide. Her attention went back to where she had last seen him. He had vanished, there wasn't a clue as to where he was holed up, yet she knew that he was there. Astonishing skill she thought.

Her radio came to life once more.

'Hello all stations this is Zero...Tango one is on his way, arrival is imminent and he is armed...Over.'

'Eagles Nest copied...Over.'

'Ground Hog copied...Over.'

'Trident copied...Over.'

'Zero Out.'

Gruff could see the entrance to Tiger's Croft and about five yards either side. It wasn't a great view, but if everything went to plan, that was where any action would take place. He had to trust in the motion sensors that were to his left and right and slightly behind him and of course to Brown's timely reactions to any movement. His earpiece volume was turned down to minimum and any reply by him to Brown from now on in, would be via his radio pressel switch. One click for yes two for no.

He saw Tiger push his motorcycle behind the Croft and enter the front door, leaving it slightly open.

Old habits.

He had been in this position many times before, lying in a hide for days was sometimes the norm, and he'd never seen it as a hardship In fact after Brown's last radio message it would appear that he wouldn't be in this position for too long at all and that was something of a bonus. He felt pretty safe and had a good protective view of his best friend's blind spot. Things could have been worse.

Tiger tidied up the kitchen. The lengths of wire and electronic bits and bobs were useless now and were placed in the bin. The map had been folded and placed neatly on the table and the cups and plates following breakfast had been washed and dried and placed in their respective racks.

He checked his Browning one last time. It was fully functional, the magazine had thirteen rounds of deadly nine millimetre ammunition and one already in the chamber. The weapon had been cocked and was ready to fire. He had a further twenty rounds loose in his jacket pocket.

He sat back on a chair in the lounge and watched the front door in total silence, wholly aware that he was to be the last person to actually see Stone arrive, that any plan put in place would be worth dog toffee as soon as there was contact with an enemy, and the fact he was reliant on Anna, Brown and Gruff for information over a radio set. He could do nothing now but wait.

The whole team waited.

~ONE HUNDRED TWENTY TWO~

'We are going to play a little game Sheila. It's called. 'You drive me to Fort William.' It's a really easy game but there are rules, nod your head if you understand.'

Charlie nodded her head. Stone was calling her Sheila. He didn't know who she really was.

'That's good Sheila, now start the car and pull off nice and steady and I'll explain the rules as we go.'

Charlie put the vehicle into gear and as she pulled out of the little service station, she made eye contact with the cashier hoping perhaps he'd seen something, but he just waved and looked away.

'Rule one. If I think that you are trying to attract anybody's attention I will shoot you in the head. Rule two. If I think you are going to do anything stupid with this vehicle, like maybe crash into a barrier, I will shoot you in the head. Rule three. If you accelerate or brake more than I consider necessary, I'll shoot you in the head. All pretty simple really. Do. You. Understand?'

'Yes Sir.'

'Excellent, you'll be free to go in thirty minutes or so. Enjoy the drive and try not to get shot in the back of the head.'

After twenty minutes they arrived at the southern outskirts of Fort William. The main street through the town was busy with traffic but not really a concern, and anyway, Charlie now had no intention of angering her unwanted passenger. He'd already jammed his weapon into her head three times during the short journey, even though she'd obeyed the rules.

'Do you know where Cameron Croft Lettings are?'

Charlie saw an opportunity to stall for time.

'No Sir. I've never heard of them.'

'Pull over and ask that bloke standing at the kerb. If I'm not happy with the conversation I'll shoot you both.'

Charlie slowed her vehicle and indicated left as she pulled over to the kerb. She powered down the front passenger window and asked for directions to Cameron Croft Lettings. The man was a local and in a thick brogue gave her the directions that of course, she already knew. She thanked the man and drove on. They passed the Flint Hotel and Charlie's thoughts went briefly back to the previous evening and she wondered if she'd ever see Anna again.

Five minutes later a large sign on the left advertised the fact that Cameron Crofts were down the next road on the left, less than one hundred yards away.

'Where would you like me to stop Sir?'

'Keep going Sheila. Take the left turn and slow down.'

Charlie nodded and looked straight ahead, although every nerve in her body was screaming at her to look around and scan the area, she knew where everybody in her team were located, surely one of them should have spotted her car by now and know that something was wrong.

'Stop here.'

Charlie brought her vehicle to a gentle stop.

'Can you see any motorcycles?'

'What?'

'It's a simple fucking question Sheila. Can you see any motorcycles?'

'Charlie powered the driver's window down and made a show of looking around.

'No, no I can't.'

'Take the keys out of the ignition and hand them back to me.'

Charlie complied.

'Now. I'm getting out. You stay right where you are until I get around to your door.'

Charlie had seen nothing when she had looked around. Perhaps the plans had changed, she knew how fragile the whole thing was. Perhaps her team, her friends, her lover had abandoned her?

For the first time in her life, Charlie was now truly frightened, and felt utterly and completely alone.

~ONE HUNDRED AND TWENTY THREE~

Charlie had been seen. Anna had been tracking her vehicle for the last mile.

'Hello Zero...This is Eagles Nest...Situation report...Over.

'Zero...Go ahead...Over.'

'Eagles Nest, something's wrong. Babbage is two minutes away. Driving slowly. No sign of Tango One...Over.'

'Zero...Copied...Is it definitely Babbage driving? Does Babbage have a passenger? Over.'

'Eagles Nest, It's too far...I'll know in thirty seconds...Wait Out.'

Tiger and Gruff had heard the call from Anna and wondered what had happened. Stone should have arrived first, Charlie should have been at least 30 minutes behind him and then she should have waited in the town.

'Hello Zero...This is Eagles Nest...Over.'

'Zero...Go ahead Eagles Nest...Over.'

'Eagles Nest...Babbage is driving...No Passengers...Wait...Babbage is turning left left left onto the plot...Wait...Babbage is stopping. Drivers window is coming down...Babbage looks terrified...Something is very wrong...Over.'

'Zero...All copied....Keep me informed, all call signs are to stay at their posts...Zero Out.'

Brown was thinking fast. There was no way Charlie would have deviated from the plan, and in an emergency she had a phone. Unless the emergency meant that she couldn't get to the phone, and that meant Stone, or someone else, was somehow in her vehicle, with her as a hostage. If that was the case his personal plans would start to unravel. He couldn't let that happen.

His train of thought was interrupted...

'Hello Zero...This is Eagles Nest...Over.'

'Zero...Go ahead Eagles Nest...Over.'

'Eagles Nest...Tango one is out of the vehicle, walking around the front to the driver's side...Wait...Babbage is out of the vehicle...Tango one has a short pointing at her head and they are moving towards Tridents position...Two hundred yards...I have a clear shot...Over.'

Anna was referring to Stone,s pistol as a 'short.' Unidentified barrelled weapons were described by length, a rifle would have been a 'long'.

'Zero...I copy all that Eagles Nest, but you are observation only at this point. I say again observation only Hold your fire, we go with the plan, everybody stay at your posts... Zero Out.

'Ground Hog... This is Zero...Do you copy? Over.'

Gruff pressed his send pressel once.

'Click.' Yes.

'Zero...Copied...Three clicks when you have eyeball on Tango one...Over.'

'Click.' Okay.

'Copied Ground Hog...Zero Out.'

'Hello Zero...This is Eagles Nest...Over.'

'Zero...Go ahead Eagles Nest...Over.'

'Eagles Nest. One hundred yards and moving slowly...I still have the shot but will observe...Ground Hog should have the eyeball in seconds figures twenty...Over.'

'Zero, copied. Ground Hog standby...Zero Out.'

Tiger was sat listening to the radio traffic, it was good, it was professional and although there was nothing he could do at the moment he knew precisely what was going on and was happy that he could deal with Stone and his hostage as soon as they entered his part of the stage.

'Click, Click, Click.' Gruff could see the target.

'Ground Hog this is Zero...Is Tango one at the door? Over.'

'Click.' Yes.

'Zero... Copied... Is Babbage still in front? Over.'

'Click.' Yes.

'Trident this is Zero do you copy? Over.'

'Trident...Affirmative...Over.'

'All call signs this is Zero...There may be more Tango's out there. Stay in position and stay alert...Zero Out.'

Stone stood at the open door to Croft number two. His pistol was aimed at the back of Charlie's head. He called out.

'Tiger!'

There was no reply. He tried again.

'Tiger! It's Taff Stone. Are you in?'

No reply.

'I'm coming in Tiger...I have a friend with me.'

Stone reached a leg around Charlie's and pushed the door slowly all the way in with his foot. He then jabbed her in the back of the head with his pistol for emphasis as said,

'After you Sheila.'

~ONE HUNDRED TWENTY FOUR~

Although his view from his hide was not great, Gruff had managed to slowly clear away some bracken to give him a slightly better arc. He watched as Charlie and Taff Stone entered the Croft when a sudden movement caught the corner of his eye.

Brown had left his Croft and was ducking around the side, appearing to run at a crouch. He was not holding a radio. It took Gruff a moment or two to realise that this wasn't in the plan. Brown's Croft was supposed to be the operations centre for want of a better word, and he should be glued to his radio set, not running around without it.

He had to make a decision. Tiger, he was sure could handle himself with Stone in the Croft, he'd get up and follow Brown.

Brown ran across the main road, the A82 and scrambled over a flimsy wire fence. He was heading for Anna's position up the slopes of Ben Nevis. The Eagles Nest. Anna would have her eye glued to the optics on her rifle, there was no way she could see Brown heading up from below unless she relaxed her view and as a Sniper she wouldn't be doing that.

Gruff reached for his radio, and then paused. Tiger was in the Croft with an armed man, and a hostage. A radio call could easily compromise his position. No radio calls. He followed Brown over the fence.

Brown had fifty yards on him as he picked his way over the small boulders and scrub that made up the base of the Nation's highest mountain, but he wasn't looking back, he obviously wasn't expecting a tail.

Brown made the small ridge that housed Anna. Gruff was only thirty yards behind and closing when a shot rang out.

Small calibre, low velocity possibly nine millimetre. The shot echoed across the mountain before fading quietly away.

Gruff was five yards away from the lip of Eagles Nest when Brown reappeared. Brown's eyes opened wide at the sight below him, a figure in a camouflaged ghillie suit scrambling towards him. He jumped, catching Gruff full in the chest with both feet and tumbled away.

Gruff slid downwards on his back, it was a short but painful journey. His chest was bursting and he banged his head on a rock as he came to a halt.

Brown recovered from the impact quicker and continued down the lower slopes, zigzagging though the rocks.

Gruff shook his head, he still felt dizzy but after sitting up he realised that there was nothing seriously wrong with him. He wiped dirt and gravel from his mouth with the back of his hand and turned on his belly to see Brown over one hundred yards away.

His priority was Anna. He climbed the last few yards to her position and hauled himself over the lip. Anna looked to be unconscious, and was breathing with difficulty. Loud rasping gulps of air. Gruff knew a serious chest wound when he heard one.

'Anna, it's Gruff, can you hear me?'

Anna's eyelids opened briefly as she made an attempt to talk.

'Can't…Breathe…Brown…Shot…Please…Breathe…Gruff…'

Gruff glanced around Anna's hideaway, the Sniper rifle but now without a magazine, a water bottle and the radio that looked intact, but nothing in the way of a first aid kit. He grabbed Anna and turned her over. He couldn't see any sign of blood on her back.   He gently turned her around to face him and ripped open the front of her jacket and blouse. Just below her bra on her left side was an ugly looking hole, heavily bruised around the perimeter and oozing frothy blood.

Sucking wound to the chest. There didn't appear to be an exit wound. He'd dealt with worse and he could sort this. He tore a large strip from her blouse, poured some water on it and applied it to the hole in her chest. He removed his belt and wrapped it around her frail body, buckling it back up at the side. It was a temporary fix - it would do for now. He shuffled around and managed to lay her in a recovery position with her damaged side lying on the rock; there wasn't much else he could do.

He picked up the sniper rifle and operated the bolt action to expose the brass casing of a NATO seven point six two bullet. Brown may have removed the small magazine but he hadn't counted on Anna having one 'up the spout.'

He brought the rifle up to the aim position and looked through the scope.

Brown was approaching Tiger's Croft at a full run.

One thousand yards. One shot.

Gruff placed the centre hairs of the optical sights graticule on the back of the running Brown's head then moved his aim off slightly to account for the downhill slope and a very slight breeze; he breathed in slowly and halfway through the expiration he squeezed the trigger and followed through the trigger.

Travelling at eight hundred and eighty meters a second, the deadly copper round would take just over a second to reach its intended target. Gruff saw Brown dive around the corner of Tige'rs Croft at precisely the same instant that the bullet should have killed him.

The booming report of a high velocity round screaming over the A82 echoed around the mountain, a group of birds screeched and in a flurry of wings headed for safety. The noise subsided into an eerie silence and was broken only by the sound of a dismayed Gruff.

'Bollocks.'

~ONE HUNDRED TWENTY FIVE~

Charlie's eyes took a few seconds to adjust to the dimness in Tiger's Croft so this meant that Stone's eyes would have to do the same. She was itching for an opportunity to turn the tables on him. She was a petite computer nerd and he was a large, solidly built ex Special Forces soldier; however she'd attended various self-defence courses and done rather well and she knew that surprise was a massively useful tool, but so was timing.

So she waited.

Tiger was laid back in one of the chairs in the lounge, to a casual observer he looked totally relaxed but there were no casual observers in the room, only trained professionals.

'Hello, Stone. I see you have indeed brought a friend, would you care to take a seat? Oh! You can put the gun away as well, I'm not armed.'

Stone held Charlie by the back of her collar and pointed his weapon at the seated Tiger.

'Stand up, Tiger, and do it slowly.'

Tiger stood up, real slow.

'Now un-tuck your shirt, lift it up high and turn around full circle.'

Tiger complied and asked.

'Can I drop my shirt now? Do you want tea or coffee? Maybe a dram of something stronger?' He made a move to enter the kitchen.

'Stand still...Sit back down, Tiger, and not in that chair,' he pointed his pistol at another chair.

'I've told you, Stone, I'm not armed.'

'Maybe not but that chair might be. I'm not an idiot, Tiger. Unlike you. Leaving your name lying around and giving out forwarding addresses, if I didn't know better, it was like you wanted to be found.'

Stone shuffled to one side keeping Charlie between them. He slowly crouched down, bringing Charlie with him, and scooped out the base cushion from the chair. There was no gun. He turned and letting go of Charlie's collar, he pushed her into the chair.

'You said you'd let me go once I drove you here, please let me go.' Charlie pleaded.

'Shut the fuck up, Sheila.'

Sheila? Tiger thought. Stone obviously didn't know who he had taken as a hostage, perhaps he could use that information to his advantage.

'Who is she? Tiger asked pointing at Charlie. Is this all necessary? Let her go, Stone.'

'Just a greedy, money-grabbing receptionist, Tiger, and my key to get in here.'

'Well you're in now, let her go.'

'Ha! You are a bloody fool. What? Let her go? The Police would be here in ten minutes if I let that happen, Tiger old son, so that's not going to happen.'

'Just thought I should mention it, out of politeness to Sheila.'

'Yeah, well forget it, she's staying. So Tiger, this is all very cosy, what's it all about then?'

'I'm having a break, Stone. After a bereavement.'

'Ah. I heard about that. Was she close?'

'You know damn fine well who she was, and what she meant to me, Stone.'

'Well a little birdie has told me that you are up here for other reasons, Tiger. Reasons that involve me.'

'What? Why would I come all the way up here for you? That doesn't make sense. You know I don't like you, Stone, it's never been a secret, same as you don't like me, and it's been that way for years.'

'My little birdie has a name.'

'Really? What would that be?'

Tiger wasn't expecting an answer, and anyway he knew it was the traitorous Adrian.

'Steve Brown. I expect you know him quite well after a couple of tranquil days up here, except that you don't know him Tiger. You don't know him at all.'

Tiger was momentarily stunned, he saw Charlie tense up at the name and hoped she wouldn't say anything.

'I don't believe you, Stone. Steve Brown is renting the Croft next door, we've had a chat and coffee as neighbours do, so I don't believe you.'

'Did he tell you about his gambling debts when you were having these neighbourly chats?'

'No of course not, why would a complete stranger tell me that?'

'Well, perhaps he wouldn't. But he's told me and I used to be a complete stranger as well, Tiger, but then I suppose you haven't got the sort of money to give away that I have.'

'You've paid off a stranger's gambling debts? Why would you do that?'

'I don't pay off debts Tiger, I buy information, what a person does with that money is beyond my control, and quite frankly, I couldn't give a rats arse what they do with it.'

'So what lies has Brown told you in order to pay off his debts?'

'Hardly lies old son, because with the information at my disposal, here you are, right in front of me.'

'Have you been looking for me? Why couldn't you just call?'

'Stop being a clever prick, Tiger. You. Sheila. Get in the kitchen pour a couple of Jack Daniels, I'm sure there will be some not far away, and stay where I can see you otherwise...'

'You'll shoot me in the back of the head?'

'You're a clever girl, now up you get, steady now.'

Charlie stood up slowly and took a couple of paces into the small kitchen. A bottle of Jack Daniels was on a shelf at eye level and a couple of whisky tumblers were on the drying rack next to the sink. She picked up the bottle of Jack and turned, placing it on the table next to the folded map, and turned to get the glasses.

She'd noticed that the map looked a little bulky, and her heart started to hammer. Tiger's pistol! She was sure it was under the map. She picked up the two heavy crystal tumblers and placed them on the table next to the bottle. She gently nudged the map with the back of her hand as she did so, and there was the gun.

From somewhere outside there was the sound of a high velocity rifle being fired. The sharp crack followed by a distant bang was unmistakable to the two ex-soldiers sat in the lounge of Tiger's Croft.

'What the fuck!' Exclaimed Stone looking at Tiger and then his world turned black.

'

~ONE HUNDRED TWENTY SIX~

Anna was trying to speak again, it was a faint whisper. Gruff put his ear close to her mouth.

'Gruffff...Backpppack...Phone...Code seven one, double one...'

Gruff opened Anna's daysack and picked out her SatPhone. He'd used them before but they were prototypes, this was slightly different but the buttons looked self-explanatory. He pressed the green button and was presented with a menu, it took a couple of seconds to figure out where the scroll button was and he pressed it.

There were only half a dozen numbers listed and none of them meant anything to Gruff. He highlighted the first number and hit the green call button. Nothing happened for about ten seconds but he kept his ear jammed to the earpiece.

'Identification.' A woman's voice. Calm.

Gruff paused. What had Anna mumbled?

'Seven one double one.'

There was a pause at the other end of the connection.

'This isn't seven one double one...'

'I know, I'm a friendly. She is lying next to me with a golf sierra whisky.'

'Gunshot wound?'

'Yes. She needs urgent medical help. I am at grid reference...'

'I can see where you are.'

'It's a chest wound, collapsed lung, it's urgent.'

'Who are you?'

'Wetherspoon, I'm ex two two...'

'Stay on the line.'

Gruff's attention was suddenly interrupted by the sight of Tiger's croft rising slowly in the air. Before he could comprehend what he was watching, the sound of a massive explosion rocked the side of the mountain.

Wattle and daub was used to make small buildings, small buildings like a Croft, the wattle being thin strips of wood filled with daub, an aggregate of clay, limestone and straw. The buildings were made to last tens of years and were extremely robust.

However, they were not a challenge for a fertiliser and oxide mix that was built to last milliseconds. The Croft just disintegrated, vapourised, and a tall mushroom plume of black and grey smoke rose high above where there was once a habitable building.

'Jesus Christ.' hollered Gruff, putting down the SatPhone and grabbing the radio.

'Hello Trident this is Ground Hog...Over.'

There was no reply.

'Trident, this is Ground Hog. Babbage this is Ground Hog... Over.'

Hissing static was the only reply.

'Tiger, this is Gruff. Tiger, answer me. Tiger. Tiger!'

Gruff slowly put the radio down. The scene below was of utter devastation, Tiger's Croft, gone. Tiger's motorcycle gone. Half of Brown's Croft was missing and so were Tiger and Charlie.

Gruff jammed the SatPhone back to his ear.

'Hello?'

'What was that noise?'

'An explosion about a thousand yards away.'

'Was that you?'

'No. We need help up here. Your operative needs help. Urgently, what's with the questions?'

'Help will be with you in a couple of minutes. It'll be a civilian chopper, they have been briefed by us but under no circumstances are you to give the crew any information whatsoever, do you understand?'

'Yes.'

'Good. There is to be no mention of gunshot wounds, no mention of explosions and no names, you will mention nothing. You will accompany our operative in the chopper to our base in Oban, the lives of both of you are in your hands. Do you understand?'

'Oban?'

'Yes, Oban. It's about a twenty minute flight. You'll be met by a medical team. You must stay with our operative at all times. Is that clear?'

'Yes.'

'Thank you Gruff. We may speak again.'

The call ended. Gruff! The woman had called him Gruff. He hadn't mentioned that to her, they must have checked him out when he mentioned that he was ex two two. Bloody hell that was quick, he thought.

He saw the chopper before he heard it, mainly because there was a bit of a din going on below him. Fire trucks, an ambulance and a Police car were screaming along the A82 towards the Croft site. Two tone sirens hammering through the afternoon.

Gruff started preparing the site. He quickly packed away the rifle in its hard case, stuffed his Browning pistol, the SatPhone, radio and water bottle into Anna's backpack and secured it. He lay down next to Anna, she was still breathing, but very quietly and in a ragged fashion. He couldn't do anything more for her but whisper close to her ear that she was going to be okay.

~ONE HUNDRED TWENTY SEVEN~

It was the Glencoe Mountain Rescue helicopter. It hovered above Gruff and Anna whilst a rescue man was winched down with cage like stretcher. Gruff helped the rescuer gently strap Anna into the stretcher, she looked very pale.

The crewman looked up at his winch man and raised a gloved finger rotating it in a small circle. The winch rope slowly tightened. The rescuer winked at Gruff.

'Back in two minutes pal.'

'I'm not going anywhere mate.'

'Are you okay?'

'I'm fine, just send down the wire, I won't need a hand.'

The winch reeled the rescuer and Anna's stretcher up and into the body of the hovering helicopter. Twenty seconds later the winch man looked over the side of the machine and down at Gruff. He raised a thumb. Gruff returned the thumbs up, strapped Anna's bag to his back and picked up the rifle case.

A quick glance around the area showed that there was nothing to indicate that they'd ever been there. He looped the rescue cable under his armpits and was hoisted smoothly into the air and pulled into the helicopter as it made a banking turn to the left and headed south.

Gruff noticed a second crewman was working on Anna. It took him a couple of seconds to realise that it was actually a woman. She had the words 'Medic' patched onto the rear of her flight suit.

The rescuer handed him a airman's fluorescent helmet and pointed to the wall indicating a plug in point. Gruff squeezed the helmet on, plugged it in and lowered the boom microphone.

'Do you have a name?'

'No, sorry.' Said Gruff.

'No, not you, your lady friend here.

'Not a clue mate.'

'What about you?'

'No.'

The rescuer shrugged and turned to talk to the medic. They were obviously on a different channel as Gruff couldn't hear the conversation. The rescuer turned to Gruff again.

'It's a gunshot wound.'

'It's a rock fall.'

'No. it's a gun...'

Gruff leaned over and grabbed the rescuer by the front of his winch harness and looked him directly in the eye.

'It's a rock fall...Very similar to a gunshot wound. Okay?'

'Of course. Rock fall.'

Gruff moved to his right and looked over the side of the accelerating helicopter. Although they were fairly low, he saw no sign of Tiger or Charlie among the small groups of uniforms that had started to gather amongst the vehicles and their blue flashing lights.

'Anything to do with you?' The winch man asked over the headset intercom.

'I've no idea what that's all about mate.'

The remaining fifteen minutes of the flight were spent in comparative silence. Only the wind rushing past the open doors of the helicopter and the noise of the two jet engines interrupted Gruff's thoughts as he shed a tear for his friend.

~ONE HUNDRED TWENTY EIGHT~

The helicopter landed with a soft bump on the helipad at a small military enclave just south of Oban on the West coast of Scotland. A dozen people were waiting to greet it including a crash team with a stretcher on wheels. Gruff removed his helmet and tried to exit but was held back by the winch man who pointed at Anna.

'She goes first,' he shouted.

Gruff just nodded and sat back down on the deck of the chopper. There were no seats.

The winch man gave a thumbs-up signal to the waiting crash team and the four person team wheeled the stretcher to the helicopter door. The chopper medic and the rescue man gently pushed the stretcher cage to the edge of the door and Anna was carefully manhandled onto the stretcher.

Gruff noted that this was a slick manoeuvre and had obviously been done many times before. For the first time in over thirty minutes he now knew that Anna was in good hands and would be okay. The crash team disappeared from view and once again Gruff tried to exit the helicopter and once again he was held back. What now?

Two men in matching blue suits, white shirts open at the neck and wearing sunglasses approached the door. One them pointed at Gruff and then pointed at the floor in front of him. The engine noise was getting louder and the speed of the rotor blades had increased noticeably. The helicopter was obviously not staying, it was too loud for conversation, even shouted ones.

Gruff got the message. He climbed down from the helicopter and turned to pick up Anna's bag and the rifle case and saw the winch man handing them to another blue suited man through the opposite door.

'Hey! Hey,' his shouted words were lost in the noise as the turbine engines increased in noise. The helicopter was now lifting slowly.

The two suited men grabbed Gruff firmly by the arms and wheeled him around, striding purposely towards a low roofed building beside the helipad. Gruff was pretty sure he could take down at least one of the men, probably both, but what would be the point? He relaxed into their care.

Only once the chopper had roared away to the north and the three men had entered the building was it quiet enough to talk once more. They entered a large room with desks and chairs, much like a classroom. There was even a blackboard on the far wall.

'Okay. Where am I? Who are you? Am I under some sort of arrest?'

The older of the two suited men replied.

'Please take a seat, Mr Wetherspoon.'

'And how come everybody knows my name, yet I don't know anybody else's?'

'Please Mr Wetherspoon, take a seat, we're not the enemy, we're friendlies but we do have some questions.'

'If you ask me about Marmalade I'll fucking punch you.'

The two suited men looked at each other and shrugged. The younger man continued.

'Nobody is going to be punching anybody, Mr Wetherspoon.'

'Where's my bag? And my rifle?'

'Is the bag yours? Is the rifle yours? If they are you can have them back right now.'

'I'm looking after them, they are technically mine.'

'Wrong, Mr Wetherspoon, there is nothing in the bag which is yours, the bag, and its contents, and the rifle belong to us. Thank you for looking after them, but now we're good.'

'Are you with Anna and Brown?'

'I don't know Anna and Brown.'

'Anna is the one in the stretcher, the one who was shot, lung damage. You saw her being taken away on that stretcher.'

'Ah. Is that the name she gave you? Well I guess we'll continue to call her that.'

'Who are you?'

'All in good time, now sit down, calm down and we'll get you a brew sorted and then we'll have a chat. Perhaps things will become clearer then. Anyway, that's where we stand now. Okay?'

'I am supposed to be with Anna. I've been told to stay with her and not talk to anybody. About anything. So, that's where we stand about now. Okay?'

'Who told you not to talk to anybody?'

'A lady on the SatPhone. The Satphone in the bag.'

'Ah. Okay, I can clear that up for you right now, Mr Wetherspoon. Hang on.'

The younger man left the room and returned about two minutes later, he was holding a SatPhone that he passed to Gruff.

'Here you go. Call the lady again.'

Gruff turned the phone over in his hands, it looked the same but he couldn't be sure. He powered it up and scrolled through the short menu. The numbers appeared to be the same. He highlighted the first number and hit the green dial button.

Nothing for ten seconds.

'Identification.' A woman's calm voice. The same one as earlier.

'Seven. One. Eleven.'

There was a pause at the other end of the connection.

'Mr Wetherspoon. How may I help?'

'You asked me to look after your operative, to stay with her and not talk to anybody, but...'

'Our operative is in safe hands now, Mr Wetherspoon, The facilities at Oban are first class, you have saved her life and we thank you for that, a couple of our people will want to debrief you over the next couple of days, I do hope you'll oblige?'

'Two days?' Spluttered Gruff.

'You didn't have any other plans did you? No, I thought not, I believe your debrief has already started, please be as cooperative as you can Mr Wetherspoon, you are in good company, you have nothing to fear.'

The call ended and Gruff handed the SatPhone back to the younger man who immediately went back out of the room with it.

'Okay,' said the older of the two men, 'I hope you're a bit happier now?'

'A bit,' admitted Gruff. 'But I still have questions.'

'We all have questions, Mr Wetherspoon, but the way it works is, we ask them first, that's how a debrief works. I am sure you have been part of many such meetings.'

'Couple of points before I agree to anything.'

'Okay, fair enough, what?'

'I get updates, regular updates on Anna, and I get to see her when she gets out of theatre.'

'No problems with that. What else?'

'There was an explosion at the Croft site North of Fort William, a friend of mine was there and a girl, the Police and what looked like the entire Scottish emergency services were on scene, they will know something, speak to them, speak to them now, your lines of communication have looked pretty fast to me up to now and I want to know what happened to my friends.

'I shall make enquiries on that issue, Mr Wetherspoon, because I really don't know anything about that. Is there anything else, or can we make a start?'

'I'm hungry and would like to eat and a cup of tea would be fantastic, a change of clothes would be good, I am beginning to hate this bloody Ghillie suit, oh, and not a blue suit like yours either, something casual, I am sure

you know my sizes. And you can stop calling me
Wetherspoon. My name is Gruff.'

~ONE HUNDRED TWENTY NINE~

Gruff was sat drinking tea at Anna's bedside. He was wearing green casual fatigues, all ex-Army but brand new, and of course they fitted.

'How long has it been, Gruff?'

'Since we got here? About forty hours.'

'Crikey! Has anybody told you what happened? Why did Brown go rogue? Why the fuck did he shoot me?'

'No Anna, no one has told me anything. I am not sure that they know.'

'How come you are still here? Have you been waiting to see me?'

'Yes, I have been waiting to see you.'

'Ah, that's so sweet, thank you Gruff.'

'Don't mention it Anna, if in fact that is your name, and don't read anything else into my apparent caring side either. I had no choice. I'm not allowed to leave so it's you or nobody.'

'Are you a prisoner?'

'Sort of. My room isn't locked and I can wander about, but I can't leave the facility, whatever it is.'

'We're in Oban. It's an Army adventure training facility, we use it a lot.'

'Okay. What I don't understand is why I can't leave. I've been debriefed, I've given up everything. The reason I came to Scotland, who I came with, meeting you and that Brown wanker, the whole nine yards, now everyone is going quiet on me.'

'I wish I could help, but I can't. Look at the state of me.'

'I'm not asking for your help and you look fine now, you'll be up and running about playing sniper any day now Anna.'

'Thank you Gruff.'

'For?'

'Well saving my life for a start.'

'It's sort of what I do Anna.' Gruff paused and took a deep, sad breath,' or it used to be, but I failed him this time.'

'Failed who? Tiger?'

'Yes. Tiger.'

'I wish I could help.'

'I made a decision when I saw Brown running but my orders, such as they were, were to stop any bad guys escaping once they'd passed me. Now it didn't look like there were any more bad guys other than Stone, but I should've stayed. I disobeyed orders and now my best friend is dead.'

'You saved my life because you disobeyed orders, and as much as I respect the friendship, the love, the brotherhood between you and Tiger, I'm glad you left your post. I'd be dead if you hadn't. What more can I say? It sounds dreadful, Gruff, but that's the truth.'

Gruff reached out his hand and gently squeezed Anna's.

'I know Anna, and I am glad you're alive. I really am. You're a brave woman who I'd work with again no question, but some things will never sit right with me. Do you understand?'

'I do Gruff, I am so sorry for your loss, but I don't know what else to say.'

Gruff was openly crying. Tears were streaming down his face without a shred of embarrassment or shame. Just a release of pressure following the last forty eight hours of adrenalin fuelled activity. Anna squeezed his hand that bit harder as she started to cry with him.

~ONE HUNDRED THIRTY~

Gruff was back in the classroom. The questions had been endless and repetitive, he'd been involved in hundreds of after action military debriefing sessions, he knew how the system worked but it was still exhausting work all the same but he knew it was nearing the end. The questions were less intense, there were bigger breaks and it wasn't so monotonous. He was even starting to admire the two blue suited men, they were very switched on, very professional, even if he didn't know their names, who they worked for or what they did.

It was during one of the breaks that a new man entered the room. Older than the first two and although he was wearing a similar blue suit, it looked just that little bit more lived in, and he was wearing a tie.

'Good afternoon, Mr Wetherspoon.'

A posh voice, educated, he had a military bearing. He had to be a Rupert, an Army Officer, Gruff guessed.

'Good Afternoon. I suppose it's pointless asking your name?'

'Not at all. I should have introduced myself. Brigstock. Brigadier Brigstock.'

'Thank you. Good afternoon Sir. Whoa there, I know you, that name, I bloody know you Sir.

You should do, I was your Commanding Officer for a very short time, at Hereford. Now back to business, firstly I want to thank you for your actions on Ben Nevis. First Class.'

'Thank you Sir, there wasn't much else I could do to be fair.'

'Nonsense, a lesser man would have flapped all the way back down the bloody mountain.'

The Brigadier chortled at his own little joke. Gruff couldn't see anything to even smile about.

'Secondly I want to talk about the man you know as Brown.'

'I've told your men already Sir. A dozen times.'

'This is true, Wetherspoon, but you might want to hear what I've got to say Hmmm?'

'Sorry Sir, but it's been so bloody frustrating. I've been here for two days, I need to get out, go home, try and sort something out for my friend...'

'I understand. Now, if you'll let me finish…Thank you. Our man Brown died at the scene of the Croft. He didn't die in the gas explosion…'

'Gas explosion?'

'Yes. Gas explosion, unfortunate gas leak from a faulty system in Croft number two I've been told. Anyway, Brown actually died following a NATO seven point six two millimetre round entering the back of his head. Then he was incinerated, by the, er, gas explosion. Terrific shot from one thousand yards I must say, Wetherspoon.'

Gruff remained silent. The cover up had started. Gas explosion? Tiger had died in a poxy gas explosion…

'Hang on sir, the explosion at the Croft was massive. Nothing could have survived that. Nothing. So how do you know about Brown?

'We have a witness. Correction we have two witnesses, Mr Wetherspoon.'

Gruff looked utterly confused. More smoke and mirrors? More cover-ups?

'I don't believe you Sir. Who are they?'

A broad grin crossed the Brigadiers face as he stood up and crossed the room to open the door.

'If you don't believe me, then ask them yourself, Mr Wetherspoon, ask them yourself,' and he left the room.

~ONE HUNDRED THIRTY ONE~

Tiger pushed Charlie into the room, she was in a wheelchair. Tiger was grinning from ear to ear and Charlie looked just as happy despite some sort of disability. Gruff was stunned. Surely to God this can't be happening. Nothing could have survived that explosion. It was massive, and Tiger and Charlie had been right in the middle of it.

'Tiger? Really? How the… excuse my French Charlie, but just, what? How the bloody hell are you still alive?'

Tiger walked around Charlie's wheelchair and grabbed his friend in a bear hug. They both stood in the middle of the room hugging. Two grown men slightly swaying and tears running down their respective cheeks.

'Get a bloody room the pair of you,' Charlie may have been carrying an injury but she hadn't lost a sense of humour.

Tiger and Gruff separated, Gruff wiped the tears from his eyes with the back of hand.

'Are you crying, Gruff?'

'Yes, you've just broken two of my ribs you stupid tosser. Are you crying?'

'Not at all, it's just a bit dusty in here.'

Both men laughed. It was a joyous reunion, a miraculous reunion.

'Bloody hell mate, I honestly thought you were...'

'So did I mate. It was a terrific bang wasn't it?'

'It bloody was mate, far too much oxide in that mix. I'll give you a hand with the next one.'

'Next one?' Charlie asked.

Both men looked at each other again and in unison said, 'there is always a next one,' and once more they burst out laughing.

One of the younger blue suits brought in a tray of hot drinks and some delicate looking cakes, set them on the table and walked out without saying a word.

Gruff acted as Mum and started pouring out the tea.

'Right, you go first, Tiger. What the bloody hell happened? Where have you been?'

'Stone came into the Croft with his gun at Charlie's head...'

'I know that Tiger, I was watching. How did Charlie get in that position?'

Charlie put her cup down and said.

'Everything went to plan at the Glencoe Inn Hotel. I even made forty quid for the Mountain Rescue Team. I left some fifteen minutes after Stone but I stopped for fuel. He slipped into my car when I was paying. He wasn't waiting for me, he was going to use the first single person who chanced along. It was just bad luck.'

'It was bloody good luck Charlie, as it turned out. After Stone and Charlie came in there was a bit of chat, nothing serious, I couldn't do anything immediately because he kept a gun pointing at Charlie.

Stone obviously had me checked for weapons but I was clean. I'd hidden the Browning under the map in the kitchen and needed an opportunity for Stone to relax a bit, get Charlie out of the way and then get in the kitchen.'

'All sounds like a long-winded plan mate. Why didn't Stone just kill you there and then?'

'I have no idea. The man was a coward, we know that but he was also extremely egotistical, perhaps he was waiting to tell me his grand plan. I really don't know.'

'What was Charlie doing when all this was going on?'

'I was sat in a chair next to Tiger' Interrupted Charlie. 'With a gun pointed at my face trying to think of way I could help, a distraction or something. You know scream like a girl and let Tiger spring into action with some Kung-Fu stuff.'

'Then Stone' must have had a brain fart or something,' Tiger continued. 'He asked Charlie to go into the kitchen and make him a drink, a bloody Jack Daniels would you believe?'

'And when I was in the kitchen I noticed the bulge in the map and saw the gun,' continued Charlie.

'That's when we heard Anna's rifle going off.' Tiger said.

'That was the distraction I needed. I grabbed the gun, prayed it was ready to fire, pointed it at Stone and pulled the trigger,' Charlie added.

'So. You killed Stone?' Asked Gruff, looking at Charlie.

'I don't know,' answered Charlie. 'I certainly hit him and he dropped his pistol. That's when Tiger leapt from his chair and dropped him. It was all very quick.'

'I punched him in the throat, he hit the floor unconscious,' Said Tiger. 'But he was still breathing. I have no idea where he was hit. I was more concerned about the rifle shot from the mountain. Something wasn't going to plan and we had to get out of the Croft.'

'Where the hell did you go? It was less than one minute from me firing the rifle and the Croft turning into matchwood?'

'We legged it from the Croft and I nearly tripped over a body lying by the front door, dressed like Brown with half his head missing, so I knew something had gone horribly wrong. I assumed that Stone's kill team had somehow spotted you and killed everyone. We jumped into your hide fully expecting you to be in it dead, and praying to every God under the Sun that you'd dug a deep enough hole for three people.

'Jesus Tiger! That was a one man hide, I doubt if I dug down more than ten inches, the rest was heather and scrub.'

'You're telling me it was cramped, but Charlie is tiny and I made a bit more room by lobbing your grenade stash towards the Croft before we hunkered down, they were taking up too much room. I then made another assumption that you had been dragged away as you weren't in the hide so I just hit the remote switch.'

'That's bloody mental mate, I cannot believe you survived!'

'Well my theory was that the blast would go upwards. Remember the training we had on the grenade ranges whilst serving? Lie down next to a grenade, big bang and the horrible bits go up in the air?'

'That was bloody stupid as well mate. It got banned.'

'Aye it was, but it worked and this was the same, only on a bigger scale. We were one hundred yards away, not a couple of feet.'

'Still bloody mental. How did Charlie get injured?'

'Shrapnel from the fall out,' responded Charlie quietly, 'a slice of metal through my right thigh.'

'What? Metal in the Croft? It was all mud and straw wasn't it?'

'My Triumph wasn't mud and straw was it mate? It was part of my own bike's side panel. What were the chances of that?'

'So you somehow survived the biggest blast since Hiroshima...'

'Nagasaki,' interrupted Charlie.

'Eh?'

'Nagasaki was after Hiroshima and therefore...'

'Okay. Okay, whateve,r Babbage... It was a turn of phrase, and you have no room to talk. One of the few people I've ever met that doesn't own or ride a motorcycle, yet gets involved in a serious accident with one.'

Charlie smiled, 'you're funny, Gruff.'

'Can I move on? Thank you, as I was saying Tiger, the bloody wheels fall off the plan, there is a massive burning crater where a Croft once stood, your ears are ringing you've got a seriously injured girl in a shallow trench, you're armed with an illegal nine millimetre firearm, there are dead bodies everywhere and the place is crawling with cops. How did that work itself out?'

'We lay in the hide for ten minutes, the fall out was just as bad as the explosion, and we had no idea if there were any more bad guys out there. When the emergency services turned up we just handed ourselves over to the nearest Fireman, told him it was our place, I smelt gas and we left to get to a phone and thirty seconds later kaboom! He handed us over to a local Copper, we said the same thing to her and I was taken to the Cop Shop in town to make a statement, Charlie was stuck into the back of an ambulance for immediate treatment and then taken to hospital for a check-up. She found me four hours later still with the Police and made a brief statement herself. We were never under arrest.'

'What about your Browning pistol?'

'Charlie had left it on the kitchen table after shooting Stone.

We were in the nick drinking bloody awful coffee wondering what to do next when a uniformed Superintendent came to see us. He informed us that a helicopter was on its way to pick us up. We were to take our original statements with us and he had been told that he'd never seen or heard of us.'

'Nobody can blackmail or pay off a whole Police Station, Tiger.'

'I have no idea what was said, but that senior cop was very happy to see us get on that helicopter.'

'Where did you go?'

'We landed at RAF Northolt in West London and were picked up by car. We then got the silent treatment, all the way to an underground car park somewhere in Central London. Charlie and I were separated but I think that was for ablution reasons, nothing sinister. I was taken to a cell, open door and debriefed on the whole thing. It was fairly obvious that they knew the basics, they even knew why I was up there in the first place.'

'Christ. How do they know so much?'

'Christ knows mate. You got mentioned a few times.'

'By you?'

'No, by them. They knew a lot about you. They let me know on the second day where you were and what had happened on the mountain. They are very pleased with you mate. Everywhere you go you seem to be saving a life.'

'I should have been looking after your back, Tiger. That was the plan, not running up bloody mountains, leaving my post, disobeying orders.'

'Nobody had orders, Gruff, and it was a loose plan. You know what happens to plans on contact with the enemy?'

'Of course I do, but all the same...'

'Listen to me Gruff. If you hadn't followed Brown, you wouldn't have saved Anna. If you weren't up a mountain saving Anna, Brown would have been interfering with me and I would have a huge problem dealing with him and Stone. If you hadn't shot Brown, there wouldn't have been an unexpected diversion and last, but certainly not least... Charlie and I wouldn't have fitted in a low hide with you already in it.'

'Well if you put it like that...'

'I do put it like that, because that is how it was.'

'Okay mate, I'll buy myself a congratulatory pint on the strength of that. Thanks. What's happening about Stone?'

'Brigadier Brigstock has told me that following Stone's removal from Office by the Oversight people, he took an unofficial flight up to Scotland in the Service helicopter, was dropped off in Glencoe where a he drove off in a hire car and hasn't been seen since. Severe depression and possible suicidal tendencies are being mooted.'

'No gas explosion for him then?'

'Nope. And talking of explosions…Mrs Cameron is being paid an almighty sum from her Insurers, enough for her to retire on, probably to a midgeless country of her choice.'

'And Brown? What was he about?'

'Money as far as can be ascertained, big gambling debts now all paid.'

'But to shoot your team mate in the chest, then leaving them to slowly die on the side of a bloody mountain? A woman to boot.'

'I suppose that what happens when you're taking money from the bad guys. You end up turning bad.'

'And us?'

'We are free to go mate. The Brigadier is kindly laying on transport of our choice to anywhere we wish to go, me personally? I'm getting a train to Derby, I have some unfinished business with a mutual friend and I have a funeral to attend.'

'I'm going to say cheers to Anna and give her the good news, and if it's okay with you I'll join you on that train mate,' he turned to Charlie and took hold of her wheelchair. 'C'mon Hoppity. I'll give you a spin over to the hospital wing.'

Brigadier Brigstock entered the room as Gruff was about to leave.

'Wetherspoon.'

'Yes Sir?'

'Make a point of seeing me before you go won't you. Your train warrants can be picked up from the guardhouse, but I'll need to speak to you before then. Say twenty minutes back here?'

'Certainly Sir.'

Gruff looked at Tiger who just shrugged.

.

~EPILOGUE~

The rain was coming down in sheets and the bitter wind flapped the sodden hem of the Vicar's white robes. His grey hair was plastered down one side of his face and although his prayer book had been laminated for such weather it was still heavy going. There were three mourners in attendance. None of them had given their names but the charity box at the nearby church had been handsomely loaded.

One was tall, handsome wearing a black suit and tie covered by an expensive Barbour coat. He was well-built with a shock of thick hair greying at the sides.

The other man was shorter, close cropped hair and more casually dressed although an attempt had been made with a black tie, obviously knotted in the dark, by a blind assistant. The third was a young woman in a wheelchair smartly dressed, in black with a large hat and with a black lace veil covering her face.

All three obviously knew each other well and yet none of them had spoken to each other since arriving at the Church some forty minutes earlier. They had sat at the back of the Church during the service and although the men had stood during the relevant sections of the service, none them had bowed their heads in prayer. Not one had come forward to read a eulogy; the Vicar hated it when that happened, and on this occasion he had to say a few kind words about a Miss Kelly, a young woman he'd never heard of before that rainswept afternoon. That was wors than the loneliness of singing two hymns on his own, but the tiny congregation of three didn't seem to mind.

Halfway through the service the Vicar was having his doubts about the Christian sincerity of these three mourners.

Outside, none of them seemed to notice the rain. It was if they'd been in harder straits recently and a bit of bad weather was nothing to worry about.

The Vicar had just reached the end of the burial service as the tall man in the Barbour coat stepped forward and dropped an item into the open grave. He paused for a second or two, muttering something unheard, before he turned to the vicar and offered his hand.

'Thank you Vicar, an excellent service.'

The smaller of the two men took a grip of the wheel chair and pushed it past the grave, stopping for a second to crouch down and grab a handful of soaking earth and dropping that into the grave.

On the way along the gravel path to a waiting car, all three passed the two gravediggers who removed their sodden caps and bowed their heads reverently.

The Vicar closed his prayer book and nodded at the two gravediggers, giving permission for them to finish their work, and then he too stepped forward and took a long look into the grave.

Lying on top of the wooden coffin, next to the single clump of earth was what looked like a large wooden fish.

'Ah!' He muttered, 'they were committed Christians after all.'

THE END

Printed in Poland
by Amazon Fulfillment
Poland Sp. z o.o., Wrocław

60436483R00317